A Time of End

A Medieval Romance

By Kathryn Le Veque

Book Four in the Executioner Knights Series

© Copyright 2019 by Kathryn Le Veque Novels, Inc.
Print Edition
Text by Kathryn Le Veque
Cover by Kim Killion
Edited by Scott Moreland

Reproduction of any kind except where it pertains to short quotes in relation to advertising or promotion is strictly prohibited.

All Rights Reserved.

The characters and events portrayed in this book are fictitious. Any similarity to real persons, living or dead, is purely coincidental and not intended by the author.

KATHRYN LE VEQUE
NOVELS

WWW.KATHRYNLEVEQUE.COM

ARE YOU SIGNED UP FOR KATHRYN'S BLOG?

You'll get the latest news and information on exclusive giveaways, exclusive excerpts, coming releases, sales, free books, cover reveals and more.

Kathryn's blog followers get it all first. No spam, no junk.

Get the latest info from the reigning Queen of English Medieval Romance!

Sign Up Here

kathrynleveque.com

Kathryn Le Veque Novels

Medieval Romance:

De Wolfe Pack Series:
Warwolfe
The Wolfe
Nighthawk
ShadowWolfe
DarkWolfe
A Joyous de Wolfe Christmas
BlackWolfe
Serpent
A Wolfe Among Dragons
Scorpion
StormWolfe
Dark Destroyer
The Lion of the North
Walls of Babylon
The Best Is Yet To Be

The de Russe Legacy:
The Falls of Erith
Lord of War: Black Angel
The Iron Knight
Beast
The Dark One: Dark Knight
The White Lord of Wellesbourne
Dark Moon
Dark Steel
A de Russe Christmas Miracle

The de Lohr Dynasty:
While Angels Slept
Rise of the Defender
Steelheart
Shadowmoor
Silversword
Spectre of the Sword

Unending Love
Archangel

Lords of East Anglia:
While Angels Slept
Godspeed

Great Lords of le Bec:
Great Protector

House of de Royans:
Lord of Winter
To the Lady Born
The Centurion

Lords of Eire:
Echoes of Ancient Dreams
Blacksword
The Darkland

Ancient Kings of Anglecynn:
The Whispering Night
Netherworld

Battle Lords of de Velt:
The Dark Lord
Devil's Dominion
Bay of Fear
The Dark Lord's First Christmas

Reign of the House of de Winter:
Lespada
Swords and Shields

De Reyne Domination:
Guardian of Darkness
With Dreams
The Fallen One

House of d'Vant:

Tender is the Knight (House of d'Vant)
The Red Fury (House of d'Vant)

The Dragonblade Series:
Fragments of Grace
Dragonblade
Island of Glass
The Savage Curtain
The Fallen One

Great Marcher Lords of de Lara
Lord of the Shadows
Dragonblade

House of St. Hever
Fragments of Grace
Island of Glass
Queen of Lost Stars

Lords of Pembury:
The Savage Curtain

Lords of Thunder: The de Shera Brotherhood Trilogy
The Thunder Lord
The Thunder Warrior
The Thunder Knight

The Great Knights of de Moray:
Shield of Kronos
The Gorgon

The House of De Nerra:
The Promise
The Falls of Erith
Vestiges of Valor
Realm of Angels

Highland Warriors of Munro:
The Red Lion
Deep Into Darkness

The House of de Garr:
Lord of Light
Realm of Angels

Saxon Lords of Hage:
The Crusader
Kingdom Come

High Warriors of Rohan:
High Warrior

The House of Ashbourne:
Upon a Midnight Dream

The House of D'Aurilliac:
Valiant Chaos

The House of De Dere:
Of Love and Legend

St. John and de Gare Clans:
The Warrior Poet

The House of de Bretagne:
The Questing

The House of Summerlin:
The Legend

The Kingdom of Hendocia:
Kingdom by the Sea

The Executioner Knights:
By the Unholy Hand
The Promise (also Noble Knights of de Nerra)
The Mountain Dark
Starless
A Time of End

Contemporary Romance:

Kathlyn Trent/Marcus Burton Series:
Valley of the Shadow
The Eden Factor
Canyon of the Sphinx

The American Heroes Anthology Series:
The Lucius Robe

Fires of Autumn
Evenshade
Sea of Dreams
Purgatory

Other non-connected Contemporary Romance:
Lady of Heaven
Darkling, I Listen
In the Dreaming Hour
River's End
The Fountain

Sons of Poseidon:
The Immortal Sea

Pirates of Britannia Series (with Eliza Knight):
Savage of the Sea by Eliza Knight
Leader of Titans by Kathryn Le Veque
The Sea Devil by Eliza Knight
Sea Wolfe by Kathryn Le Veque

Note: All Kathryn's novels are designed to be read as stand-alones, although many have cross-over characters or cross-over family groups. Novels that are grouped together have related characters or family groups. You will notice that some series have the same books; that is because they are cross-overs. A hero in one book may be the secondary character in another.

There is NO reading order except by chronology, but even in that case, you can still read the books as stand-alones. No novel is connected to another by a cliff hanger, and every book has an HEA.

Series are clearly marked. All series contain the same characters or family groups except the American Heroes Series, which is an anthology with unrelated characters.

For more information, find it in **A Reader's Guide to the Medieval World of Le Veque**.

Alexander de Sherrington, the man affectionately referred to as "Sherry" by his friends, is off on the greatest adventure of his life… and his target is Lady Christin de Lohr.

Lovely and vivacious, Christin is as headstrong as her mother but born with her father's innate sense of politics. She fostered in the finest homes and proved herself to be smart, intuitive, and calm under pressure. Unbeknownst to her father, William Marshal recruited Christin into his network of spies and even as she serves a de Lohr ally, the House of de Winter, as a lady-in-waiting for Lady de Winter, she completes missions at The Marshal's directive.

Enter Alexander de Sherrington.

He is intrigued with the beautiful new spy, and he and Christin are thrown together due to necessity. But Alexander soon realizes there is something very special about the daughter of Christopher de Lohr. As a romance blossoms, King John has his own plans for Christin – marrying her to his bastard son to undermine Christopher's power.

The only one who can stop the marriage is Christin herself.

Join Alexander and Christin, Christopher and David, and the rest of The Marshal and de Lohr allies in this epic adventure of intrigue and romance that pushes the bonds of trust between allies. It's Medieval Mayhem in 13th Century England!

AUTHOR'S NOTE

I've got to say... I love me some Sherry!

Finally – his story is here. And his leading lady? None other than Christin de Lohr.

This book is set between the last chapter and the epilogue for *Starless*, Book 3 in the Executioner Knights series, and what a story it is. The Executioner Knights series is growing by leaps and bounds, with so many awesome knights who are part of William Marshal's spy ring. I originally wrote about the spy ring in the novel *The Whispering Night*, and then in *Lord of the Shadows*, so it's been a lot of fun to expand on that particular aspect of England's political underground.

If you're wondering why my original spy from *The Whispering Night*, Garren le Mon, isn't in any of these books, the reason is simple – at the end of his story, he fled to France, so he's over in Gascony while all of these adventures are going on.

But back to the tale – for those of you keeping track of the de Winter aspect of this series as it ties into another novel, *High Warrior*, I have to explain something – we have two Daveigh de Winters. The first Daveigh was mentioned in the novel *High Warrior*, and I only mention this because the hero of that novel, Bric MacRohan, has also made appearances in the Executioner Knights series.

Bric serves Daveigh de Winter of Narborough Castle, while Daveigh's uncle, also Daveigh de Winter (and the brother of Daveigh's father, Davyss de Winter the First) is the garrison commander at Norwich Castle and the father of Lady Delesse de Winter, who was mentioned in *Godspeed* as having broken Dashiell du Reims' heart. We met Delesse, briefly, in *The Mountain Dark*, Book 2 in the Executioner Knights series. For those keeping track, Davyss de Winter – hero of *Lespada* – is the son of Grayson de Winter, half-brother of Daveigh de

Winter of Narborough Castle. They both share the same father, Davyss I.

Confusing, I know, but those de Winters really aren't original when it comes to names. They're all named after each other – Davyss, Hugh, Grayson, and Daveigh. That's what you'll see the most of. In fact, a heroine in the Reign of de Winter series even comments on it. You can actually find the House of de Winter family tree on my website.

Back to the House of de Lohr – I've never fully outlined the children of Christopher and Dustin, but we know they had a bunch of them. The first time I gave a full accounting was in *A Blessed de Lohr Christmas*, so here it is again:

The children of Christopher and Dustin:
Peter (Christopher's son with Lady Amanda)
Christin
Brielle
Curtis
Richard
Myles
Rebecca
Douglas
Westley
Olivia Charlotte (the future Honey de Shera)

Now, aside from the de Lohr family, lots going on in this story. William Marshal has spent the past few years in and out of England, mostly in Ireland, for a variety of reasons, not the least of which was the fact that he and John were at odds, and also because some English lords were trying to take over his Irish properties. In this story, he's only recently returned home again, back to serve John.

Something else to note – this takes place about four years before *Lord of the Shadows*, and Sean de Lara once again plays a fairly major role in this book. I've loved writing the Executioner Knights series and one of the reasons is because we get to see Sean in action over the years and why he was called Lord of the Shadows. We also get to see some poignant scenes between Sean and his brother, Kevin.

No pronunciation guides in this book because there are no odd names (surprising, I know!). Castles such as Norwich are real, but Lioncross is fictional. This is such a fun story, so enjoy it. I know I did!

Hugs,

Kathryn

HIC FINIS DAT DEUS
(GOD ENDS HERE)

Year of Our Lord 1211
Ramsbury Castle
Seat of the Duke of Savernake

THE TARGET WAS on the move.

This night was the culmination of intelligence, of rumors and whispers. A miasma of information had swirled for months like the fogs that often settled in during the winter – thick, like stew, masking the ingredients therein. It was the night when the information had finally become clear and spies from William Marshal's stable would catch the double agent who had been carefully cultivated, lured into believing this was the night when all of France's dreams would come true.

William Marshal's men had been clever. The agent was an English nobleman, one Lord Prescombe, with ties to the French king. He'd pretended to ally himself with William Marshal, offering his army and money to help the English king, John, regain his properties in Normandy. John had lost Normandy some time ago but had spent the past year building up money and ammunition in order to take an invasion force over the channel and gain back what he believed was rightfully his.

But the French king, Philip, wanted those plans.

To catch the French spy, this night of nights had been created.

It was a feast that would live in legend for years to come. The Duke of Savernake, Edward de Vaston, was a great supporter of William Marshal and the host of the event. The Savernake army was one of the largest armies in Southern England with the exception of the Earl of Canterbury's army. David de Lohr, the Earl of Canterbury, shared the distinction along with his brother, Christopher, of having one of the largest and best-equipped armies in all of England.

Armies that William Marshal depended heavily upon.

In fact, both Christopher and David de Lohr were at the great feast tonight, meant to celebrate the marriage of the heiress to the de Vaston dukedom, Lily, to a somewhat minor but wealthy nobleman named Clayton le Cairon. That was the premise, anyway. The truth was that Lily and Clayton had married the month before, so this celebration was conveniently late.

But it had been a perfect excuse for William Marshal to call together his network of spies in the hunt for the French spy. Along with Christopher and David de Lohr, other notable agents included Alexander de Sherrington, known as Sherry to his friends. If there was ever a perfect agent, Alexander was it. The man was the perfect combination of knightly skill, experience, and intelligence. He was also the most deadly assassin in The Marshal's arsenal, a man who preferred to work alone but was no less comfortable leading a contingent, which he was now.

A contingent of some of William's finest agents.

Also at the top of that contingent were Maxton of Loxbeare, Kress de Rhydian, and Achilles de Dere, the original Executioner Knights, men with great and vast reputations that had been established in The Levant with Richard's Crusade. All three men had settled down and married since their return to England, and Achilles had brought his wife, Susanna, who had been an agent for William Marshal before marriage and motherhood had taken priority.

Even as William looked over the enormous great hall of Ramsbury Castle, he found satisfaction in knowing Susanna was once again primed for action. She was one of his best. In fact, she was playing the proper wife even as her husband and his friends were pretending to become drunk. William saw Susanna remove Achilles' drink on more than one occasion, which gave William a good laugh. Achilles was a big, fearsome knight, but it was clear who was in charge of that relationship.

Along with Maxton, Kress, and Achilles was Dashiell du Reims, the commander of the army for the Duke of Savernake and an agent for William when he was needed. He sat at the same feasting table with the original Executioner Knights, and Susanna, along with Bric MacRohan, the commander for the Narborough Castle's de Winter armies. Bric was Irish to the bone and one of the most frightening, most deadly men William had ever known.

Another perfect assassin.

The Marshal's group rounded out with Sir Kevin de Lara, Sir Cullen de Nerra, and the eldest son of Christopher de Lohr, an outstanding young knight by the name of Sir Peter de Lohr. Peter came into the service of William Marshal a few years before and was already one of The Marshal's best agents, much to his father's distress. Peter was smart, cunning, talented, and deadly. But he wasn't the most talented spy in the de Lohr family. That title went to Christopher's eldest daughter, and Peter's sister, Christin.

She was the one they called The Ghost – there one moment, gone the next, and no one was the wiser until it was all over.

William watched Christopher as the man sat with his daughter and son. He often wondered what the man would say if he knew his daughter had taken to the spy business like a duck takes to water. William lived in fear of that moment, actually, because he knew Christopher would not react well. Nor should he – he had a lovely daughter to protect. William's gaze moved to Christin. She had long, dark hair and enormous gray eyes. She looked like an angel. In fact, there were few women in the world with Lady Christin de Lohr's beauty.

She was young, well-spoken, charming, and quite witty in all conversation except that she came across as rather naïve. But that was what made her such an exceptional agent – no one realized she was assessing them and analyzing information until it was too late. William knew for a fact that she had killed at least three men she'd been sent to draw information from. She served Lady de Winter from Norwich Castle as a lady-in-waiting, but that was a cover. Her liege, old Daveigh de Winter, sent her off at The Marshal's command.

And her father knew nothing about it.

Christin was here tonight, along with the rest of William's agents, but her directive was specific – she was to make herself agreeable to the spy and get him drunk so the men could remove him from the hall and make him disappear.

She was the perfect weapon.

But she hadn't had the chance. The French spy had arrived with a woman on his arm, a woman who had showed great aggression towards Christin when she approached Lord Prescombe, so Christin had been forced to back off and reassess her strategy. They'd all seen the man depart the great hall several minutes earlier with his companion, presumably heading for the garderobe, but neither had returned to the hall yet. Dashiell, who had been out patrolling the wall, had seen the man heading around the side of the keep to the kitchen entrance, but not the woman. She was missing.

It was time to mobilize his agents. With a nod of his head to Peter, the young knight was by William's side.

"My lord?" he asked.

William's gaze was over the room. "Lord Prescombe has decided to re-enter the keep through the kitchen entrance," he said. "Spread the word. Everyone knows what they are to do."

"Aye, my lord."

Peter was off, very casually, as if nothing were amiss. As he approached the table where his father and uncle were speaking with his sister, he nodded slightly to Maxton, who casually stood up himself. He yawned, feigning drunkenness, which had Kress on his feet to steady him. Big, bearded Maxton gripped Kress, his tall and blond companion, and the two of them staggered out of the hall, presumably to find the garderobe as well.

But their act had Achilles and Susanna on their feet, with Achilles deliberately picking a fight with his wife and storming off because she kept taking his drink away. But it was all an act. Susanna, looking wounded, watched him walk away as Kevin and Cullen joined him, all three of them staggering out of the hall under the guise of being drunk.

Christin, seeing that Susanna appeared as if she were about to cry, broke off from her father.

"Papa," she said, holding up a hand to interrupt the conversation. "I think Lady de Dere requires my comfort. Please remain and enjoy your meal. I will return shortly."

With that, she rounded the table and went to Susanna, who appeared properly injured by her rude husband. As Susanna and Christin headed out of the hall through a door that led into the heart of the keep, presumably to engage in womanly conversation, Bric MacRohan finally stood up from the table and, with cup in hand, made his way over to Peter.

"Time to move, young de Lohr," Bric said in his heavy Irish accent. "Make it good."

Grinning, Peter threw his arm around Bric's neck and the two of them departed the hall in a chummy fashion. With the table cleared of almost everyone, Christopher and David sat there, realizing they were very much alone.

"Was it something I said?" David wondered aloud.

Christopher shook his head, pouring himself more of Savernake's fine Spanish wine. "Probably," he said. He watched Peter and Bric disappear through one of the smaller doors in the hall. "You know, it is quite disturbing to me to see Peter make such great friends with MacRohan. He could find better companions."

David snorted. "You adore Bric," he said. "The man is as fine as they come. It's good to see that Peter has been accepted by all of The Marshal's men."

Christopher looked pointedly at him. "You mean he has been accepted by all of The Marshal's agents," he muttered. "He thinks I do not know, but I do. He is a spy like the rest of them."

David didn't react to that. He simply took the pitcher of wine and poured himself more as well. "Who told you?"

"That is of little matter. Did *you* know?"

"They call him The Ghost."

"I know."

Christopher sat back in his chair. "Did you notice how they all left at the same time?"

"I did."

"Something is afoot."

"My thoughts, as well."

"Evidently, I must look stupid if they do not think I noticed."

"You don't look any more stupid to me than you usually do."

Christopher cast his brother an exasperated look but was prevented from replying when he spied William Marshal making his way over to their table.

"Look," he muttered, putting his cup to his lips. "The Puppet master himself. The man is making an assassin out of my son."

David grinned. "Peter can take care of himself," he said. "If I were you, I would pretend that I still didn't know. Give the old man the illusion that he knows more than you do."

Christopher simply lifted his cup to William when the man came to join them. The three of them indulged in Savernake's fine drink, each man pretending there wasn't something going on around them, something that involved The Marshal's finest agents.

And one agent Christopher knew nothing of.

A curious evening was about to get interesting.

"WE MUST HURRY," Christin said to Susanna. "We are to cover the duke's solar where the map decoys are."

Susanna was right behind her. "Do you know this keep well?"

"Well enough," Christin said. "On the day we arrived, I had one of the duke's daughters show me around. I pretended to be impressed with the place so she showed me everything. I'm confident I know where we're going."

Susanna stayed close to her, considering she hadn't been anywhere in the keep other than the great hall. The corridors were dark, with closed doors, and barely a hint of light except for occasional torches in their iron sconces. They rounded a corner and were faced with great double doors ahead, shadowed and dark in the dim light. The corridor here was lined with wooden panels, elaborately carved, and Christin took Susanna by the hand.

"Quickly," she whispered. "Come this way."

Susanna followed, though her free hand was on the hilt of the small sword she kept sheathed on her hip. A large cut in the fold of her skirts allowed her to get to the sword easily. Susanna was a tall woman, and strong, and had trained at the infamous Blackchurch knight's school in Devon. Only the best of the best were accepted and only the very best in the world managed to finish the training.

Susanna had been one of those.

Therefore, she was the perfect weapon in a fight, meant to both protect and assist Christin as the woman took the lead. Christin pushed on one of the carved wooden panels and the thing gave way, revealing a hidden servant's corridor. It was pitch black so she grabbed one of the torches lining the corridor before they entered, shutting the panel behind them.

"What *is* this place?" Susanna hissed.

Christin put her fingers to her lips to silence her. "A servant's passage," she said. "De Vaston's daughter took great delight in showing it to me. She said that this is where she and her sisters spy on their father. Look."

She was pointing to two panels that, when removed, provided a peep hole into the chamber beyond. Putting the torch well away from them so the flickering light wouldn't be seen when they opened the panels, they carefully slid out two small pieces of wood, revealing tiny holes in the wall.

But they were enough to see by.

The great solar beyond was dim except for the fire in the hearth, giving off a nominal amount of light. Almost immediately, they could see that there was someone in the chamber, standing over the great table that had the decoy maps on it. Christin and Susanna watched, trying to see who it was, when the figure picked up a one of the maps and brought it over to the firelight to see better.

Christin let out a hiss. "That is Lord Prescombe's companion."

Susanna could see the woman, too. "Then it wasn't him we had to worry over."

Christin shook her head and replaced the panel very carefully. "Nay," she said. "He is leading the men on a wild goose chase while his companion gathers the information. We must move swiftly."

Susanna replaced her panel, too, and unsheathed her sword. "I will cover the main entry," she said. "You enter through the servant's entrance."

Christin nodded quickly. "I will flush her to you."

Susanna was on the move, swiftly and quietly exiting the servant's hall, as Christin went to the small servant's door that led into the solar. She was armed with a bejeweled dagger, one she always kept on her person. It was long and thin and quite dangerous, sheathed against her right thigh. Lifting her skirts, she unsheathed her weapon and silently opened the door.

Prescombe's companion was still by the hearth, reading the map. She hadn't noticed Christin as the woman entered from the shadows. Even as Christin drew closer, the woman still didn't look up and when Christin was about ten feet from her, she came to a halt. To go any closer would be dangerous.

"You will not make it back to Philip with that information, you know," she said quietly.

The woman gasped, startled, and the map fell into the hearth. As it began to catch fire, she stood up and faced Christin.

"I suppose that remains to be seen," she said. "Who is going to stop me? You?"

Christin smiled thinly. She was smaller than the woman, but she was also as fast as a cat and armed with a dagger that could do a great deal of damage. She wasn't afraid to use it.

"Aye," she said simply. "Me and several of William Marshal's agents. In fact, they should have Lord Prescombe in their custody now. He is not going to be able to tell Philip anything, either."

The map in the hearth was beginning to flame, dark smoke billowing up. The woman stepped away from the hearth, keeping her attention on Christin.

"I know you," she said. "You are the one who approached Lord Prescombe and then you sat at that table with The Marshal's allies. Whose whore are you?"

That brought a genuine smile from Christin, a dazzling gesture. "Because you are a whore, you assume that I am, also," she said. "I am sorry to disappoint you, but I am no one's whore."

The woman, up until that point, had held a calm and composed expression, but with Christin's sharp tongue, it was beginning to tighten.

"I cannot let you leave this chamber alive," she said. "You know that, don't you?"

"I was about to say the same thing to you."

The woman looked her up and down, sizing her up. Then, she gestured to the hearth. "Your map is burning," she said. "There will be no invasion. Everything is going up in smoke and your plans are finished, at least for now. I accomplished something this night."

"You would have had that been the correct map."

The woman's eyes widened. "Do you mean to tell me...?" she said, torn between surprise and outrage. "I saw what was on that map. It was greatly detailed."

"You saw a decoy."

The woman's mouth popped open as outrage won over. "That is a lie!"

Christin shook her head. "Do you truly believe the real map with the real plans would be laying out for anyone to see? You're dumber than you look and a poor spy in any case. You deserve to be caught."

The woman stiffened. "And your tongue is reckless, little girl," she snarled. "You have no idea what is happening, do you? Even as you make plans against Philip, he is already ten steps ahead of you. You have already lost but you do not know it yet."

Christin remained cool. "There is nothing Philip could do to defeat the English. That is clear by the caliber of the spies he sends."

The woman clenched her teeth. "Stupid girl. You do not even know that the danger, for England, is already here. It is right under your nose. God will see you all punished."

With that, she suddenly charged at Christin, who was far enough away that she had time to bring forth the razor-sharp dagger. Just as the woman was upon her, she shoved it deep into the woman's chest, grabbing her by the hair and slipping a foot in front of her. With a cry, the woman tripped with a great deal of help from Christin, who yanked her right down to the ground.

The woman was mortally wounded, but she managed to grab hold of Christin by the hair. Enraged, and fearing for her life, Christin removed the dagger and stabbed the woman again, twice more, until she stopped fighting.

Blood sprayed onto her, marking her, but she wisely tossed the dagger away, far away, so the dying woman couldn't take it from her and try to use it against her. Instead, she ended up in a dominant position over the woman, her hands around the spy's neck, squeezing the life from her as the woman bled out all over the floor.

"Speak not of God and punishment," she grunted, using all of her might to squeeze. "For in this room, God ends here."

At that moment, the door to the solar burst open and Susanna charged in, fully prepared for a fight but quickly seeing that Christin had already subdued the spy. She saw that Christin was also covered in blood. Seeing this, and believing that Christin must have been hurt, Susanna lifted her sword and cut the woman's head off. Blood splattered everywhere.

The battle was instantly quelled.

"Christin?" Susanna said with great concern, pulling the woman off of the decapitated body. "Are you injured? Where did she hurt you?"

Christin shook her head. Her manner was as cool and hard as a rock, as if she'd not just been in a fight for life and death.

"I am not hurt," she said. "This is her blood. She attacked me and I was forced to kill her."

Susanna breathed a sigh of relief, looking over at the woman's body on the ground. "Thank God you are not hurt," she said. "But that woman…"

At that moment, Alexander rushed into the chamber, sword in hand. He, too, was ready for a battle. One look at the decapitated corpse on the floor and his shocked gaze moved to Christin and Susanna.

"What happened?" he demanded.

Christin's gaze lingered on the bloody mess. "Prescombe leaving the hall was a ruse," she said. "He did it to lure all of you out so his companion could look for information on John's invasion."

Alexander sheathed his sword, bending over the body and visually examining it for a moment before he began to pat down her skirts, looking for anything she might have on her possession.

"We figured that out," he said. "Prescombe is in custody and The Marshal wants to interrogate him. He wanted to interrogate his companion, as well, but that is clearly not going to happen."

Christin watched Alexander frisk the woman's undergarments, looking for secret pockets or anything else that might be hidden. He was silent and efficient, doing what needed to be done.

Calm, cool, and collected.

Christin didn't know Alexander de Sherrington personally. The first time they'd met had been tonight, with brief introductions. She knew him by reputation, of course. She'd heard her father talking about the man everyone called Sherry. Her father had said that he was an enigma, a man until himself, and one of the most elite warriors in all of England. According to Christopher, they didn't come any greater or any smarter than Alexander de Sherrington.

In truth, she'd been intimidated by him the moment she met him.

He was very big, and very tall, and quite handsome. He had close-cropped black hair, and dark eyes, and a trim, dark beard that embraced his square jaw. When he smiled, which she'd seen tonight, he had big white teeth in great contrast to that dark beard. His smile was infectious and his laugh booming, but it was all a deception. According to her father, he was one of the more deadly men in The Marshal's arsenal.

An assassin beyond compare.

Now, that handsome assassin was focused on the body in front of him and as he rolled the dead woman onto her stomach, Christin broke away from Susanna and went to find the dagger she'd tossed across the chamber. More men were entering the solar now; Bric, the big Irishman, and Cullen, a tall and handsome knight she had seen at Norwich Castle before. He was a friend of her brother, Peter's. Both Bric and Cullen were standing over Alexander as he thoroughly searched the body. Bric looked over at the women.

"What happened?" he asked.

Susanna looked at Christin as she rejoined them, her dagger in her hand. "Susanna and I caught her in here, reading the map we'd left out as a decoy," Christin said. Then, she pointed over to the charred map in the hearth. "She burned that map on purpose, thinking it was the plan's for John's invasion. When I caught her, she told me that she could not let me leave the room alive."

"And she attacked you?" Bric asked.

Christin nodded. "I had no choice but to defend myself."

At that point, Alexander stood up, pointing at the detached head. "Who did that? You?"

"I did," Susanna said. "Christin came in through the servant's alcove and surprised the woman. I was waiting at the entry doors for Christin to flush her out, but the woman attacked Christin instead. By the time I entered, they were on the floor struggling, or at least I thought they were. Christin had blood on her and I assumed she was injured, so I disabled her adversary."

Alexander took a few steps towards Christin, looking at the blood on her hands and the splatter on her bodice. Those dark eyes were piercing. "You're going to have to change your clothing," he said. "You cannot return to the hall like that."

Christin glanced down at herself. "I know," she said, looking up to Alexander, who was quite a bit taller than she was. "Before she attacked me, she said something strange. She told me that I did not know that the danger, for England, was already here. She said it was right under my nose."

Alexander's dark-eyed gaze lingered on her. "She could have just said that to throw you off," he said. "But it's equally possible she meant it."

"You may want to ask her companion about it."

Alexander nodded. "I will, indeed," he said, looking at the body on the floor. "It is a pity she had to attack you. She might have told us what she meant had she not been so foolish as to advance against a woman unafraid to use a dagger."

He was voicing a regret and nothing more, but Susanna stepped up to defend her.

"Christin fought bravely," she said. "She kept her head in a difficult situation. She did what she had to do."

Alexander looked at Susanna, whom he knew well. He'd been on many an adventure with the lady warrior. "I know," he said. "She confronted the spy we were all looking for and is to be commended for her actions. I did not mean to intimate otherwise. But she must return to the hall as if nothing has happened and she cannot go covered in blood. I doubt her father would appreciate that."

"Sherry." Peter was suddenly in the doorway, looking at the carnage with some shock. "The Marshal is looking for you. Is *that* the other spy?"

He was pointing to the body and Alexander nodded. "Aye," he said, glancing at Christin. "She made the deadly mistake of attacking a de Lohr."

There was a twinkle in his eyes as he said it and even Susanna flashed a grin, looking to her young friend. Christin may have looked like an angel, but she was a de Lohr to the bone. But Peter took one look at his sister, covered with gore, and nearly came apart.

"Cissy," he gasped, coming into the chamber. "What in the hell happened? Are you injured?"

Christin could see that Peter needed reassurance and she went to him, taking him by the arm. "Not to worry, dear brother," she said soothingly. "'Tis just a little bit of blood. It will wash right off."

But Peter wasn't convinced. "Are you hurt?"

"I am not hurt. It is her blood, not mine."

Peter sighed heavily. "Christ, you gave me a scare," he said. "We must get you cleaned up before Papa sees you. He is already wondering what has become of you."

Christin let go of him and quickly gathered her skirts. "Then I had better clean up in a hurry," she said. "It would not do for Papa to see me covered in blood. I might have some explaining to do, which I do not wish to do at this time."

She bolted from the chamber with Peter right behind her. Once she was gone, Alexander shook his head as he returned his focus to the body. "I suppose I should not have expected less from a de Lohr," he said. "I had heard tale Lady Christin was fearless. I suppose the proof is at my feet."

He was referring to the body. Susanna nodded. "Christin may be young, but she is mature beyond her years," she said. "She has the makings of a great agent."

"But only if her father doesn't find out."

"Precisely."

"I feel as if we are all keeping a very big secret from de Lohr. He will not be happy if, and when, he finds out."

"I am sure he will not be. Would you?"

"Hell, no."

The subject of Christin de Lohr dropped as Alexander, Bric, and Cullen removed the body and its head, leaving Susanna to find something to clean up the blood with. When she finished, it would look like nothing was ever amiss in Savernake's great solar.

All evidence wiped clean.

William Marshal's agents would make sure of it.

No trace.

CHAPTER ONE

Farringdon House
Two days later

"AND THAT WAS what she said to you?" William Marshal asked. "There was no mistake?"

Christin was sitting in William Marshal's lavish solar, the one that covered nearly half of the second floor of The Marshal's opulent London townhome. The walls were painted wooden panels, with scenes from Greek mythology, perhaps more lavish than a man like The Marshal would like, but his wife had insisted. It was the fashion of the season last year when Savoy artisans had been brought in from France. Therefore, he sat beneath the watchful gaze of Zeus and Hera and Ares, all of them lending judgment to the man's activities as he controlled the power of England.

Christin had been in the chamber before, several times. She had come with her father once or twice when she had been younger, and then with Peter when the man brought her to The Marshal because Christin had expressed interest in serving England's greatest knight.

Because she was a de Lohr, The Marshal had permitted her to help Peter when he went about his duties for The Marshal, but Christin took to covert activities very quickly. Faster than Peter had, in fact. Within a year of her first meeting with The Marshal, she was undertaking her own missions on his behalf.

Therefore, sitting in William's solar was nothing new. But in this case, she was explaining what happened that night in the Duke of Savernake's solar. Surrounded by most of the men who had been there that night, she tried not to feel intimidated by the situation, as if she'd done something wrong by defending herself.

"There was no mistaking what she said, my lord," she said steadily. "The woman told me that the danger was already in England, right under our noses."

William's gaze lingered on her, pondering that statement. "But she did not say what?"

"Nay, my lord."

"Go over the conversation with me once more."

Christin thought back to that night. "She seemed to know what she was doing, my lord," she said. "She was reading the map quite ably when I entered Savernake's solar. When she realized I had found her out, she told me she could not let me leave the chamber alive. I knew she meant to kill me, which is why I was forced to kill her when she attacked me."

"Go on."

Christin shrugged. "She burned the decoy map intentionally," she said. "She told me that there would be no invasion now. When I told her that she'd burned the wrong map, she became enraged. She said, exactly, that I have no idea what is going on and that even as we make plans, Philip is already ten steps ahead. She said that we have already lost, but do not know it yet, and that the danger for England is already here and under our noses."

"And that is everything?"

"It is, my lord."

William sighed heavily, sitting back in his chair and mulling over what his young agent had told him. She was quite composed and very much like her father in that respect. She had only seen eighteen years, but she had a maturity that went well beyond that. His gaze moved to the men standing back in the shadows of the chamber, listening.

"Sherry," he said. "You heard none of this?"

Alexander stepped out of the darkness. "Nay, my lord. I came into the chamber after Susanna had cut the woman's head off."

Susanna wasn't there to confirm his story because she and Achilles had already headed home, back to their very small children whom they did not like to leave without both mother and father for too long. Cullen had also departed for his garrison at Rockingham Castle and Dashiell had remained at Ramsbury. But Peter, Kevin, and Bric had come to London, along with Maxton and Kress. It was Maxton who spoke next.

"Prescombe has proved useless," he said. "It is my assessment, and Sherry's, that he was led around by the woman Christin killed because he truly seems to be a dullard. The woman appears to have been the driving force behind his actions."

Maxton was the unofficial leader of the Executioner Knights, a man of little humor, of serious demeanor, and of deadly intentions. He wasn't a man to cross, but he was fair and honest in all things. William's focus shifted to him.

"Where is Prescombe now?" he asked.

"In your vault," Maxton said. "I am surprised you cannot hear him screaming from here."

William smiled, humorlessly. "I cannot, but I am grateful my wife is not in residence. She can hear a rat squeal a mile away, yet she cannot hear me when I tell her something important."

Maxton lifted a dark eyebrow. "Prescombe is going to be trouble," he said. "The man has money and a reasonably-sized army, and if we release him, he will run right to Philip and tell him what has happened."

The Marshal's expression was unapologetic. "That will not happen because he will never leave here alive," he said. "But nothing will happen to him until we are finished with him. There may be more he is not telling us."

"We have interrogated him for nearly two days," Kress said, coming out of the shadows to stand next to Maxton. "He is either the most resistant spy alive or the dumbest. With everything we've done to him, he has not spilled anything of note."

With everything we've done to him. That bespoke of nasty interrogation methods the Executioner Knights had learned in The Levant. William wasn't squeamish by any means but he didn't ask for details, especially with Christin in the chamber. He trusted Kress at his word.

"Then give him a few more days and every opportunity to tells us what he knows before you end his life," he said. "But I am interested to know if, indeed, he is holding back. His companion spoke of danger already being in England. I want to know what that means. See if you can find out."

Maxton and Kress nodded, glancing at Alexander before quitting the chamber, but Alexander stopped them.

"Wait," he said. "It occurs to me that keeping Prescombe alive might work better to our advantage."

"Why?" William asked.

"Because we can feed the man false information and he can report that back to Philip," he said. "Certainly, he will report the death of his companion, but he doesn't know the circumstances. In fact, he doesn't know anything at all. Only what we tell him."

William was listening with great interest. "Excellent point," he said. "We can tell Prescombe anything. Mayhap we can even lead Philip's armies into something to greatly diminish them."

"An ambush?"

"Or worse."

That suggestion had the approval of Maxton and Kress. "Then we must figure out what to tell him," Maxton said. "We can make it so the man can escape back to Philip and tell him everything we want Philip to know."

As Kress and Alexander nodded in agreement, William held up a hand. "Indeed, we can and we will. But at this moment, I am more concerned over the cryptic words of danger that the woman spy spoke of," he said. "Forget about John's plans of invasion in Normandy for a moment. I have said this before and I shall say it again – John may be a thorn in the side of every Englishman, but he is still our monarch. It behooves us to keep him alive because our alternative is a six-year-old heir. The only real danger in England is a direct threat to the monarchy. That is the only real way England herself would weaken. Would you agree?"

Everyone nodded to certain degrees and William continued.

"The woman said that danger was right under our noses," he muttered thoughtfully. Then, he looked to Alexander. "What does that mean to you?"

Alexander shrugged. "Something obvious that we do not realize."

William looked to Maxton expectantly. "The same," Maxton said.

William moved to Kress. "And you?"

Kress cocked his head thoughtfully. "Mayhap something that we cannot see more than it is something obvious we do not suspect," he said. "That would make more sense to me. Subversion under our noses that we simply cannot see."

"Someone we would never suspect," Christin said softly.

Her voice was soft, unexpected, and the men all looked at her. "Speak up, my lady," William said. "You have the de Lohr mind. I will listen. You said someone we would never suspect?"

After a moment of hesitation, Christin nodded firmly. "If danger is under our noses, then it would make sense it would be someone we would never suspect," she said. "Wouldn't the greatest danger be from someone we trusted who was not who we thought he was?"

It was an astute observation from a young woman who had not spent years in the espionage game. William nodded faintly; he agreed with her for the most part. But he wasn't a man to pin everything on one theory.

There was more to this situation than met the eye.

"That would make sense," he said. "But it could be any number of things, so we must not focus on one thing only. I will stand by my opinion that, somehow, John is under threat and that threat is in this country. Something greater than all of the other threats we face. We will reach out to our network to see if anyone has seen or heard anything, but until we receive answers, it is important that John is watched. I believe he is attending a feast in his honor at Norwich Castle in a fortnight. Lady Christin, you would know this to be true."

Christin nodded quickly. "Aye, my lord," she said. "Lord de Winter is having a feast in celebration of the king's birthday, which is next month. He has invited all of his allies to attend."

"A threat under our noses," Alexander murmured thoughtfully. When everyone looked at him, his gaze moved to Christin, sitting straight in the chair opposite The Marshal. "It could be one of the allies."

Christin didn't want to agree or disagree. These men were the greatest minds in the land, just like her father, and she wasn't so arrogant as to believe she could match wits or opinions with them. So, she simply smiled, without humor, the flash of a smile that was noncommittal because, truly, she had no business giving Alexander her opinion. But as she stared at the man and he stared back, she realized one thing –

His eyes were hypnotic.

She was looking into greatness. She knew that. Alexander de Sherrington was a name she'd heard for the past year, solidly, to the point where even Peter had built Alexander up into something legendary. She didn't know what to expect when she finally met him, perhaps a marble god from the top of the Parthenon, but she'd never expected the man to be such a handsome beast. It had been difficult for her to take her eyes from him since the moment she met him.

Something about him was dark, delicious, and enticing.

But he was far beyond her reach. She knew that. Men like Alexander de Sherrington didn't attach themselves to women in any way because their vocation was their wife and mistress. They were men of warfare and death, and what was she?

Absolutely nothing.

In fact, Christin knew that she'd probably said too much already in this meeting even though The Marshal had been kind about it. Still… throughout this entire gathering, she had the distinct feeling that she'd made a mistake when she killed the French agent. Perhaps a more experienced agent would not have, realizing the French agent would have been a valuable prisoner.

It was a mistake that was starting to haunt her.

As she sat there and pondered the greater implications of her actions, The Marshal suddenly barked.

"Bric," he said sharply.

Bric stepped out of the shadows. "My lord?"

William turned to look at him. "You are heading back to Narborough, are you not?"

"Aye, my lord."

"Then you will ride with Peter and Lady Christin back to Norwich first," he said. "I want you to inform Old Daveigh de Winter of what we have discovered so he knows what is happening. The king will be under the man's roof and he should know if we suspect turmoil. Then you will continue on to Narborough and tell his nephew, Young Daveigh, what is happening. When John's feast occurs, I expect you and your liege to be there."

Bric nodded shortly. "Aye, my lord."

With that directive given, William turned to speak to the last knight in the room. "De Lara?"

Kevin de Lara stepped forward, almost hidden back in the recesses where he'd been waiting. He wasn't as tall as some of the men around him, making it easier to overlook him, but that was a mistake. He had the strength of Samson. There wasn't a man in that room who would voluntarily tangle with him, trained assassins included. Kevin wasn't an assassin or a dirty dealer like Alexander or Maxton; quite the contrary. He was a knight to the bone, pious and noble.

Kevin was the group's white knight.

"My lord?" he answered.

William's gaze lingered on the powerful knight. "You will be going with them, as well," he said. "Along with Sherry and Peter and Bric, I will need your eyes and ears on what is going on at Norwich. This means you may be forced to interact with your brother. Can you do this?"

Kevin's expression didn't change, but those who knew what William meant were all thinking the same thing – beneath Kevin's professional facade was the fact that his older brother, Sean de Lara, had defected into the service of King John had built himself a frightening and brutal reputation as a knight known as Lord of the Shadows.

At least, that was what everyone thought. But those in The Marshal's inner circle, including Kevin, knew the truth.

Sean was The Marshal's greatest weapon.

It was no secret that Kevin was greatly disappointed in the path his talented brother had taken, choosing to damage the family's reputation by taking on such a brutal task. It was something Kevin disagreed with wholeheartedly but, professional as he was, he never spoke a word of it. He would die before revealing what he knew about his brother, so the secret was safe.

But the pain of the estrangement was real.

Therefore, no one really spoke of Sean de Lara to Kevin, so for William to bring it up openly was something that simply wasn't done. Alexander, in particular, was close to Sean, though not unsympathetic with Kevin, and he watched the knight's reaction as William brought up the forbidden subject.

"I will, and can, do all that is required of me, my lord," Kevin said easily.

Not that there had any doubt, but William still wanted to hear it from Kevin. "Very well," he said. "You will go with them to Norwich. Stay sharp. In fact, all of you stay sharp. If there is a threat under our noses, we must discover what it is."

Those heading to Norwich nodded, but it was Alexander who spoke for the group. "Aye, my lord."

"Leave us now," William said, waving his hand at them. "I will be following shortly to Norwich, but do not wait for me. I will see you there. Sherry, this is your mission. You are in command."

As Alexander nodded and headed out with the others, William turned his attention to Maxton and Kress.

"Now," he said. "Pull up a chair and let us discuss what to do with Prescombe."

With that, his attention was diverted and those heading to Norwich quit the chamber. Alexander, Peter, Kevin, Bric, and Christin headed down the mural stairs to the lower level of the great townhouse, which was a fortress unto itself. It was big and square, with the lower levels being the kitchens and a dormitory for visiting knights and soldiers, and the upper floors being where The Marshal and his family lived.

"I will take my sister to The Duck and Dribble over on Lombard Street," Peter said. "I've already sent our baggage on ahead, so you can find us there in the morning."

Alexander was right behind him. "Very well," he said. "We'll head down to The Pox on Ropery Street. That will give us a bit of entertainment before we have to head north into the wilds of Norfolk."

Bric put a hand on Alexander's shoulder, yanking the man back as they headed for the fortified entry of the manse. "The Marshal does not like us to go to that place," he said. "If he finds out, there will be hell to pay."

Alexander cast Bric a long look. "He will not know we've been there if a certain Irishman keeps his yap shut," he said. "I do not intend to engage in anything untoward. Mayhap a bit of gambling. I also have not eaten anything all day and they have the best food in town. If you want to go with Peter and the lady to the inn on Lombard, be my guest. But I am going to The Pox."

They were out on the street now with a crisp autumn night overhead. The stars were brilliant, like a blanket of diamonds, and the streets were dark enough so that most people were already in for the night.

But Christin didn't notice. She had been looking forward to a meal and a quiet evening, or perhaps something a little more thrilling considering she didn't get to London often. Given that there was no excitement in Norwich, Alexander's comment about The Pox had her attention.

"The Pox," she said, picking up her skirts so they wouldn't drag in the mud on the street. "It sounds like a lively place. I think I've heard Lord de Winter speak of it, but his wife becomes irritated when he does. It has a bad reputation, doesn't it?"

Alexander grinned, his big teeth flashing in the dim light. "That depends on who you ask," he said. "They have beautiful women, excellent food, and any game of chance a man could want for."

Christin was watching the street, making sure she didn't step in a smelly puddle. "What about women?"

"I said they had the most beautiful women."

"That is not what I meant. Are there games of chance for women?"

"Not that I am aware of."

"Can a woman play with the men?"

"I have seen a few."

"Then I want to play."

Alexander's smile vanished. "It is no place for you, Lady Christin."

She looked at him as if his words meant nothing. "Even so, I would like to accompany you. It sounds like an exciting place."

"The Pox?" Peter said, aghast. "You cannot go there. Papa would eviscerate me if he knew I let you go into that place."

"He will not know," Christin said as she looked at her brother. "As long as a certain de Lohr sibling keeps *his* yap shut."

Alexander's words were reflected in her statement and, walking behind them, Bric and Kevin started to laugh. Peter turned, scowling at the pair.

"You think this funny, do you?" he demanded. "If she was *your* sister, would you find it so funny?"

"If she was my sister, I would throw her over my shoulder and cart her into The Duck and Dribble without delay," Bric said. "But, then again, my sisters have not learned to kill on command or function in a man's world. Lady Christin has."

Peter sighed sharply, looking at his sister. "You may *not* go to The Pox," he said. "It is not for you and if you go, I will tell Papa."

"How are you going to tell him and explain why I was in London in the first place?" Christin asked smoothly. "He will want to know because I am supposed to be safe back at Norwich right now. What will you tell him?"

Peter was licked. He knew that before the conversation ever really got going because what Christin wanted, she got. That had started in childhood. She was a most determined, cunning, and smart young lady. With her father's drive and her mother's intelligence, it was a combination that had put her where she was now. Christin had everything she ever wanted, and if she wanted to go to The Pox, Peter knew that, short of binding her to the bed and locking the door for good measure, she would go.

Therefore, this entire conversation was a losing battle. He thought that if she took in her fill of The Pox and saw what a nasty, dirty, corrupt place it was, she would forget all about wanting to play games of chance there.

Perhaps the only thing to do was let her see it.

"Very well," Peter said, frustrated. "If you want to go, then I will take you. But do not say I didn't warn you. It is no place for a woman."

Christin merely grinned at him before turning to Alexander. "Will you lead the way, my lord?"

Alexander looked at her like this was all a very bad idea. "Are you serious? We have explained to you that The Pox is not for a woman of your breeding."

Christin maintained her smile. She had her father's grin that saw the ends of her mouth turn up slightly, something very lovely and charming. It had been a gesture that had fooled many a man into thinking she was a sweet and innocent thing.

But that was not the case.

Headstrong didn't even begin to cover it.

"I appreciate your concern," she said. "Please do not bother, then. I can find it myself."

With that, she turned on her heel and headed south on the nearest street, one of the smaller alleyways that crisscrossed the city. As she darted down it, Peter ran after her and grabbed her by the arm simply to assert himself as her escort. He wasn't going to stop her.

With a shrug, Alexander, Bric, and Kevin followed.

CHAPTER TWO

THE POX WAS packed to the rafters.

Filled to the brim with mostly men but a few women, Christin took one look at the common room and thought it was all rather exciting. Every kind of human imaginable was there; men in tattered clothing, sitting on the floor with their drink because the tables were full, knights in expensive protection, and well-dressed merchants who had just come off of their cogs along the river. Serving wenches mingled among the tables, bringing food and drink.

It was a busy place.

A thin layer of blue smoke hung near the ceiling from two hearths that were blazing on this night as men huddled around tables, some only to eat, but some to roll dice or play cards. Stacks of hand-painted cards were on several of the tables, well-used wooden panels, as dealers shuffled and dealt them out to those willing to gamble on a game of chance.

Christin was fascinated by all of it. A wench passed her bearing trenchers that contained meat and vegetables, reminding her of how hungry she was. The games would have to wait. She turned to her brother.

"May we find a table?" she asked. "I would like to eat."

Peter had his eyes on everyone in the room, suspicious of every man regardless of dress or obvious wealth.

"Fine," he said shortly. "And then we will leave. Do you understand me?"

Christin nodded, but it was simply to appease him. Whether or not she would leave after she ate was still up for debate as far as she was concerned. She could see a mostly empty table midway deep in the room, against the wall, and she pointed to it.

"There," she said. "There is only one man at that table. Surely he will share it with us."

Before anyone could answer her, she charged off into the room. Peter rolled his eyes at his headstrong sister, but Alexander was right behind her. He wasn't going to let any lady move unescorted in this room because he knew what kind of men frequented this place. Before he could caution her, however, she spoke to the lone man at the table.

"May we share your table, good sir?" she asked politely. "The inn is very crowded tonight."

The man turned to look at her. He was older, dressed in outdated and damaged mail, with a well-used tunic that Alexander noticed before anyone else did. He recognized the red and gold standard of William d'Aubigney, an enemy of the crown and of William Marshal.

"I am waiting for my friends, girl," the man told Christin. "Find another table."

He was decidedly unfriendly and Christin opened her mouth to plead with him, but Alexander touched her on the arm, getting her attention. When she looked at him, he shook his head faintly and motioned her away. Curiously, she followed him.

"What is it?" she asked.

Alexander had her by the elbow now as if afraid she'd run back to the table. By this time, Peter and Bric and Kevin had caught up to them and Alexander sandwiched Christin between him and Peter.

"D'Aubigneys men are here," he said quietly. "I am not willing to face hostilities with your sister present."

Peter looked over his shoulder to the man bearing the d'Aubigney tunic. "I did not see him when we entered," he said. "We should leave."

Christin knew the name d'Aubigney and she further knew that he was an enemy of William Marshal and his allies. Though she very much wanted to remain and enjoy this terrible and interesting place, she'd been in The Marshal's service long enough to know what enemies meant to one another, especially enemies of William Marshal. She'd seen it too many times before.

In truth, she was a little disappointed at having to depart so soon, but much like Alexander and Peter, she didn't want a fight. Too many men with too many weapons could spell disaster, especially in these turbulent days. So without an argument, she let Peter take hold of her and head for the entry. She'd have to return to The Pox at another time. They were halfway to the door when someone grabbed her arm, yanking her away from Peter.

"C'mon, lass!" A very drunk man had her by both arms. "Give us a dance!"

Peter was on the man in a second, driving his fist into the man's face. As he fell back, Peter yanked Christin from the man's grip.

"Go," he commanded. "Quickly. To the door."

Christin began to move swiftly, but it was difficult given that the inn was so packed. She ended up shoving people out of her way, kicking one slow-moving man in the arse. Just as she reached the door, the panel flew open and several heavily-armed men entered.

Christin, being that she was in the front of their group, saw the men first. She noticed that they were wearing the same tunics as the man they had so recently turned away from. *D'Aubigney.* Christin came to a halt but before she could say anything, the knight in the front spied Bric, whom he evidently knew.

And didn't like.

"MacRohan!" he roared. "You foul Irish bastard! I told you what would happen if I saw you again!"

Christin didn't have time to step out of the way before the unruly knight shoved her aside, using his arm in a big sweeping motion that shot her over a table and saw her crashing to the floor on the other side.

Horrified, Peter couldn't go to her aid because he found himself swept up in an attack by at least six d'Aubigney knights.

It was a brawl of epic proportions from the start.

As Christin struggled to her knees, shaking off the stars dancing before her eyes, everyone in the front section of the inn began screaming and running. Christin ended up rolling under a table, gripping the legs for dear life as people scattered all around her. The table was hit a few times, buffeted from side to side as the floor cleared.

But after that, she was up.

Six against four was nearly fair odds in d'Aubigney's favor. Already, three enemy knights were down as Kevin, Bric, and Alexander pummeled those trying to attack them. Without a fight of his own for the moment, as he had already dispatched one man, Peter headed in Christin's direction.

"Are you hurt?" he asked her in a panic.

Christin shook her head. "Of course not," she said. Then, her eyes widened. "Look! That knight has thrown something into Alexander's face! He's blinded!"

Before Peter could stop her, she grabbed one of the chairs around the table and rushed to the knight trying to kill Alexander, swinging it with all her might against the back of his skull. When that only made him falter, she leapt on his back, grabbing her pretty bejeweled dagger from its sheath at her waist and plunging it into the man's neck.

Down he went and Christin right along with him. Alexander was on his feet now, using the edges of his tunic to wipe the hot wine out of his eyes. When the vision in one eye cleared, he could see Christin removing her dagger from the man's neck.

"Bloody Christ," he muttered, pulling her to her feet. "My lady, did you do that?"

She nodded without hesitation. "He was going to kill you," she said. "Look in his left hand. I saw the flash of a dagger. If the sword did not kill you, the dagger would as you tried to clear your vision. He was coming at you with both hands armed, my lord."

Blinking his stinging eyes, Alexander could, indeed, see that the man had a weapon in each hand. He wasn't entirely sure the man would have killed him, but he was still having difficulty with his vision, so it would have been a problematic battle.

Perhaps he might have, indeed, found himself in trouble.

But it was a battle that a brave lass had quickly ended. When Alexander should have been grossly irritated, he found that he couldn't muster the will. He found himself looking into Christin's doll-like face and seeing utter calm there. No hysteria, no fear. Simply the expression of one who did what needed to be done, just like she'd done with the French king's spy. Truly, it was remarkable for a woman to be so composed in the face of death.

A seed of respect for her sprouted.

"Are you well, Sherry?" Bric, winded, came up beside him. "We should leave. *Now.*"

Alexander was still wiping his face and eyes, but he was already heading for the door. "We shall return another day when the company in this place is better," he said. "Let us depart."

He was through the entry when he realized he had Christin by the wrist, pulling her along to ensure she followed him and didn't somehow rush back in and start braining men. He wouldn't have put it past her, courageous as she was. Peter was right behind his sister, followed by Bric and finally Kevin covering their rear.

Once outside in the damp night air with the smell of fish and the river heavy in the air, Alexander let go of Christin when he realized he probably should.

"Take your sister and go, Peter," he said. "We will meet you at the livery across from The Duck and Dribble at dawn, so be ready to depart."

Peter had hold of Christin, much like Alexander, as if afraid she might run off to do battle again. "Come with us," he said. "London abounds with danger tonight, Sherry. We should stay together."

Alexander waved him off. "If there are more d'Aubigney knights, I will keep them off your tail," he said. "Take the lady and hurry. Get into a room at the inn and remain there. I will be on the streets tonight, making sure no danger follows you."

Peter nodded and hurried off, towing Christin by the arm. But her gaze was on Alexander, and his on her, and for a moment, they couldn't seem to tear their attention off one another. There was just something about the woman that made Alexander take a second look. He only pulled his attention from her when Bric and Kevin came up on either side of him.

"Let's get out of here," Bric said. "I think the only knight killed is the one Lady Christin took down, so his friends will be out for revenge."

Alexander knew that. "That one is a spitfire," he said, shaking his head. "I've never liked working with a woman other than Susanna, but de Lohr's sister... I've not yet decided."

"She probably saved your life," Kevin said. "You were in no position to fight that knight as he took the offensive. I tried to get to you but I had my own problems."

Alexander lifted a dark eyebrow. "I was in perfect control," he said, which was probably true. Alexander was always, and completely, in control. "And no woman is ever going to save my life. Come on, now. We need to separate. Bric, you take the wharf. Kevin, get over to Bridge Street but stay out of sight, both of you. When d'Aubigney's men move, see where they're going and make sure they stay away from The Duck and Dribble. As for me... I'm going in through the rear of The Pox. I'll watch them from there."

They had their directives, so they began to move. The primary objective was simply to make sure the d'Aubigney men remained away from Farringdon House and the inns up on Ropery Street. Truth be told, Alexander might have agreed that Christin had saved his life because he'd been in a bit of a bind, but no one else needed to know that. To them, the man they knew as Sherry was never in trouble.

Except he might have been.

Saved by a slip of a woman who looked like an angel.

No matter how much he fought them off, thoughts of Christin de Lohr and her fearsome courage poked at him all night.

CHAPTER THREE

On the road to Norwich Castle

THE FIRST DAY'S journey to Norwich had been long and wet thanks to a series of storms that had blown in from the east. The roads had been marred with holes and puddles, the horses up to their ankles in mud.

It made for slow going.

But Christin didn't say a word about the discomfort of the icy conditions or vertical rain. Not a gasp, a sneeze, or a complaint as she plodded along on her robust warmblood with Alexander, Peter, Bric, and Kevin. The knights were dressed in full armor, including mail which became soaked, and by nightfall when they stopped, the armor was cold and heavy with moisture. It was a most uncomfortable way to travel, but if they weren't complaining, then she wasn't going to, either.

Even if she *was* soaked to the skin.

In fact, she already felt as if she was on some kind of probation after the events of the past few days. First, she killed a French spy and at The Pox, she killed a man who had been trying to murder Alexander. She certainly didn't enjoy killing but she'd grown up around knights. She knew their code and their sense of honor, and if someone was trying to kill you or a friend, then you had every right to fight back. She'd seen that in her father and uncle too many times to count. Even her mother wasn't afraid to use a dagger if necessary.

Lady Dustin de Lohr had instilled that fearlessness in her daughter.

Still, Christin received the distinct impression that Alexander was irritated at her for killing his opponent.

The first day's journey began before dawn and ended just as the sun sank below the western horizon. The rain had started to fall again, gently this time, by the time they reached the village Peter had been planning on. He set his sights for an inn called The Buck and Boar.

It was a rather large establishment with three stories of whitewashed walls and brown cross-beam architecture. The second and third stories were larger than the first story, giving the building a substantial overhang onto the street.

Light emitted from the shuttered windows, giving the place a warm glow, as the five of them rode into the livery around the side. The livery was mostly full but a few coins from Peter had the livery master shoving horses out of the way to pull the big warhorses in so they could be dry. Confident the animals would be well-tended, the group entered the establishment through the rear kitchen yard.

The Buck and Boar was different from most inns in that it catered to a higher class of clientele. The serving wenches were dressed in clean clothing and were somewhat groomed, and the place didn't reek of the usual vomit and smoke and unwashed bodies. It smelled like fresh bread and baking apples.

It smelled inviting.

Even the common room was different. There was a small common area with tables and chairs that were in good repair, a massive hearth that was blazing against the wet night, and several alcoves that had tables and chairs, lamps for light, and curtains that could be closed for privacy.

Peter led them into one of those secluded alcoves that could accommodate at least eight people. In this alcove were a clean table, two lamps, and an iron brazier with glowing coals to warm the area. There was even a window with precious diamond-glass panes looking out over an alley, but part of the window was open to let out the fumes from the brazier. As soon as the group entered the alcove and began settling in, serving women came on the run.

Rags to dry off with were brought along with hot wine. The knights began to strip off their tunics to let them dry in the warmth of the room but they stopped short of removing mail or any protection. When in a public place, they maintained their uniform appearance at all times, especially for protection.

But for Christin, it was different.

No protection and no armor meant she was soaked through to the skin. As the knights dried off, she sat as close to the brazier as she could get, removing her cloak and gloves, wringing out the skirts of her traveling dress and hoping the heat would dry it somewhat. She was shivering, and her teeth were chattering, and she was quite certain that her lips were blue, so she kept her head down so no one would notice. Peter handed her a cup of hot wine, but she kept her head down as she accepted it so he wouldn't see her face.

The food began to come. Stewed beef, an onion tart, a pottage of cabbage and turnips, plus bread and butter and stewed fruit. It was a veritable feast and the knights sat down, taking the flat trenchers provided and filling them from the bowls of steaming food.

Christin sat on the end, next to the brazier still, and remained quiet as the men served themselves. She was so determined not to be a bother that all of the food except for the bread was gone before the men realized she had absolutely nothing. Chagrinned, it was Alexander who rose from his seat and went to the kitchens, demanding more food for the lady since she had been cheated out of a meal by four hungry men.

Christin could hear him in the kitchens, barking.

"What is he doing?" she hissed at Peter. "He does not need to go through so much trouble."

"Let him," Bric said from across the table, mouth full. "If you give him a free rein long enough, he may very well end up confiscating this entire inn just for you."

His pale blue eyes twinkled as he said it, leading Christin to believe that he was jesting with her for the most part, but given Alexander's reputation, there was probably some truth to it.

"That is truly not necessary," she said. "I did not mean for him to go to the trouble. I could have easily gone to the kitchens myself."

Bric shook his head, shoving more food into his mouth. "Do you not know when a man is being polite to you?"

Christin looked at Peter, who simply lifted his shoulders. "I fear that she does not," he said, answering Bric. "She has fostered in the finest homes, trained with the finest teachers, but she is the kind of woman who would rather do for herself. Chivalry does not mean very much to her."

"That is every man's dream," Bric snorted. "Every man dreams of a woman who does not make demands of him. Lady Christin, you should fetch the best husband in all of England with that attitude. In fact, if I thought your father would not grind me into mincemeat, I might offer for you myself."

Christin flushed a dull red, embarrassed by such talk even though she knew he was teasing her. "And what would you do with me?" she asked. "Keep me locked up at Narborough? I do not suppose you would let me continue serving The Marshal."

Bric looked at her as if she had gone mad. "Never," he declared. "The woman I marry will know her place and that will be to make *me* happy. And anything else I can think of."

He exaggerated his heavy Irish accent, which made it both humorous and threatening. As he chuckled at his own wittiness, Christin went along with his joke.

"Then God help the woman you marry if that is as much as you think of her," she said. "Women have minds and opinions, you know. They do very well for themselves."

Bric pointed his knife at her as he chewed. "You are an exception," he said. "But, then again, you are a de Lohr. The entire family is full of exceptional people. But women, for the most part, are cattle. They want to be herded, fed, kept warm and safe. Once in a while, they do something useful."

He and Kevin laughed in agreement. Even Peter grinned until Christin pinched him. "Ouch!" he yelled, rubbing his arm as he looked at her. "What was that for?"

"For concurring with them," she said, lifting an eyebrow in a gesture that looked very much like her mother. "You think more of women than they do – *right*?"

Peter made a face at her but didn't answer, fearful of another pinch. He continued eating as Alexander returned to their table with two serving wenches in tow. The women had two big trenchers full of food and both of them ended up in front of Christin.

Her eyes widened.

"That is a great deal of food," she said, looking to Alexander. "Truly, my lord… you did not need to go to the trouble, but I am most appreciative."

Alexander eyed her a moment before digging into his own food. "It is the least I can do for the woman who saved my life," he said. Then, he looked at the others. "There are three rooms on the top floor and I have confiscated all of them. One is for the lady and the other two are for us. Peter, you and I shall share a chamber because I do not wish to be kept up all night by Bric's snoring. And if you snore, I shall throw you out of the window."

Peter snorted in reply, shoveling food into his mouth just like they all were. Even Christin began to eat the stewed beef and carrots boiled in vinegar and cinnamon, but she was still so cold and so wet that she shivered the entire time. The hot food helped but with her wet clothing, even the heat from the brazier against her amounted to little more than hot, damp clothing. She was just drinking the last of her hot wine when she heard Alexander's voice.

"Peter," he said quietly. "Look at your sister."

Christin's head shot up, looking at her brother with wide eyes, wondering why on earth Alexander should say such a thing. Even Peter looked at her curiously, his mouth still full of food.

"Why?" he finally asked.

Alexander set down the cup in his hand. Those dark eyes were fixed on Christin as he stood up and came around the table. She was looking at him with great curiosity, and perhaps even some fear, when he reached out and lifted her left arm by the wrist.

"Feel her clothing," he said. "The woman is soaked to the skin and none of us has noticed."

Peter looked at Christin in horror, touching her sleeve and even her skirts. Alexander was absolutely correct; she was soaked.

"Why didn't you tell me?" he demanded. "You are going to catch your death."

Christin looked at him, at the others, contritely. "It is nothing of concern, truly," she said. "I am sitting by the fire. I will dry out."

Peter didn't believe that for a moment. "You are going to get sick and Mother will blame *me*. You really should have told me, Cissy."

He started to get up so he could tend to her, but Alexander shoved him down by the shoulder.

"Sit and finish your meal," he said. "I am finished already. I will see to our martyr."

With that, he crooked a finger at Christin, motioning for her to come with him. She was on her feet in an instant, grabbing her satchel and her wet cloak as she followed Alexander from the alcove and into the common room beyond. She trailed behind the man as he moved through the inn, towards the stairs that led to the upper floors, snapping orders to the serving wenches as he went. He ordered a bath and more food to be taken up to the lady's chamber.

Although Christin wasn't one to let men that she didn't know take charge of her, Alexander was different. It wasn't as if she had any choice; he was leading and there was nothing she could do to stop him.

But it was more than that.

She'd been in awe of the man from the moment she met him and, if she was being perfectly honest with herself, she was flattered that he would take the time to assist her. He made her heart flutter, just a little, and speaking to the man made her feel the least bit jittery. Completely out of character for the normally confident young woman who had never met a man yet who intimidated or interested her.

But Alexander de Sherrington had... and did.

Even as she walked behind him, she found herself looking at the sheer size of the man. He was tall, though she'd seen taller, but the width of his shoulders and the size of his arms had her attention. There was enormous physical power there. She wasn't even really listening to what he was saying. All she could think of was the fact that she was walking with Alexander de Sherrington.

Sherry.

Aye, she was starstruck.

She could admit it.

Alexander took the stairs to the second floor and Christin followed closely behind. Once they got to the landing, there was a smaller staircase that led to the third floor, a staircase that seemed to lean slightly, and they took that one to the top floor. Once there, Alexander took her to the smaller chamber that overlooked the stable yard.

There was already a fire in the hearth because the room was rented for the night and the servants had prepared the chamber. There was even a warming pan for the bed propped up against the hearth. Alexander entered the room and lit the taper that was on the small table next to the hearth, bringing more light into the space. The warm glow made it feel safe and cozy as the storm raged outside.

"You should be comfortable here," he said, looking around the chamber. "They are bringing you a hot bath and wine. Is there anything else you need?"

He was being quite attentive and Christin wasn't sure why. "If there is, I can send for it," she said. "Truly, you needn't have gone through so much trouble. I am sorry to have taken you away from my brother and your friends."

"It was no trouble," he said, his gaze finally falling on her. He gestured to her clothing. "You had better get out of those wet things immediately."

"I will, thank you," she said. "I am ashamed to have been such a bother. You may go if you wish. I can take care of myself."

"Are you trying to rid yourself of me?"

She looked stricken. "Nay," she said. "'Tis simply that I feel as if I have been trouble to you from the outset. I do not wish to be any further inconvenience."

He cocked his head. "Outset? Explain."

She gestured in a general southerly direction. "At Ramsbury," she said. "And then in London. Truly, my lord, I am very sorry if I offended you by dispatching your opponent at The Pox. It's just that you had wine in your eyes and I could see that… well, I thought that he had you at a disadvantage. Just for the moment, of course. I only wished to help."

Those dark eyes took on a glimmer. Looking behind him, he noted a chair and planted his big body on it. With the door open, and Christin still standing in doorway, there was nothing improper about him remaining, at least for the moment.

"Firstly, there will be no more of this nonsense with a formal address," he told her in a rumbling tone, though not unfriendly. "My friends call me Sherry. Since you have killed on my behalf, I will grant you that privilege. It is the least I can do."

Christin's pale cheeks flushed in the dim light. "Thank you, my… I mean, thank you," she said. "I am honored that you would consider me a friend. Well, not a friend. A comrade. Oh… not a comrade, either. God's Bones… I don't know what I am, but thank you, anyway."

By the time she was finished, he was grinning at her with those big, white teeth set against the black beard. "You are a female associate," he said. "There is only one other female I will allow to call me Sherry. You know Susanna de Dere, of course. She is the only other one. I like the woman."

"So do I."

"And she likes you," Alexander said. He settled back in the chair, folding his enormous arms over his chest as he gave her an appraising look. "Tell me about yourself, Lady Christin de Lohr. I know your father well, and your uncle, but I have only heard about you."

"What have you heard?"

His smile broadened. "That you are flawless in whatever you do, a true de Lohr to the bone. Had you been born a man, you would have been a magnificent knight."

A smile creased her lips. "That is the greatest compliment anyone could have paid me. Thank you."

"It is true, or so I have been told. But from what I have seen in the short time we have been associated, I believe the rumors."

The servants picked that moment to bring in the big, copper tub and all of the accompaniments, including buckets of hot water, a stool, and drying linens. Christin was forced to move out of their way, which put her next to Alexander. He pulled out a chair for her as the hot bath was prepared.

"You may as well sit," he said, watching her perch on the edge of the chair in her wet clothing. "You have not answered my question."

"What question?"

"Tell me about yourself."

Christin set her satchel on the table. "There is not much to tell," she said. "My life has been unremarkable. I fostered at Thunderbey Castle."

"That is East Anglia."

"Correct," she said. "Dashiell du Reims' father is the Earl of East Anglia. They are cousins to the House of de Lohr, you know. My grandmother was the sister to Dashiell's grandfather, Tevin du Reims."

Alexander nodded. "I remember hearing that," he said. "So you fostered at Thunderbey. Did you enjoy it?"

She nodded. "It was my home for about five years. I loved it there."

"Did they teach you the common female pursuits, or were you out in the yard with the men learning to fight with swords because you are a de Lohr?"

He meant it as a joke and she grinned, displaying her father's curvy smile. "They would not let me learn to fight with a sword."

"Did you try?"

"What do you think?"

He laughed softly. "I think you tried," he said, sobering. "Did you learn anything?"

"I learned enough until the earl's wife forced me to stop."

"It is their loss. But the skills I've witnessed go beyond just a few lessons. Who taught you?"

"My father, mostly."

"He taught you well."

"That may be, but he does not know that I use what he taught me."

Alexander nodded. "I know," he said quietly. "I was told your father does not know who you truly serve."

Christin nodded, watching the servants put the last bucket of hot water in the tub. They were keeping their voices low, and their words cryptic, so those around them wouldn't hear. She had learned long ago that men, and women, in the vocation of espionage don't live long if they speak openly about it.

She'd learned to hide her profession.

"It's strange, really," she said. "From the moment I began this journey, I have felt as if I belong here. As if it is what I was always meant to do. I know that sounds odd coming from a woman, but I feel as if I am accomplishing something that few women can claim."

Alexander could see the contentment in her face as she spoke. There was something about Christin de Lohr that seemed to transcend normal womanhood. Certainly, she was beautiful. Absolutely stunning. But there was steely strength below the surface. She was no simple lady, content with the role society demanded of her.

Quite the contrary.

He rather liked that.

"That is because you are," he said as the last servant left the chamber, taking the buckets with him. "It is good that you realize that. It means you will never take it for granted. You will always respect the privilege you have been given."

Christin nodded, grinning bashfully as she realized he understood exactly what she'd been trying to verbalize. She further realized that she had taken enough of the man's time.

"Forgive me," she said. "I must sound foolish. A man like you has better things to do than listen to my ramblings."

"It's not often I hear ramblings. Coming from you, it's not so bad."

Her grin turned into a giggle and she looked away, absolutely mortified that her cheeks were starting to flame again.

"Well," she said, "you have been kind, anyway. You did not have to give me your time or your attention. I am sure you would rather be with your friends downstairs."

He shrugged, lifting those big shoulders. "I already know all there is to know about them," he said. "Since you and I have seen action together twice, I thought I should come to know a little about you, too. If The Marshal permits you to serve him, then clearly, you are extraordinary."

He was showing interest in her, which was thrilling. She tried not to read too much into it, telling herself that he was only being polite. She couldn't bring herself to even consider that it might be something more.

"We are to see more action in the coming days at Norwich," she said, changing the subject because his personal questions had her uncertain. "With the king coming, it should prove… interesting."

Alexander's gaze lingered on her for a moment. He couldn't help but notice she didn't seem to want to talk about herself more than she already had, which was disappointing. Therefore, he did the polite thing and went with her change of focus.

"Have you been around the king at all?" he asked. "I mean, have you met the man personally?"

She nodded. "When I was young," she said. "I was with my father when we went to London and I met John then, but I have only seen him occasionally since. We've had no contact other than that."

Alexander sighed faintly. "You know that he has an eye for beautiful women, don't you?"

"Why should that concern me?"

"Because you are astonishingly beautiful. That will not escape his notice."

She looked at him in surprise. So the man thought she was beautiful, did he? The entire conversation had been peppered with what could easily be construed as compliments and Christin was genuinely at a loss how to respond. Either Alexander was free with meaningless flattery or he truly meant what he was saying. She hoped it was the latter. Given that she had no idea how to respond, the flush in her cheeks was back with a vengeance.

"I am no one of consequence," she said. "I do not care what he thinks."

Alexander looked at her seriously. "You cannot possibly mean that," he said, his voice low. "Surely you know that if the king sees a woman he fancies, he has been known to claim her. For his bed, I mean. It does not matter if the woman is married to an ally or the daughter of an enemy. If the king demands you warm his bed, there will be trouble."

Christin had heard that, of course. She knew what Alexander meant from the beginning. But given her status as a Marshal agent, she wasn't worried about it. Foolishly, she was confident that she would remain untouched and unnoticed.

"He will not touch me," she said with confidence. "My father will have something to say about that and he does not wish to provoke Christopher de Lohr."

Alexander lifted his eyebrows. "Mayhap," he said. "The king has a healthy fear of your father and for good reason, but still… you must take precautions. Try to stay out of his sight and never allow yourself to be alone with him. This is for your safety, my lady. If the king moves for you, there is little the rest of us can do to defend you."

"I can use a dagger. And I will."

"On the king?" Alexander shook his head. "William Marshal has spent years keeping that man alive, so you cannot use a dagger on him. You cannot kill him. If you did... the consequences to you and your family would be unfathomable. You would destroy everything your father and uncle have worked so hard for. Do you understand me?"

She looked at him with those pale gray eyes, eyes that could easily bring a man to his knees. Perhaps she knew she had the power; perhaps not. Alexander could feel the power radiating from those eyes as surely as he could breathe air. After a moment, she simply nodded.

"I do," she said. "But I could not surrender to him, in any case. I *would* not.'"

Alexander believed her implicitly. "Then that is why you must stay out of his sight," he said. "We have much to do at the gathering in Norwich and I know you do not wish to be a distraction."

"Not at all."

"Good," he said. Then, it occurred to him that those in the common room would be wondering where he was. He'd been so swept up in the conversation that he'd lost track of time and he quickly stood up. "Forgive me. I have been talking up a storm while you continue to sit in wet clothing. I will take my leave of you now. We will see you on the morrow for another thrilling day of traveling to Norwich. I am purely giddy with the thought."

His sense of humor was droll, and quite charming, and Christin stood up with a grin on her lips. "As am I," she said. "More wet roads and rainstorms. I can hardly stand the anticipation."

Alexander laughed softly. "Then we understand one another."

"We do. And Sherry?"

He paused by the door. "Aye?"

She scratched her chin nervously. "Since you have given me permission to address you informally, I must reciprocate. Please, call me Christin."

A smile flickered on his lips. "I am deeply honored," he said. "But I heard Peter address you as something else."

Her brow furrowed briefly until she realized what he meant. "Oh," she said. "*That*. Growing up, my younger siblings had a difficult time pronouncing Christin, so it came out as Cissy. That is what my family calls me – Cissy."

"May I?"

The request had her heart fluttering again. "If you wish."

"I do."

With that, he quit the chamber and shut the door, leaving Christin standing by the hearth, biting her lip because the smile on her face threatened to split it in two. She hadn't really been looking forward to the journey back to Norwich, but now she was.

Definitely… she was.

CHAPTER FOUR

H E WAS TRYING very hard not to look at her.

They were a day out of Norwich on their journey north and Alexander had never wanted a long, insufferable trip to keep going so much in his entire life.

God, he was losing his mind.

Something both frightening and wonderful was happening to him.

Since that night at The Buck and Boar, Alexander looked at Christin differently. Or perhaps it had started even before that, when he'd entered de Vaston's great solar and saw her covered with blood and a dead woman at her feet. Even then, she'd been as composed as any seasoned knight. Perhaps his notice of a strong young woman had started then.

But now, it was growing stronger.

In order to keep his attention off of her because he was fearful that Peter might catch on to his interest in her, he'd kept away from her after that first night. The trip from London to Norwich was usually a five-day trip, depending on the weather and any number of factors, but they'd made good time in spite of the rain that had come in waves.

Alexander had ridden at the head of their escort, keeping conversation to a minimum since chatty knights tended to be less in tune with their surroundings and potential threats. Therefore, travel was quiet, with Christin positioned between her brother and Bric, with Kevin watching their backs. Every so often, Alexander would hear Christin and Peter conversing quietly. Then he'd turn around, casually, and glance at the dark-haired beauty. Most of the time, she would smile politely at him. But he wouldn't smile in return. He would face forward before he'd let a smile play on his lips.

That had been the second day.

They'd spent the night at an inn that wasn't nearly the glory of The Buck and Boar, traveled all the next day in a driving rainstorm, and then spent that night in the common room of a tavern that was so full, people were sleeping in the kitchens.

It hadn't been ideal.

Alexander had remained away most of the night while Christin slept and the knights rotated in and out of sleep, keeping vigilant watch until an hour before dawn when Christin awoke and insisted on taking her turn at the watch. Alexander had declined, but she'd pressed, until finally he pretended to sleep simply to please her. She'd spent the time watching the room like a hawk, her bejeweled, sharp dagger in her hand.

He'd spent the time watching her through slit lids.

Now, they would be arriving at Norwich by nightfall and he was sorry to see it end. Once they reached Norwich, his chances to see her or speak with her would be few and far between, although he didn't know why he was worrying about it considering he'd barely spoken to her since The Buck and Boar.

Now, he was coming to regret that decision in the slightest.

The day, surprisingly, was one without rain. A bright, blue sky reigned overhead with puffy white clouds pushed along by the breeze. There was a chill to the air, however, but there was enough sun and wind to dry out the roads a little, making them somewhat easier to travel on. They'd made good time on this day, coming into the outskirts of Norwich proper as they entered a village without an official name, but the locals called it Stratton.

The daughter of the richest merchant in town had been married earlier in the day and the entire village had been invited to the feast. People were out in droves, drinking and laughing, and as the five of them headed into the heart of the village, they could see that great tables of food and drink had been laid out all over the square.

On a grassy area near the well, they had two giant spits going with two big sides of beef, and an entire area in the center of town was dedicated to barrels upon barrels of ale. The entire town seemed to be wildly drunk, which was quite amusing. They had garlands in their hands of autumn greenery, mostly evergreen branches woven with purple asters. A group of giggling young women handed a garland to Christin, who didn't look quite sure what to do with it.

"Put it on your head," Alexander told her. "It is a celebration."

She looked at him, smiling wanly as she pulled off the hood of her cloak and put the purple flower garland on her head.

Alexander's willpower to leave her alone fled.

She looked like an angel with the flowers around her dark hair, which was braided and draped over one shoulder. Alexander grinned at her, the first smile in days, and his gaze lingered on her a little longer than it should have. Realizing that he was looking at her like a besotted fool, he quickly shifted his focus and looked to the others in their group.

"Would you turn down free food and drink?" he asked them. "We have made excellent time to Norwich and, even now, the castle is less than an hour away. Mayhap we could all do with some frivolity before the seriousness begins."

Peter was already sliding off of his horse, followed by Kevin. Bric seemed a little more reluctant because he wasn't one for frivolity, but free drink was enough of a lure. With a heavy sigh, he dismounted his horse, taking the reins from Peter and Kevin, as they were nearly pawing the ground in their haste to get to the food, women, and drink. Once he took their horses, they ran off into the crowd.

"I will take your horses and sell them," Bric called after them. When there was literally no response from the overeager knights, Bric shook his head. "Oh, to be young and foolish."

Alexander dismounted and behind him, so did Christin. "Mayhap," Alexander said. "I think it is more that there is so little time for merriment given the tasks we undertake that any chance for it has us reliving our youth. There is little time for anything but duty in our lives these days."

Bric understood that. Given that he served de Winter at Narborough, he had a little more time away from William Marshal than most of them, so he forced himself to be tolerant. The crusty Irishman had that capacity, sometimes. Taking the reins of Alexander's horse and Christin's horse, he headed off towards the livery at the edge of the village.

That left Alexander standing with Christin as they watched the party going on around them. He could see her in his periphery, standing there with the garland of purple flowers around her head, and he realized that he wasn't sorry at all that Peter had run off and left his sister alone.

She wasn't alone at all, fortunately for him.

He turned to her.

"My lady?" he said, offering her his elbow. "Shall we find the food and drink?"

Christin looked at him with some hesitation, an expression that turned to confusion when he smiled at her encouragingly.

"You... want me to go with you?" she asked.

"And why not?"

Her well-arched eyebrows lifted. "Because..." she began, then trailed off. "My lord, did I do something to anger you?"

He lowered his elbow. "Why on earth would you think that?"

"Because you spent the past three days ignoring me and behaving as if I had upset you," she said frankly. "I assume you are speaking to me again? If that is the case, I must apologize for whatever I did."

He knew exactly what she meant and confusion began to swamp him. He thought he'd been quite neutral in his behavior towards her other than the fact he wouldn't look at her, but as bright as she was, she noticed. And she'd been thinking about it, concerned that she had angered him somehow. That made him suspect that, perhaps, she might be thinking of him beyond a simple working associate and that's what he didn't want.

... but he did.

God help him, he did.

"You have done nothing," he said quietly, with some resignation. "It is simply that my mind has been... elsewhere. I am sorry if you thought I was angry with you."

Relief filled her features; he could see it. "I am very glad to hear that," she said. "I thought I had said something to upset you."

"You could not upset me, I assure you."

She nodded her head in the direction of the partygoers. "Then I will find food and drink with you," she said. "And if you are not upset with me, mayhap you will tell me more of yourself. The last time, we spoke of me. This time, we shall speak of you."

His lips twisted unhappily. "Must we?"

"Is your life so boring that I will be in tears, begging you to shut your mouth?"

He burst into laughter. The elbow extended again. "We shall find out."

With a grin, Christin took his elbow, following him into a crowd that was quite drunk. There were big barrels of ale that had been brought out for the occasion and Alexander took two very large cups of ale from the man doling out the drink, handing one over to Christin. She took it, taking a big gulp of it and coughing because it was quite strong. But she took another drink because she was thirsty. Alexander laughed softly at her sputtering reaction to the ale, taking his own swallow and nearly choking on it himself. He made a face but they continued on to the food.

To their right, two dozen villagers were engaging in a dance that had the women in a circle in the middle and the men in a circle on the outside. There was a group of minstrels on instruments that needed to be tuned, but they were playing lively music. Before them was one long table comprised of several pushed together, all of the tables filled with food.

There was roast beef, pies with more meat and carrots and apples, stuffed eggs, a variety of breads, and little puddings with honey and butter drizzled on them. They ended up standing at the table and just eating off it rather than grabbing food and going somewhere to share the bounty. Christin was fond of the stuffed eggs while Alexander tore off big hunks of the beef. For every egg she ate, she downed a big swallow of that strong, terrible ale.

"Now that I know you are not angry with me," she said, mouth full, "will you tell me of Alexander the Great?"

He had to swallow the massive bite in his mouth before he could speak. "Who has called me that?"

"No one. Just me. But based upon your reputation, I am quite certain it is the truth."

He smirked. "Very funny," he said. "What do you wish to know?"

Christin took another bite of her egg as she gazed up at him quite openly. "Well," she said thoughtfully, "where were you born?"

"At a place called Ashdown," he said. "It is my family's home."

"Where is it?"

"Near Warminster," he said. "My family is a very old one. We were here before the Normans came but I had a very wise ancestor who married his daughter to a Norman lord, so we were able to keep our lands and our homes."

Christin was listening with great interest. "Does your family still live at Ashdown?"

"Indeed. My father does, anyway."

"No brothers?"

Alexander nodded. "I had two," he said. "They were both killed on Richard's Crusade."

"I see," she said, sympathy in her expression. "I am sorry if it is painful to speak of them. I did not mean to bring up sad memories."

He looked at her, warmth glimmering in his dark eyes. "You did not," he said. "It is no longer painful to speak of them, though the sorrow for their passing is still there. It will always be there. My father entrusted me to take care of my brothers and I failed, so I have not been home in many years."

There was a hint of something darker, sadder, in that comment, but Christin wasn't sure she should ask him any further questions about his family since it seemed to be a brittle subject.

"I could not imagine staying away from Lioncross Abbey," she said, drinking her ale. "I was born there, along with all of my siblings. My mother's family has lived there for centuries. They, too, are of Saxon blood."

"What is the family name?"

"Barringdon."

Alexander shoved more beef into his mouth. "I have met your mother," he said. "A beautiful woman. It is clear where you get your beauty."

So he was back to more flattery. Christin wasn't sure how to react and she could feel the familiar flush creep into her cheeks. She simply wasn't used to being paid a compliment and she abhorred the games of flirtation that men and women played. She'd witnessed enough of that at Thunderbey Castle, and at Norwich Castle, and she'd always ignored it. Any man who tried to flatter her was either verbally speared or disregarded. But she couldn't manage to do either with Alexander. All she could do was change the subject.

Again.

"My father fought with King Richard, too," she said. "Did you know my father in The Levant?"

Alexander nodded. "The Lion's Claw?" he said, speaking the nickname that Christopher had learned those years ago. "He was the king's champion. I have never seen a fiercer man, although your uncle was fairly fierce himself."

"That was so long ago," she said. "Well before I was born. You must have been very young."

He snorted. "I was," he said. "I had barely seen twenty years, but youth did not make me inexperienced. I had a great deal of experience even before I went to The Levant."

"Why?"

"Because I served John Marshal back then, who was William Marshal's older brother," he said. "I fostered at Marlborough Castle, a holding of the elder Marshal. When he was killed, I swore fealty to the king and went to The Levant."

She cocked her head thoughtfully. "If you were barely twenty years when you went to The Levant, that was almost twenty years ago," she said. "That makes you…"

"Old," he cut her off, grinning.

"And you have never married?"

His smile faded. "Nay," he said. "I have never had the time."

"Will you inherit Ashdown?"

"Someday."

"Then you should have an heir," she said firmly, looking around at all of the women with flowers in their hair. "I shall help you find a wife. Every man wants an heir."

He wasn't sure he wanted to discuss this subject, mostly because the only woman he was attracted to was standing next to him and he barely knew her. He didn't want to embarrass himself by saying the wrong things. To avoid that problem altogether, he simply shook his head.

"Thank you, but that is not necessary," he said. "When the time is right, I shall find my own wife."

"But you said yourself that you've not had the time," she said, swallowing more of that strong ale. "Look around you; there are many young maidens here that I am sure would make fine wives."

He laughed nervously, taking another gulp of that cheap ale, too, now because he needed it. He needed the fortification. She was pushing him into a corner and for a man who was always in control, always sure of everything in his life, he was feeling unsteady with the conversation.

But it wasn't just the subject.

He went to take another drink of the ale but realized he'd drained it. It was a very big cup. Christin had drained hers, too, and she was becoming quite animated. And pushy. It occurred to him that the strong ale was stronger than he thought because he felt like he did when he had four or five big cups of the more refined, better processed stuff.

Giddy.

God help him, he was tipsy.

"I do not want to talk about wives," he said. "Besides, it is unseemly for you and me to discuss such a thing. We are both unmarried. Did that not occur to you?"

She looked at him in horror. "Now you *are* angry with me."

"Nay, I am not, but no more talk of wives."

"I am sorry. I did not mean to be forward."

He shook his head, taking the cup out of her grip and setting it on the table. Then, he took her hand and began pulling her towards the dancing, something he would not have ordinarily done had he not been feeling his drink.

"Come," he said in a voice that could very easily be interpreted as seductive. "I wish to dance."

But Christin dug her heels in. "But there are many other young women who would love to dance with you."

"I do not want to dance with them."

"But I cannot dance!"

"All young women can dance."

"Please," she begged. "Truly, I would look like a clod out there. I have never been able to dance. I will only shame myself and you."

He wasn't listening to her, smiling as he pulled her into a group that had already started to dance. "Hush," he said quietly. "Look into my eyes; that's right. Look right at me. Do what I say and you shall dance beautifully."

Christin was terrified. Drunk and terrified, but thank God for the drink or else she wouldn't have been able to go through with it. She wanted to dance with him because she simply wanted to be near him. All of the resistance and inhibitions she had been feeling towards him now had an outlet and she gladly let them through. She let him put her palm up against his and pull her rather close.

"Now," he said softly. "Take a few steps back and then a few steps towards me again. That's right; well done, Cissy."

Cissy. She'd never heard her name sound so sweet. Coming from him, it sounded like the voice of angels. At that moment, Christin let everything go so she could experience something she never really had – dancing with, and being close to, someone she was attracted to. That had never happened before. Alexander had her dancing next to him, turning her around at the appropriate time to spin, then pulling her right back against him in beat with the music.

All the while, she began to giggle uncontrollably.

Once, she spun around and tipped over, falling into the woman next to her, who also laughed. Fortunately, they were all laughing, and Christin went back to Alexander, who put his arm around her waist and basically walked her through every step. She held on to him, fearful she was going to tip again, until she finally came to an unsteady halt and put her hands to her head.

"I am not usually so giddy or so clumsy," she said. "That terrible ale has made me drunk."

Alexander looked at her, amused. "It has," he said. "It has made everyone else drunk, too, including me. Whatever that drink was, it is was very strong."

"And terrible."

"*And* terrible."

"Can we dance some more, then? I fear being drunk is the only way I am brave enough to do it."

Alexander immediately put his arm around her waist again, turning her in beat with the music. At one point in the dance, the women broke off and went to the center of the dance area, looping arms and moving in a circle. Alexander had to walk Christin right up to the women so she could loop her arms, but the moment the circle started to move, she lost her balance and they ended up dragging her. Laughing hysterically, she simply lay in the dirt, staring up at the sky, as the circle moved around her.

"What's wrong with my sister?"

Alexander turned to see Peter standing next to him, a knuckle of beef in his hand, as he peered curiously at Christin laying in the dirt. Alexander pointed at her.

"She's drunk," he said. "She drank that bitter ale too fast and now she cannot keep her balance."

Once Peter realized what was going on, he started to laugh. "Good," he said flatly. "It is good to see her loosen up. Honestly, she's so serious all of the time. Jesus, Sherry, she's killing men as if she were born to do it. What maiden does that? She needs to get drunk and have some fun."

With that, Peter took a big bite from his beef knuckle and wandered off, leaving Alexander standing there, watching Christin as she tried to get up. But she couldn't seem to sit up, so she rolled into her belly and rocked onto her hands and knees. By that time, he pushed through the circle of women and lifted her up underneath her arms.

"Come along, my lady," he said. "Let's go find a place for you to sit down. Or lay down. Whichever you prefer."

Christin was still giggling as she tried to walk but she wasn't doing a very good job, so Alexander swept her up into his arms and carried her away from the dancing.

"Where are we going?" she asked, arms around his neck. "Truly, I am fine. I can walk."

She probably could, but Alexander thought she felt quite good in his arms so he didn't want to put her down.

"You must not drink very much, very often," he said.

They walked past the food table and Christin ended up hanging over his shoulder, watching the food longingly as Alexander walked further and further away.

"I am very careful with what I drink," she said. "Usually, it's watered down or boiled. But I was thirsty."

"I know," he said. "I saw."

She pointed to the food table as they moved away from it. "I want more of those eggs, please. Can we go back?"

Alexander saw a stone bench beneath a yew tree that was next to a small church. There were people around, but no one sitting on the bench, so he deposited her onto the cold stone surface.

"Sit," he commanded softly.

"But can I have more eggs?"

He put up his hands. "I will get you more eggs. You remain here. Do you understand?"

"I do."

He held a finger out to her, silently commanding her to remain where she was, as he headed back to the food table to collect more stuffed eggs. By the time he returned, both hands full of eggs, she was simply sitting there, staring off into space.

"Here are your eggs, my lady," he said. "Eat them in good health."

She looked at him before looking at the eggs. Taking one, she simply stared at it for a moment.

"May I ask you a question?" she said.

"Aye."

"Why are you being so nice to me?"

Alexander wasn't nearly as tipsy as she was, but tipsy enough to loosen his tongue. He sat down next to her, closer than he should have simply because he wanted to. He'd just spent the past several minutes watching a thoroughly charming and exceedingly beautiful young woman have the time of her life.

He was enchanted.

"Because."

"Because why?"

"Can't a man be nice to you without you asking him foolish questions?"

Christin looked at him in surprise. "I do not think so," she said seriously. "I think that I must know everything because no man has ever been truly nice to me."

"What is that supposed to mean?"

"Because of my father," she clarified. "He terrifies everyone and no man is brave enough to be nice to me. You heard Bric. He said that he might offer for me if he was certain my father would not grind him into mincemeat. That is very true, you know. My father chases all of my suitors away. Well, if I had any. No one will come near me."

Alexander still had eggs in his hand. She finished the one he'd handed her and now she took another from him.

"Not all of them," he muttered.

She had a mouth full of egg. "Who?" she demanded. "Do you know of someone he cannot chase away? It does not matter, anyway. I will be like you and Peter and Bric and the rest of them. I will be a career agent for William Marshal and I shall never marry. My work for him shall be my husband. Besides... no one wants to marry a woman who kills on command. Even I know that."

Alexander watched her stuff more egg into her mouth. "I think I may know one."

She stopped chewing, egg on her lips. "*Who?*"

"Finish your egg. When he is ready to tell you, he will."

Her eyes widened. "Do you actually know someone who might... well, God's Bones, man, who is it? Is it Bric? I do not want to marry that loud-mouthed Irishman. You can tell him I said that."

Alexander started to laugh. "Nay, it is not Bric, and I will not tell him what you said. It would hurt his feelings."

"Ha!" she said, biting into the last egg. "That is not possible."

"It is. He is very tender."

She started laughing, full mouth and all. But she stood up to brush the excess egg from her traveling coat and the moment she did so, she suddenly stopped chewing. As Alexander watched, she spun away from him, grabbed the tree, and proceeded to vomit out all of the egg and ale she'd been eating and drinking. It had been a horrific combination, anyway. All of it came spewing out until there was no more.

Embarrassed, Christin hugged the tree, trying to catch her breath, as Alexander stood up behind her.

"Breathe, Cissy," he said softly, putting a surprisingly gentle hand on her back. "Then sit back down. I will go find you some boiled fruit juice and some bread. That should help calm your belly."

Christin wiped her mouth with the back of her hand. She couldn't even reply to him. All of that lovely food and conversation had been destroyed in an instant, all because she wasn't used to such strong ale.

And she'd done it right in front of Alexander.

Mortified, and still drunk, she staggered off towards the church, hoping to find a dark, cool place to hide.

She could make it the rest of the way to Norwich on her own.

CHAPTER FIVE

The Royal Procession
Somewhere on the road to Norwich

IT SMELLED LIKE rain.

The sky was full of pewter-colored clouds and the road was already puddled from a rainstorm that morning. The trees were heavy with moisture and the foliage was thick all over the land.

The rainy season had started early in Norfolk, an area that seemed to have its own weather patterns that were separate from the rest of England. It could be a wild land, with dense forests and settlements that were still reflective of the Danes that used to populate the area. Some said there were doorways to other magical lands in Norfolk, through a stone ring or a fairy mound.

He didn't believe in magic doorways or mythical lands, but he knew that hell existed because he lived it every single day.

Sir Sean de Lara rode very close to John's carriage because that was his job. As the king's personal bodyguard, he maintained close physical proximity to the monarch at all times. The carriage was a heavily-fortified cab built on top of a wagon chassis, lined with iron and a reinforced door that nearly doubled the weight of the carriage itself. There were small slits up at the top of the cab for ventilation, but little more. They hardly emitted any light. Inside, it smelled like a pigsty because the king lived and ate and slept and pissed in it.

It wasn't the most pleasant form of transportation.

Sometimes John chose to ride like a mounted knight and in those instances, his escort moved much faster. But he'd wanted to take the carriage this time and it had been painfully slow going out of London on their way to Norwich Castle.

With the stormy weather, the roads had been rough and the heavy carriage fell into ruts, which exhausted the team of horses pulling it. There were six heavy-boned horses lugging that wagon and the days were cut short because they were often just too weary to continue.

In fact, in the last town, Sean had purchased two more big-boned horses so they could rotate out a pair and give them a rest. He'd always had a soft spot for horses, including the magnificent beast he owned, so he watched the carriage horses carefully and made sure they were well tended. Fortunately, the drivers were sympathetic and the horses were given massages and plenty of food when the entourage stopped for the night.

But it didn't make this journey any less difficult or taxing, for all of them.

Even now, Sean tried to stay upwind of the carriage as he rode. He could hear the king inside, playing a citole, a musical instrument he had no real talent for. He had two of his advisors in the carriage with him, including a Marcher lord, Evan Monnington. Monnington Castle and the Lords of Dorè were relatively small and insignificant Marcher lords who had been deeply allied with Christopher de Lohr in the past since their lordship bordered his lands.

But that all seemed to change three months ago when the old Lord Dorè passed away, leaving his young son, Evan, as his heir. Evan had barely seen eighteen years and had fostered in the finest homes but, from what Sean could see, he was an idiot. Now, he was as thick as thieves with John and Sean knew why – it was because John was hoping to glean information on de Lohr and also station crown troops very close to de Lohr's earldom.

The entire de Lohr alliance along the border was impenetrable, or at least it had been until Evan Monnington decided to become the king's pet. Unfortunately, the king hadn't much confided in Sean about what Evan had told him, so he could only guess. Even now, Evan was in the king's carriage, speaking on God only knew what.

Sean suspected he would find out soon enough, considering John couldn't keep a secret from him. Whatever it was, John liked to boast to Sean, his most trusted bodyguard and confidante. Advisors and courtiers came and went, but Sean remained constant.

The man known as the Lord of the Shadows.

Off to the east, a storm was brewing. They could hear the thunder and see flashes of lightning light up the sky. They could also see sheets of rain pummeling the earth, knowing that the storm would soon be upon them. There was a village up ahead, one that was fairly large, so they knew they could find shelter there for the men. The entire contingent, however, was looking to the east, wondering if they would be able to beat the storm.

That would have been a possibility had the carriage not slipped into another rut. The men knew the drill; as the drivers snapped the whips at the weary team of horses, two dozen men surrounded the wagon and pushed until it lurched out of the hole. By that time, the rain was starting to pelt them, meaning they'd be soaked by the time they reached the village.

But it couldn't be helped. Sean bellowed commands to get the army moving forward, hauling that dreadful carriage the last mile or so. As he fell in behind the carriage, keeping an eye on the axels, which seemed to be folding under the strain of the bad road, the fortified rear door opened, spilling out Monnington.

"De Lara!" he shouted over the rain that was beginning to pound. "His Grace wishes to speak with you!"

Sean wasn't particularly thrilled that Monnington addressed him so informally. The man hadn't earned the privilege. But he dutifully dismounted, handing the reins over to the nearest soldier before sloshing his way through the mud to the carriage. Sean was an enormous man, big and powerful and intimidating, far superior to the mortal men around him. Reaching the door, which was still swinging open as the carriage swayed, he heaved himself into the carriage.

The smell of urine and body odor hit him in the face and he fought off the urge to wrinkle his nose in disgust. But the Lord of the Shadows never outwardly reacted to anything. He was, if nothing else, enigmatic. It was part of his mystery.

The carriage before him contained a bed near the front, right behind the drivers, and then two cushioned benches on either side. There was one advisor sitting on the cushioned bench, looking ill because of the sway of the carriage, and the king in the bed at the front.

Bracing himself against the wall so he wouldn't fall, Sean made his way towards a man covered in furs against the cold weather. A short man but strong for his size, his auburn hair had mostly turned to gray and one droopy eyelid gave him a rather dense appearance, but there was nothing dense about him. He was clever, crafty, bold, and without boundaries of any sort, as he had proven many a time. King John of England had been raised with wolves and behaved like one. Every time Sean was summoned, he wondered what fresh new hell he was going to face.

John didn't keep him waiting.

"How long until we stop for the night?" John asked.

"The village of Scole is not too much further, your grace," Sean said. "About an hour."

John nodded, hitting his head against the side of the cab when the wagon lurched. He grunted unhappily, hand to his head.

"I think I shall ride tomorrow," he said. "The roads have not been kind to us."

Sean felt some relief in that directive. "Nay, your grace, they have not been," he said. "We can leave the carriage in Scole and move much swifter on horseback. We will collect it when we return to London."

John nodded, but it was an absent gesture, as if his mind were elsewhere. "Monnington and I were just discussing the coming festivities at

Norwich," he said. "It has been at least two years since we were last there."

"Two years last August, your grace."

John lay back on his cushions. "Norwich Castle has always been a particular favorite of mine," he said. "The only problem is that the House of de Winter has taken it over. It belongs to them more than it belongs to me."

"That is because your ancestor who came to these shores with the Duke of Normandy was given stewardship of the castle, your grace," Sean said. "The crown may hold Norwich, but it has never been out of de Winter hands. The only time it has even fallen was when the garrison was weakened by a disease that swept through it and the Earl of Norfolk was able to capture it when you and your brothers revolted against your father. Had the garrison been at full strength, it would have never been captured."

John lifted his shoulders. "It is of no matter now," he said. "It belongs to me. Or, to Old Daveigh de Winter. I could not take it back if I wanted to."

"That is true, your grace."

"At least I am paid well for the privilege of having de Winter as my steward."

"Aye, your grace."

John scratched his head thoughtfully. "Do you think all of the de Winter allies will be in attendance?"

Sean braced himself as the carriage bumped over a particularly bad rut. "I would think so, your grace. This is to be a very special feast in your honor."

"Du Reims? Summerlin? De Vaston? Even de Lohr?"

"More than likely, your grace."

"Those men are not my allies, you know."

Sean nodded. "It puts them in an awkward position, your grace," he said. "De Winter serves the crown but has always and historically been allied with those houses. With them attending this feast, it will be like attending a feast with a disagreeable old grandfather. You know you should go and tolerate him purely out of respect, but the awkwardness of the event is almost unbearable."

"And I am the old grandfather?"

"To them, I would imagine so, your grace."

John fell silent as he looked up at the ceiling, mulling over the situation. "Monnington told me something interesting," he said. "Christopher de Lohr's eldest daughter, Lady Christin, serves at Norwich."

A warning bell went off in Sean's head. Whenever John began to speak on women, there was usually trouble ahead, so he proceeded carefully with the conversation.

"I do not know, your grace," he said. "I do not bother myself with details that do not concern me."

It was a lie; he knew very well that it was true. Christin de Lohr did serve at Norwich Castle. But John was oblivious to the change in his tone.

"I have been thinking on something," the king said. "Monnington gave me the idea. Christopher de Lohr was my brother, Richard's, champion. In fact, he held the title of Defender of the Realm until my brother's untimely death. After that, he allied with me for a time but that relationship turned sour. I believe I know how to bring the man back into the fold."

"A brilliant idea, your grace?"

John rolled onto his side so he could face Sean. "I have a son in need of a wife."

Sean's eyebrows lifted. "Young Henry, your grace? But he is only six years of age."

John shook his head. "Not him," he said. "Robert."

Sean understood. Robert FitzRoy was the illegitimate son of the king, born almost thirty years before from the daughter of John's old tutor, Ranulf de Glanvil. Ranulf's daughter, the fair Isabella, had died in the birth and John's father had insisted the boy be raised as part of the royal household, so he'd had every advantage.

Another spoiled Plantagenet offspring.

When his father became king, Robert had been given land in Norfolk and a title, Lord Brimington. He even had a fine manor home in Bishop's Lynn called Fairstead. The problem was that Robert was just as cruel, ruthless, and immoral as his father, or so Sean had heard. He didn't know the man and didn't want to, so for John to bring him up was curious. John usually didn't give much thought to his first-born.

"I would have thought Robert to have married by now, your grace," Sean said.

"Not yet. But I believe I have the perfect match."

"Who?"

"Lady Christin de Lohr."

Sean struggled not to react outwardly, realizing he should have seen that coming. John had brought up Christopher's daughter and Robert in the same conversation, so it was only logical he'd meant to merge the two subjects.

But this merger was worse than anything Sean had imagined.

"I see," he said, hoping his shock wasn't evident. "And Monnington gave you this idea, your grace?"

John nodded. "He knows de Lohr's family," he said. "Monnington's father was close to Christopher, so Evan knows the children. He mentioned Lady Christin and her younger sister, Lady Brielle. He says they are both beauties."

Sean shrugged, trying to appear casual. "Given their mother's comely looks, I would believe that, your grace," he said. "But marrying Robert to de Lohr's eldest daughter? Have you spoken to anyone else about this idea?"

"A few."

"And what did they say, your grace?"

John shook his head. "It does not matter," he said. "I want to know what you think."

Sean eyed him. "The truth, your grace?"

"I would expect nothing less."

"Then I would not consider that plan if I were you, your grace," Sean said. "Christopher de Lohr probably already has his daughter pledged. Or, at the very least, you will never gain his permission, so it would be futile."

"Not if you whisk her from Norwich and take her to Bishop's Lynn," John said pointedly. "Robert can marry her before de Lohr can regain her and once consummated, not even the church will dissolve the marriage. With de Lohr's daughter married to my son, we will be family."

It was a horrific plan. Even Sean thought it was a horrific plan, and he'd heard many a horrific plan coming from John. But this one… it was absurd as well as outlandish. He struggled to remain neutral.

"May I further give my opinion, your grace?"

"Of course."

Sean didn't hold back. "Should you marry your son to de Lohr's daughter without his permission, that will not create an alliance," he said. "It will create civil war. De Lohr will march on you, and bring his allies with him, and he will wash over you like a wave upon the sand. You would destroy England with this plan, I fear."

John eyed him. "Not if I threaten to harm his daughter should he act against me."

"So you would use her as a hostage disguised as a bride, your grace?"

John had an intense look about him, as if everything in his entire future hinged on the vile scheme he was about to spew.

"If I bring de Lohr to his knees, then I remove not only him, but David de Lohr from any affront against me," he said. "With the House of de Lohr subdued, do you realize what that means?"

"I realize what you *think* it means, your grace," Sean said steadily. "But the reality could be very different. De Lohr is well-respected; even if he stands down because you threaten his daughter, his allies more than likely will not. That will put you in a precarious position."

"Explain."

"If you make a threat against Christin de Lohr and de Lohr's allies move against you, then you will have to act on your threat," he said. "If you do not, you will be viewed as weak. But if you do and you harm her, kill her even, then you remove the restraints on her father and he will destroy you. He may even ally with Philip. Imagine thousands of Frenchmen flooding England, allied with de Lohr and his supporters. You will not be able to stand against that."

Sean painted a bleak picture that was very truthful. Nothing he said was fabricated or imagined; all of it was true. John was astute enough to know that. Still, he didn't like to be denied his wants. That had historically been an issue with him. What John wanted, Sean would always, with rare exception, provide. The only way Sean would discuss an order with the king is if he believed it would hurt John beyond repair.

This was one of those times.

Unfortunately for Sean, John's quest to restrain or otherwise control Christopher de Lohr was stronger than his fear of the consequences.

"De Lohr would not ally with Philip," he finally said. "He would never support France on these shores, not even to destroy me. But I still want his daughter for my son because, as the son of the king, he commands the best bride in England. It will create an alliance that will benefit me. The man would not side against his kin and his daughter would be a duchess."

Sean was genuinely trying not to argue with the man because it would only look suspicious, but he was greatly troubled by the king's intentions. The last word in the man's statement had him confused.

"I was not aware your son was a duke, your grace," he said.

John shook his head. "He is not at the moment," he said. "But when he marries Lady Christin, that will change. My wedding gift to them will be the Dukedom of Dersingham. Surely de Lohr cannot object to his daughter becoming a duchess."

There was so much wrong with that statement that Sean truly didn't know where to begin. All he knew was that they were headed for some terrible trouble and Christopher knew nothing about it.

Not yet, anyway.

Sean wasn't certain if he was going to be at Norwich but he knew William Marshal was, and he further knew that William would not be happy to hear this in the least. Years ago, John had set his sights on Christopher's wife, Dustin, and it seemed that eighteen years later, the man was going after the woman's daughter. They were traveling down a road that would only take them to ruin because as fiercely as de Lohr had fought for his wife, he would fight even harder for his daughter.

Desperately, Sean tried to salvage the situation.

"Then mayhap you should propose the marriage to de Lohr, your grace," he said. "Mayhap if you ask him to enter into negotiations for his daughter, or send a liaison to negotiate, it might be a much more civilized way to go about it rather than abducting a bride for your son. That will set the situation on end from the very beginning and given your history with the House of de Lohr, mayhap that is not the best way to go about it. De Lohr will kill you and more than likely kill me to get to you, so you will put us both in an impossible situation."

John did nothing more than lay back on his bed again, arm over his forehead. "Possibly," he said. "Faithful Sean; always trying to save me from myself. It must be a difficult task."

Sean smiled weakly. "I serve at the pleasure, your grace. It is an honor."

John snorted as if he did not believe him. "You are a gracious liar," he said. "We will speak on this subject again when we arrive at Norwich and I get a look at Lady Christin. But for now, let us speak on this evening."

"What is your wish, your grace?"

John was looking at him again. "Lord Edward Needham lives not far from here, I believe," he said. "His seat is Elsdon House. Do you remember him?"

"I do, your grace. An older man with bags under his eyes. He has a look of illness about him."

"That may be true, but he has a new wife," John said. "He brought her to the masque at Westminster this past summer. Do you recall?"

"I believe so, your grace."

John wagged a finger. "He tried to be clever and keep her out of my sight, but I saw her," he said. "She is quite a beauty. Rumor has it that he's in love with the girl, although he is old enough to be her father."

"A woman with red hair? I do recall, your grace."

John lay back again, closing his eyes as the carriage rocked and bumped. "Go to Elsdon and bring her to me," he said. "If Needham stands in your way, do what you must to subdue the man. It will be a cold, wet night and I wish for a warm, soft body to fill my bed."

It wasn't an unusual command. Sean had carried out dozens of them over the years. He'd learned not to become outraged or upset by them, as barbaric as they were. He had to push his personal feelings aside.

"Aye, your grace."

"Needham has a daughter, too. She's young, but I hear she's pretty enough. Bring her, too."

"Anything else, your grace?"

"That will be enough."

Sean quit the carriage without another word, mostly because he now had orders to head to Elsdon House and steal a man's wife and daughter away for the king's pleasure. It was part of the hell he'd condemned himself to when he'd accepted this mission from William Marshal those years ago, a mission that saw him embed close to the king to watch the man's every move and report back to William Marshal. But it was with directives like these that made him question his loyalty to the Marshal, to England in general. He knew there would be a special place in hell for him and all of the things he'd done in the name of the king.

It was something he tried not to think about.

Lady Barbara Needham was young, pretty, and very much in love with her older husband, who begged Sean not to take her away when he showed up with about thirty of the king's soldiers. The man wept and pleaded as Sean yanked his wife right out of their marital bed and handed her over to another of John's bodyguards, a bear of a man named Gerard d'Athee. When Lord Needham lunged for Sean, trying to physically reclaim his weeping wife, Sean slugged Lord Needham so hard in the head that it knocked the man unconscious in an instant.

It was a good thing that Needham had been rendered immobile, deaf, blind and dumb to what was going on around him, because once d'Athee took Lady Needham down to his waiting horse, Sean went to find the man's daughter, locating a thirteen-year-old girl who was cowering in her bedchamber at all of the screaming. Looking at that tiny, weeping girl, Sean knew she would not survive a night with the well-endowed and lusty king.

He simply couldn't do it.

Telling her to be silent and locking the door behind him, he shut the panel and headed down to the servants' quarters where he located a rather bold serving wench, who claimed she had seen eighteen years, and dragged her out into the night. Under penalty of death – her death – Sean told her that, for the night, she was to pretend that she was Needham's daughter. When he caught up to the hysterical Lady Needham, he managed to get her alone for a few moments to tell her the same thing – unless she wanted to see her stepdaughter violated, she would confirm that the serving maid was Needham's young daughter.

Poor Lady Needham was facing horrors beyond belief, but she understood.

She agreed.

Sean felt very sorry for her.

Before dawn the next day, Sean personally returned Lady Needham and the maid to Elsdon House. Fortunately for Lady Needham, the king seemed to be more interested in the maid, who had turned out to be virgin, so Lady Needham had been forced to mostly watch what had happened rather than actively participate. The maid hadn't been particularly bothered by the event, thinking it a badge of honor to have been bedded by the king, but Lady Needham had been devastated by the entire event. When Sean brought the women home before sunrise, Lady Needham had actually thanked him for sparing her stepdaughter.

But that didn't make Sean feel any less dirty or dishonorable.

On the ride back to the village, all he could think of was Christin de Lohr and what was going to happen once John reached Norwich. God help him, he was going to have to make sure Christin stayed out of sight. He had never come close to blowing his cover in the entire time he'd served John, but if Christin de Lohr's life and future was on the line, Sean knew he'd have to make some hard decisions.

Ruin eight years of hard work or put his friend and ally's daughter in grave danger.

Would he choose the greater good of England or the greater good of one family?

And that was the dilemma facing Sean de Lara as the king's escort rolled towards Norwich.

CHAPTER SIX

"THE KING IS approaching." Peter caught up to Alexander as the man stood at one of the food tables. "Where is my sister?"

Alexander had a cup of boiled apple juice in one hand and a few slices of bread in the other. All around them, the wedding feast was going on but Peter's words had him on alert. He immediately turned to the road that crossed through the town, the same road they had come in on. Other than people dancing on it, or otherwise going about their business, nothing seemed amiss.

"Are you certain?" he asked, straining to catch a glimpse. "Who told you that?"

"There are people arriving in town from the countryside for this feast and they said that John is approaching," Peter replied. "I heard some of them talking."

Alexander didn't want the king or his retinue to see him or the others. In fact, it was best that they weren't seen at all until the time was right. He set the food in his hands down.

"Go find Kevin and Bric," he said. "Get your horses and get to Norwich. I will find Christin."

But Peter shook his head. "I will find my sister," he said. "It is more important that you get to Norwich ahead of the king and let Old Daveigh know of the man's impending arrival."

Alexander wanted to argue with him; he really did. He wanted to be the one to retrieve Christin, but he was afraid that if he argued the point with Peter, that the man might think it strange. Suspicious, even. Alexander wasn't even sure what he was feeling for Christin, but he didn't want to tip her brother off before he was ready to face it himself. All he knew was that he wanted to be near her.

He couldn't seem to let it go.

"You heard me," he said, pointing to the crowd of revelers. "Get going. I'll find your sister and bring her along."

"But –!"

Alexander had already turned away at that point. He wasn't going to argue with Peter, who simply took off running in the opposite direction when Alexander shut him down. The man had his orders and was moving to carry them out.

Alexander had the stone bench in his sight and instantly saw that it was vacant. Suspecting that Christin wouldn't have gone far in her state, he jogged over to the bench, all the while looking around to see if he could locate her. The festivities were still going on around them as rumors of the king's approach spread, but he didn't see her anywhere. Puzzled but not panicked, his gaze moved to the small church.

The doors were open.

That gave him an idea.

Alexander made his way over to the church with the small and crowded churchyard built against it. It was a beautiful church, in truth, with a tall steeple that looked like it had once been a castle tower, built from dark granite. He passed into the cool, quiet sanctuary, looking into the dark recesses for Christin, and noticing that there were backless stone benches against the walls, tucked into the darkness. He hadn't taken ten steps when he immediately spied Christin laying on one of the stone benches.

Quietly, he made his way over to her.

She was dead asleep, her mouth open as she snored softly. Alexander stood there a moment, smiling faintly, thinking that he wasn't going to wake her. Since he'd become acquainted with her, she'd had quite a time of it – the French spy, the near-dressing down by William Marshal because of it, the fight at The Pox, and then riding to Norwich in horrible weather and hardly sleeping for it. No wonder that strong ale had hit her so hard.

She deserved a bit of a rest.

Therefore, he let her sleep. Quietly, he sat down by her head, leaning back against the stone wall of the church and feeling his own fatigue. He was weary also. To the soft sounds of her steady breathing, he closed his eyes.

Sleep came almost instantly.

The next Alexander realized, someone was speaking. His eyes rolled open and he could see that it was quite dark in the church now. It didn't occur to him that he, too, had fallen asleep until he lifted his head only to see that Christin's head was now in his lap, using his thigh as a pillow, and his left arm was draped over her body protectively. He froze, confused and groggy, as he watched her sleeping peacefully, curled up against him.

"My lord?"

There was that voice again. Alexander looked up to see a tall, thin man in priestly robes bent over, peering at him curiously.

"My lord?" the man said again. "You cannot sleep here. Vespers has begun. If it is a hostel you seek, there is one on the edge of town."

Alexander rubbed his eyes, yawning. "Vespers," he muttered, thinking on how long he could have possibly been asleep. They came into the village around midday, so they'd been asleep at least five hours, possibly more. Looking down at Christin, still sleeping soundly, he shook her gently. "My lady? Christin?"

She barely stirred and he could see that she had drooled all over his breeches. The sight actually made him grin. He shook her again.

"Christin, wake up," he said quietly. "We must move on to Norwich."

Christin took a long, deep breath and opened her eyes. Alexander could see the long lashes fluttering. She stared out into the sanctuary for a few moments before putting a hand up, feeling where her head was resting. He could see that she was trying to figure it all out and it was rather amusing. Then, she wiped her mouth, lifted her head, and looked at the big wet patch on the leather breeches.

Slowly, *very* slowly, she turned to see who she had been passed out on. When their eyes met and she saw who it was, she closed her eyes briefly as if to ward off the sight.

"Bloody Christ," she muttered, wiping at her mouth again to wipe away the remains of the saliva. "I do not even know what to say. To apologize does not seem sufficient."

"Apologize for what?"

She looked at him then. "*That*," she said, pointing to the wet patch on his breeches. "When I laid down on this bench, you were not here, but now I wake up and find myself… well, *laying* on you. It is unforgivable."

He grinned. "Don't take it so hard," he said. "I fell asleep sitting up, if it is any consolation. I came in here to find you but you were sleeping so peacefully that I did not have the heart to wake you. So, I sat down beside you and here we are."

Christin put her hand to her still-fuzzy head. "What *was* in that ale we drank?"

Alexander sighed wearily, rising to his feet. "Something I shall never drink again," he said, turning to her and holding out a hand. "Come along, my lady. Your brother will be wondering what has become of us."

Christin eyed his outstretched hand. Then she looked up at him, her expression one of disbelief and confusion.

"Are you truly so patient with fools?" she asked.

"What fools?"

"*Me*," she said. "I simply do not understand why you should bother with me. You are an important man. The Marshal put you in command of this escort and we should have been at Norwich several hours ago from the looks of it. It is dark outside, meaning we have slept away the entire afternoon. Where are my brother and the others?"

"At Norwich Castle," he said. "The king arrived this afternoon so they went ahead to announce the arrival to de Winter. I went to locate you and, finding you sleeping here, I simply let you sleep. It was better than taking you to Norwich and showing them all how drunk you were. I am certain you would not have preferred that."

Her eyes widened and her mouth popped open. "You did it to save me?"

"I did it so you could be rested and sober when you arrived."

Christin shook her head in awe. "Again… I do not know what to say," she said. "I am so ashamed with what happened. It seems that nothing has gone right since we were introduced. You must think I am an utterly ridiculous woman."

His hand was still outstretched and he reached out, taking her arm and pulling her off the bench. "I think you are a unique young woman and I am honored to know you," he said quietly. "Shall we go on to Norwich now?"

Christin didn't say a word. Perhaps it was best that she not say anything because he held her by the hand, leading her out into the night beyond. She found herself looking at his enormous hand as it held hers, wondering when he was going to let it go, but he never did.

He held it quite firmly.

The feast was still going on, even as night fell, with torches lighting up the evening. Alexander led her through the crowds, shoving aside a man who tried to give them more of that powerful ale, and continued down the road until they came to the livery where their horses had been stabled. Collecting the beasts, they took off up the road towards Norwich.

And that was the only time he let go of her hand. If Christin didn't know better, she would say his hand holding went beyond polite concern. It was just a feeling she had.

God, she hoped so.

NORWICH CASTLE WAS lit up like a beacon against the night sky, a massive place in a dominant position over the cosmopolitan city of Norwich. The architecture was purely Norman, a great box structure with smooth stone facing, making it unique in the structures of castles throughout England.

The castle itself was a fortress to be reckoned with. The massive keep sat atop a motte, but there were three additional mottes in a line beside it, each one smaller in size, and each one linked by a retractable bridge so in times of trouble, each motte would serve as its own separate fighting platform.

The military attributes were almost too long to list. The castle had only been breached once in known history, but it was a miracle as to how that had even happened. Alexander was impressed anew every time he saw the place, for it was truly a marvel. It belonged to the crown, but the House of de Winter had been garrison commanders since the times of the Duke of Normandy, so it was more of a de Winter castle than anything else. Everyone referred to it as a de Winter castle and the House of de Winter was deeply entrenched in Norfolk as a result. They held most of the northern part of Norfolk and into Lincolnshire.

The House of de Winter was truly a powerful and distinguished family.

As Alexander and Christin entered the first of a series of gatehouses built upon the mottes, the de Winter men recognized Christin and greeted her, and she introduced Alexander. His name alone was legendary with most fighting men and if they hadn't heard of him, then they'd certainly heard of William Marshal. It was a name that opened doors.

Passing through the first two gatehouses, they crossed the bridge to the third and immediately noticed that the king's entourage had set up camp on the west side of the motte with colorful tents and royal standards. Torches lit up the area as men moved about. This was also the motte where the stables were, so she and Alexander headed to the enormous stable area on the east side where grooms were waiting to take their mounts.

As Christin dismounted and untied her satchel from her saddle, her gaze kept moving to the king's encampment. The motte was quite large, so they weren't in danger of encroaching on the king's camp, but there were royal soldiers moving about. Christin hadn't been concerned with John's visit to Norwich until her conversation with Alexander and, now, she found herself watching the men who were setting up the tents, wondering where, exactly, the king was.

"Do you think John is inside the keep?" she asked Alexander.

He was just pulling his saddlebags from his horse. He glanced over at her, seeing that her attention was on the king's encampment. He could hear the concern in her voice.

"More than likely," he said. "Where will you go now?"

"The same place you are going," she said. "I must report back to Old Daveigh and then I shall seek Lady de Winter."

Alexander slung his bags over his shoulder as he came to stand next to her, but she wasn't moving. She was watching the king's encampment.

"I would not worry," he said quietly. "You know what you must do. Remain out of sight from the king or, at the very least, away from him. We are looking for a greater threat against him, meaning you will have to listen to the gossip of visiting ladies and even men to see if there is any information to glean."

Christin knew that and she nodded, drawing on that great de Lohr courage she had. "I am not worried," she lied. "And I find that men know more than the women do. I will have to find a young lord to drink with so he will tell me all his secrets."

Somehow, that statement didn't sit well with Alexander. He didn't like the thought of her sitting with an amorous young lord as she tried to bleed information from him. Alexander knew she must have done it a dozen times, given what she did for The Marshal, but hearing her say it... nay, he didn't like it in the least. He didn't like the idea of her prostituting herself like that even though it was her duty.

God help him, he didn't like her duty.

What was happening to him?

He cleared his throat softly.

"If you wish to stay clear of the king, at least for now, I would stay away from the men," he said. It was mostly the truth. "Stay with the women and listen to what they have to say. I will handle the men, along with your brother and Bric and Kevin. Let us do our duty and you do yours. We cannot, and should not, get close to the women, but you can. That is where you are most valuable."

If Christin thought his directive was coming from a jealous and confused potential suitor, she didn't give any indication. It was a command coming from her superior and she accepted it as such. She simply nodded her head and started walking. Alexander followed.

Norwich was lit up with the light from a thousand torches on this night and as they crossed the bridge towards the keep, they were seeing more and more royal soldiers. Alexander was dressed in full protection as a seasoned knight, bearing the green and white shield of William Marshal on his tunic, but Christin wasn't wearing anything other than her traveling dress and cloak. She'd lost the garland in her hair somewhere back at the feast. She wasn't hard to miss with her dark hair and pale eyes, attracting the attention of some of the king's soldiers.

Alexander could see the lascivious looks in her direction and his blood began to boil. Christin didn't belong to him; she wasn't anything to him. At least, not yet, but there was a huge part of him that was feeling overwhelmingly protective over her. He would have liked nothing better than to gouge out the eyes of the men who were mentally undressing her as she walked by.

Finally, he could stand no more.

"Hold my arm," he muttered.

She looked at him in surprise. "What did you say?"

His gaze was on the men around them on the bridge. "I told you to hold my arm," he said. "These soldiers must believe you either belong to me or have my protection so they will not try to accost you."

"But..."

"*Hold my arm.*"

He hissed at her, firmly, and she immediately grabbed his elbow, making it look as if, indeed, they were a pair. Not strangely, Alexander was coming to wish that they were. He felt puffed up like a peacock having her on his arm.

Proud as he'd never been proud in his life.

They came off the bridge and into the motte that contained the keep, which was immediately to their left. There was a yard here and several outbuildings, including a small garden, but Alexander headed straight for the keep. There was a stone staircase that led to a guarded lobby. As they headed up the staircase, Christin looked at him.

"May I let go of your arm now?" she asked.

He nodded. "You should," he said. "I would have some explaining to do if Peter saw us."

Christin removed her hand. "He is too protective," she said. "He would undoubtedly tell my father."

"I am not afraid of your father."

"You aren't?"

He shook his head as they reached the protected lobby, but he paused before stepping in. "There is something you should know, Cissy," he said. "No man frightens me and if I want something, a thousand Christopher de Lohrs could not stand in my way. In the end, I will have it."

Her lips twitched with a smile. "I believe you."

"Good," he said. "Because, at some point, I suspect we might have this conversation again. Come along now and stay close."

With that, he headed into the hall, but Christin was still lingering on what he'd just said. She rushed after him but, all the while, her mind was trying to decipher what he could have meant. She wasn't entirely certain of his message but, instinctively, it made her heart flutter in ways she'd never known before.

In the end, I will have it.

Could he possibly mean *her*?

She wondered.

Forcing herself away from thoughts of Alexander, at least for the moment, she looked out over the great hall as they passed through it. The room was crowded – *very* crowded – and men were seated around tables as servants moved about, bringing the precursor to the coming meal. Drink and cheese and bread were plentiful upon the three big feasting tables that she could see, with a massive blaze in the hearth that was belching smoke into the hall. The chamber itself was tall, with windows for ventilation at the top of it for the escaping smoke.

Alexander was heading for the secondary hall called the knight's hall. It was off of the main hall and where the lord usually feasted with his knights and senior officers. Lady de Winter had her own separate feasting chamber off of the knight's chamber, a small room that was cozy and only for the women.

As Alexander and Christin entered the knight's hall, they immediately saw Peter eating at the table along with several other de Winter knights. But there was no Bric and no Kevin.

Alexander approached the table.

"Where is MacRohan?" he asked. "And where is Kevin?"

Peter stood up when he saw his sister. "Bric and Old Daveigh are in the small solar next to the chapel," he said, his gaze mostly on Christin. "I do not know where Kevin went. He saw his brother arrive with the king and fled. Where have you been, Cissy?"

Christin glanced at Alexander, rather chagrinned she had to answer the question. "You would not believe if I told you," she said. "But because you will keep asking me if I do not, I will tell you that the ale at the wedding feast made me ill and Sherry found me sleeping in the church. Rather than wake me and bring me to Norwich drunk, he let me sleep. He has been most gracious about it but I am mortified."

Peter stared at her a moment before breaking out into a grin. "I am sure you are," he said, sitting back down. "Old Daveigh wants to see the both of you as soon as you arrive. Go to him."

Christin nodded, taking off through the maze of doors and passageways on her way to the small solar that was near the entry. In fact, they had walked right by it when they entered the keep. Alexander was behind her and as she entered Lord de Winter's solar from the servant's entrance, she immediately noticed that Old Daveigh and Bric were not the only ones in the room. There were other men, including two enormous knights wearing the crimson and gold royal standard, along with a man of smaller stature and graying hair seated at Old Daveigh's large table.

Puzzled, she came to a halt just inside the door.

So did Alexander.

Daveigh de Winter noticed them immediately. He was quite old but still strong, still bright in his waning years. He'd been big and dark in his youth, but now that dark hair had gone white and he wasn't as muscular any longer, but he was still quite formidable and he still attended his men in any skirmish or battle.

Daveigh was a legendary de Winter from a family of legendary men. He'd married one Lady Glyn de Lara and had four daughters – Delesse, Danessa, Darcy, and Dierdre – but no sons. The daughters were all married now, but Old Daveigh, as he was known since he had a nephew by the same name, was a congenial lord who treated his knights like the sons he never had. He positively adored Peter and had threatened on more than one occasion to adopt him. When the old man's gaze fell upon Christin, he immediately went in her direction.

"Ah," he said. "Lady Christin. We have been greatly anticipating your arrival."

Christin couldn't have known that Alexander was standing next to her as stiff as a board, eyes riveted to the small man seated at the table. She was focused on Old Daveigh, smiling politely at him.

"I apologize for the delay, my lord," she said. "I... I was ill and only now feeling well enough to finish the journey to Norwich. I apologize if I caused you any inconvenience."

Daveigh shook his head, reaching out to take her by the arm. He began to lead her over to the table.

"Not at all, my lady," he said. "It is simply that the king has been anxious to meet you. He asked for you as soon as he arrived and your brother informed me that you would be here shortly."

The king has been anxious to meet you.

Apprehension and confusion enveloped Christin as she looked to the table, seeing a small man seated there with one droopy eye. *I know that face*, she thought. She remembered it from long ago, as a child. A horrible face, she thought, one that made her chest tighten simply to look upon it.

The very face she'd been trying to avoid.

John, King of England, was looking straight at her.

As soon as she reached the table, she dropped into a practiced curtsy. "Your grace," she said, rather breathless from surprise. "I... I am honored."

John was drinking in his fill of her; that much was certain. He didn't have to say a word. His intense expression said everything. He looked her up and down before replying.

"Stand up, Lady Christin," he finally said.

She did, keeping her gaze averted. In truth, she didn't want to look at the man, terrified he'd see the loathing in her eyes. It wouldn't do well for the king to know just how much all of the de Lohrs hated him.

"I remember when you were born," John said after a moment. "I remember the rumors that you were Marcus Burton's daughter, but I do not see anything of Burton in you. You look like your father."

Christin had heard those rumors once, too, long ago when she'd first fostered at Thunderbey Castle. They'd upset her so badly that her mother had been forced to explain them to her. It had been a sordid tale of deceit and treachery and a love between her father and mother that could not be broken.

Even if Christin hadn't resembled her father, she still would have believed her mother. Not even Marcus Burton, one of her father's oldest and dearest friends, could destroy what Christopher and Dustin de Lohr had in a fit of youthful arrogance and insanity.

But she resented the king for bringing up hurtful and old rumors.

"I do more than resemble him, your grace," she said. "I am his daughter in every way."

"Look at me."

She immediately lifted her head, looking him in the eye. They stared at each other for a few moments before John smiled, a gesture that made the bile rise in Christin's throat.

"You are quite beautiful," he said. "I am sure your father is fiercely protective over you."

"As any father would be over his daughter, your grace."

John snorted softly. "That is true," he said. "Tell me, Lady Christin, are you betrothed?"

The question caught her off guard but she knew, instinctively, that she didn't want to tell him the truth. Something in that question made her skin crawl.

"You will have to ask my father, your grace," she said. "I have no say in his plans for me."

John nodded faintly, still eyeing her. But his eyes moved to her torso and Christin resisted the urge to turn away from him. She could feel the heat from his stare on her breasts, her torso. The man was trying to look through her clothing to see what was beneath it. Every word of warning that Alexander had given her were all flooding back to her.

"You are dismissed, my lady," John said after a moment. "But I should like for you to dine with me later."

So many replies came to her, but not one of them was polite. She didn't want to end up in Norwich's vault, or worse, so she simply nodded her head and turned away from him, fleeing the chamber.

She couldn't even look at Alexander as she went.

Everything he'd said had been true.

Christin quit the solar in a blind rush, heading to the keep entry and taking the stairs far too quickly. Once she hit the ground, she ran towards one of several small buildings that peppered the bailey. One was a chapel, but two of them were apartments. There was one for men and one for women, and Christin went towards the one for women that was tucked near the garden behind the keep. It was a two-storied stone building with a pitched roof and eight rooms – four on the bottom, four on the top, with an attic used for servants and storage.

The entry door was made from oak and iron, fortified, and usually open until later in the evening when it was locked from within. Fortunately, it was still open and she raced up the stairs to the small landing, and then straight into the room she occupied, the chamber on the northwest side.

Slamming the door, she bolted it.

The chamber was cold and dark, with a faint moonglow coming in through the shuttered window. She stood there a moment, trying to catch her breath, struggling to orient herself in the face of something terrifying and unexpected.

The king wanted her to dine with him.

Well, she wasn't going to. She was going to stay in her chamber until the king left Norwich and to the devil with William Marshal. He wanted her to do her duty. She wanted to do it, too, but that duty didn't include being molested by the king. If it was a choice between seeking out the threat against John amongst the attending allies or keeping to her chamber because it was safer for her, then she was going to stick to her chamber.

William Marshal and his spies would have to do without her.

If you kill the king... the consequences to you and your family would be unfathomable.

Alexander's words were ringing in her head. She couldn't even defend herself against a monarch who would only want to soil her and cast her aside. If that happened, her father would move against the king and the family would be at war, anyway, so perhaps the threat against the king that the French spy spoke of was far more complicated than anyone realized, including Christin.

But she realized it now.

It was a threat from within.

Perhaps it was the king's own lascivious nature. Bed the wrong woman and England would be destroyed. Bed a de Lohr daughter and the wrath of Christopher de Lohr would tear the country apart.

The French didn't have to destroy John. He would do it himself.

Now, she understood.

Sinking onto her bed, the tears finally came.

CHAPTER SEVEN

"**W**HEN WAS THE last time you saw John?"

David was speaking to his brother as the two of them plodded along on warhorses that each cost a man's salary for an entire year. The House of de Lohr was wealthy from years of service to the crown, but also because as the Earl of Worcester and Hereford, Christopher owned active coal mines and also gleaned taxes from the market city of Worcester.

For David, as the Earl of Canterbury, his income came from the pilgrims, taxes, and the levies imposed on cog traffic along the River Stour through the large city of Canterbury. Combined, the brothers had more money than the crown, as the king had pointed out several times, but both of them were very careful with it and quite financially astute.

Except when it came to high-end warhorses.

Astride that big-arsed horse and dressed in his usual armor and weaponry, Christopher wasn't thinking about money or expense. His mind was elsewhere, so much so that his brother had to ask him the same question twice. The second time, he turned to his brother irritably.

"It hasn't been long enough," he muttered. "Last year, I think. You and I were both in London to meet with The Marshal and we saw him then."

David grunted. "That's what I thought," he said. "And must we really attend this celebration given by de Winter? It's not as if we are going to celebrate anything when it has to do with John unless, of course, it's his death. I will happily celebrate that day."

Christopher chuckled. "Give the man a few more years, at least until his son is older and more malleable," he said. "Henry is only six. The child actually has a level head thanks to his upbringing. Properly molded, we may actually have a good king."

David shook his head. "Having a child-king may be better, anyway."

"You sound like my wife."

"She's right."

Christopher waved a hand at him. "A few more years," he insisted. "Then... then I will be happy to be rid of John. It will save me from trips like this one."

"To celebrate the birth of a man you hate?"

"Nay. To make sure the king and my children do not cross paths."

David looked at him. "Is *that* why we are going to this event?" he asked, incredulous. "So you can keep Peter away from the king? Jesus, Chris, the man has seen twenty years and six. He does not need his dada to protect him."

Christopher looked at him. "Not Peter," he said. "Christin. Do you remember when we were at Ramsbury and everyone disappeared out of the hall at the same time?"

David nodded. "I do."

"Even Christin left," Christopher pointed out. "With Susanna de Dere, who is a known agent for William Marshal. And then she returned to us an hour later in a new gown about the same time as everyone else returned and pretended as if nothing was amiss."

"So *what?*"

Christopher shook his head at his dimwitted brother. "Do you not see what I see, David? Christin must be working with William Marshal, too. Peter is. Why not Christin?"

"So you are coming to Norwich to get to the bottom of this?" David said. "Chris, your children are adults. If they serve William Marshal, it is their choice."

That was true, but Christopher didn't want to hear that, especially where it pertained to Christin. "My daughter is not going to be entrenched in The Marshal's spy ring," he said. "I will pull her out of Norwich and she will come home with me to Lioncross. A woman has no business playing a man's game."

"Susanna is playing a man's game and she has played it well for many years," David said quietly.

Christopher looked at him, exasperated. "She is also a Blackchurch-trained knight. Christin is not."

David sighed heavily. "You have always been the type of father to let your children shine," he said. "If Christin is an agent, then she must be very good at it if you don't even know for certain whether she is or not. You cannot force her home like a scolded child if she's been executing missions for William Marshal. How do you think she's going to react?"

Christopher knew how – not very well. Christin was far too much like her mother and he could never control her very well, either. But when it came to his children and their safety, this was different. Christopher had been stewing on this very subject since they left Ramsbury Castle.

It had him torn.

"I would just feel better if we could see what is transpiring at Norwich," he said. "Besides, most of our allies will be there. It will be a chance for us to reaffirm bonds."

"Reaffirm bonds with John?"

"Oh, shut up."

David bit his lip to keep from laughing. "I have a feeling this is going to be a very interesting celebration."

Christopher had that feeling, too.

Only in his case, it wasn't a good feeling. It was an ominous one.

CHAPTER EIGHT

Norwich Castle

THERE WAS A knock on the chamber door.
Christin was still sitting in the darkness of her chamber, trying to chase away the tears that wouldn't seem to stop falling, but she quickly wiped her face when there was a second rap on the door.

"Who is it?" she asked.

"It's me!" came a voice. "Open the door, Cissy!"

Christin recognized the voice and she rushed to the door, throwing open the panel. Lady Wynter de Royans swept in, shutting the door quickly and bolting it. She turned to Christin, eyes wide as she leaned against the door.

"The king has arrived!" she gasped. "Have you heard?"

Christin nodded. Wynter was her dear friend, daughter of her father's mentor, Juston de Royans of Bowes Castle. She had fostered at Norwich as a girl and was married at a fairly young age only to have her husband die of an illness three years into their marriage. Shattered, she'd returned to Norwich by her choice because it was a place of comfort to her. She was tall and elegant, level-headed and lovely. Christin liked, and trusted her, a great deal.

"Not only have I heard, I have seen him," she said.

Wynter's eyes widened further. "You *have*?" She shook her head in fear. "Cissy, we must not go to the hall. Lady de Winter has said so. We must remain here until the festivities are over."

Christin shook her head. "Oh... Wynnie," she said as she sank onto her bed. "The king has already seen me and he told me that he wishes to dine with me. But I will *not* do it. Where is Lady de Winter?"

Wynter was nearly beside herself. "She is in the lord's chamber as far as I know," she said. "She is in the keep. What will you do?"

Christin sat there for a moment, pondering the situation. Then, she suddenly stood up. "Leave," she said decisively. "My satchel is packed. I will go into the city and find a room somewhere and remain there until the king is gone. No one will be able to find me, least of all the king's men. If they try to take me to him, they will have a fight on their hands."

Wynter was in full agreement. "Then go," she said. "I have some money you can use. There is an inn near the cathedral. I have heard it is very nice. Mayhap they have room for you."

Christin grabbed her satchel from where she had set it on her bed. "I have some coinage."

"I will give you more."

Christin reached out and grasped her hand. "Truly, you do not need to," she said. "But you must tell Peter where I have gone. He will worry."

Wynter sighed heavily. "He will worry, anyway," she said. "Let me send for him. Let him at least escort you into town."

Christin shook her head. "He must not be an accomplice to my act of disobedience. This is something I must do alone."

Wynter understood. Christin and Peter were quite close, and cared a good deal for one another, and she didn't want to get her brother into trouble.

"Then let me go with you," Wynter said. "You should not go alone."

Christin smiled. "If you go with me, you will be an accomplice, too," she said. "I cannot do that to you, Wynnie. You already know too much. You are going to have to plead ignorance in all things or you will get into trouble."

Wynter knew that. Greatly distressed, she hugged Christin tightly. "Very well," she said. "But you must hurry. You can slip from the postern gate and take the path to the farm fields below. It is much easier to leave their gate than it is to leave ours."

Christin nodded. "I will," she said. "Tell Peter... tell him that I shall return when the king has left."

Wynter nodded, quickly going to the door to make sure there were no witnesses to Christin's flight. There were other women in this building and she wanted to make sure no one was out, wandering around. Seeing that the landing was clear, she nodded to Christin, who bolted from her chamber and headed down the stairs.

She had just made it free of the building and was rushing towards the postern gate, also known as the meadow gate, when she saw a familiar face heading in her direction.

Alexander.

"HAS WILLIAM MARSHAL arrived?"

The question came from John as he looked upon Alexander and the tunic he wore. Having just witnessed the horrific scene between the king and Christin, Alexander wasn't feeling particularly amiable towards the man. He could barely force himself to be polite in his response.

"Not that I am aware of, your grace," he said. "I know that he is planning on coming but not when he is due to arrive."

John simply nodded his head, faintly, sizing up Alexander. He knew who the man was; he knew it very well. John and William Marshal had shared a relationship with its ups and downs, but John knew that William's main directive in life was to protect the monarchy, so essentially, men like Alexander de Sherrington were allied with him. *Technically.* But the truth of it was that William Marshal and the men who served him were spies and assassins, and from what John had heard, Alexander was one of the worst.

Or the best.

Either way, John was wary of him.

"Then leave and take the Irishman with you," he said. "You are not required here."

Alexander and Bric departed the solar without another word, heading out of the keep. They needed to talk and couldn't do that with any guaranteed privacy in the keep, so they headed out into the torch-lit night, heading straight for the chapel because it would be empty at this hour.

The chapel of Norwich Castle was indeed dark and cold and empty. It had long lancet windows on either side, inlaid with precious colored glass depicting saints. The chapel wasn't very big given the size of the castle, crowded on either side with de Winter family crypts. They were all buried here, all the way back to Denis de Winter, who had come to the shores of England with the Duke of Normandy.

Alexander looked around the dark, shadowed chapel before finally calling out to see if there was anyone lingering nearby. He didn't receive an answer, nor did he hear any sounds, so he turned to Bric, keeping his voice barely above a whisper.

"How long has John been with Daveigh?" he asked.

Bric shook his head. "From nearly the moment he arrived," he said. "Peter and Kevin and I arrived about a half-hour before the king did and we were speaking to Daveigh when John simply walked in. There was no announcement; the man simply arrived."

Alexander ran his fingers through his dark hair. "Christ," he hissed. "That entire situation was a nightmare. And now he wants to sup with Christin de Lohr? We cannot allow it."

"I am not sure how we can stop it," Bric said. "The king's word is law. He is not denied."

Alexander looked at him. "She is an agent in William Marshal's service," he said. "We have some obligation to protect her, even from the king. Most of all, we have to do something or Peter will get himself killed trying to save his sister."

Bric knew that. Regretfully, he nodded. "I am glad he did not hear the royal summons," he said. "In fact, we should probably remove him from the keep. Someone is going to tell him or he is eventually going to see it for himself when John demands his sister keep him company at sup."

"Then get him out of there," Alexander said. "Tell him what has happened but be gentle with him. We must try to keep Christin away from the king until The Marshal arrives. After that… he will have to deal with the situation."

Bric nodded. "This is not something I expected. Of all the women the king could focus on…"

Alexander agreed with the irony of that statement but he was also trying not to look as if his concern for Christin was something more than simple duty. Worse than tipping Peter off would be to tip everyone else off. Alexander de Sherrington did not frolic with women, and especially not a fellow agent. He was torn between not caring what anyone thought and protecting his pride and reputation.

He was afraid that some might view it as a weakness.

"Go find Peter," he told Bric. "I will go find Lady Christin. She ran out of the chamber so fast she must be halfway out of the city by now."

"There are apartment blocks to the east of the chapel," Bric said. "She may have gone there."

It was as good a place to start as any. Alexander and Bric headed to the chapel entry, with Bric heading back to the enormous keep while Alexander turned towards the apartments, bathed in a soft moonglow. He was heading down the path, planning on checking the first building, when something at the end of the path caught his attention.

A beautiful moonlit wraith had entered his field of vision.

Christin.

"Where are you going?" Alexander asked as he came upon her in the darkness, noting the satchel in her hand. "What is happing, Cissy?"

Christin looked at him, struggling to keep the fear from her expression. "You were right," she said quietly. "The king did notice me. Now he wants to dine with me. I am leaving before he sends his men for me."

In spite of her best efforts to the contrary, Alexander could see the terror in her expression. With a heavy sigh, he put his hands out, grasping her gently by the upper arms.

"I will take you," he said quietly. "That is why I came to find you. I will take you into the village and find a place for you to hide, at least until The Marshal arrives. I fear he will want you here, but with his presence, the king is less likely to do anything… foolish."

Christin was tense. "Are you saying that he will protect me?"

"I am saying that he will do his very best."

"That is not good enough."

Alexander felt as if he had brought this on her. She had been fearless of the king's presence until he reminded her of the king's reputation. Now, she was reverting to panic; he could see it in her eyes. That confident young woman who killed on command was terrified when she knew she could not defend herself against a threat. Not that Alexander blamed her.

He was fairly upset about it, as well.

"I want you to listen to me and listen closely," he said. "You are a de Lohr, but more than that, you are an agent for William Marshal. I have seen you kill with more bravery than I have ever seen from a woman and you did it without fear. You are stronger than every woman I have ever known, Susanna de Dere included, because you have an innate sense of courage, justice, and determination. All of this without formal training. When I told you to stay away from the king, I meant it. But he has seen you now, so you must adjust your plans accordingly. If The Marshal will not protect you, then know that I will. I swear to you that I will not let John harm you."

Christin was watching him with a mixture of awe and confusion.

He'd said so many nice things in that brief declaration that thoughts of the king were being pushed aside. All she could focus on was his chivalrous affirmation. It was part of the flattery he'd been liberal with since Ramsbury. But this time, there was something more behind it.

She *felt* something more.

"You think I am stronger than Susanna?" she said. "But she is Blackchurch-trained."

He lifted his shoulders. "As I said, if you'd been born male, you would have made a magnificent knight."

"If I was born male, we would not have this situation on our hands," she said. "And I suspect you would not be so concerned for me."

"Of course I would. You are a comrade."

"I am also a woman, one you have called beautiful more than once." She watched his dark eyes shift, as if her implications were rolling through his mind, and emboldened, she stepped towards him. "Mayhap I am speaking out of turn, but there is something I must say. Since leaving London, you have shown me attention that, if I were the suspicious or romantic type, I would have taken as your interest in me. *Personally*, I mean. Alexander, I have known of you for at least a year or two, ever since I started along this path with The Marshal. Both my father and my brother speak of you as if you are some kind of legend and that it what I know of you – that you are legendary. A man who is merely concerned for a comrade does not swear to protect her in the face of a lustful king, especially when doing it would more than likely ruin him."

He was looking at her, guarded. He always had such a glimmer of warmth to his gaze that to see him looking at her as if he were wary or even defensive was quite different. In fact, he couldn't seem to look her in the eyes so he turned away.

"I have done many things in my life that are risky or questionable," he said quietly. "This would be nothing new or different."

"Then you would do this for any woman?"

"Nay."

"Why me?"

He sighed heavily. "What do you want me to tell you?"

"The truth, Sherry. Tell me the truth."

He was staring off towards the garden, mulling over her words. After a moment, he simply shook his head. "I have no right to," he finally said. "Forgive me if I was too bold or too forward. You are a de Lohr and beyond my reach. It will not happen again."

"And you are a legend and beyond mine."

He looked at her, then. "Is *that* what you think? That I am elite?"

She took another step towards him, now standing fairly close. She studied his face a moment. "Aye," she said. "But you told me once that you were not afraid of my father and if you wanted something, you would get it."

"That is true."

"Did you mean me?"

He held her gaze but it was difficult. The question hung between them and for a normally emotionless man, there were emotions rippling all across his face – longing, doubt, fear, interest – wordlessly, he was shouting them out to her, speaking of his dilemma. He was a man torn.

But he was also a man cornered.

The time had come for him to take a stand.

"Although I am not worthy of you, aye, I meant you," he murmured. "I am twice your age, Cissy. I have nothing to offer you but myself and that is not good enough for a woman like you. You deserve the most prestigious husband of the highest order, not an assassin with a past of unsavory things, a man who has wandered for the majority of his life. But you make me want to stop wandering and that is something I've never felt before."

Those were, perhaps, the most beautiful words a man had ever said to a woman. At least, Christin thought so. Her heart swelled so in her chest that she thought it was going to burst forth and as she looked at him, all she could feel was joy.

Pure, unadulterated joy.

She could hardly believe it.

"You honor me," she whispered. "You have no idea how much you honor me, Sherry. If you want to stop wandering… I will give you a reason to."

He looked at her, his eyes widening. "You will?"

With a smile, she reached up, cupping his bearded face with the hand that wasn't holding the satchel. It was the first moment of genuine affection between them, of her flesh against his, and it was not lost on either of them. At that moment, they ceased to become merely comrades.

At that moment, the relationship between them deepened.

"I do not care about your past," she said. "You are a man to be admired in spite of what you think, and since we have come to know one another, I have seen a man of compassion and thoughtfulness and caring. That is the man I want to know more of. Buried beneath that assassin's cloak, you have a tender heart, for I have seen a glimpse."

Her hand on his face was like heaven. Alexander gazed into her eyes, hardly believing what he was hearing. He'd been doubtful, and confused, but these past few precious moments had cleared all of that up. He knew what he wanted and he wanted Christin de Lohr.

There was no doubt in his mind.

"No one has seen that but you," he said, an embarrassed grin on his face. "I would like to keep it that way, so do not tell anyone."

"Your secret is safe."

Alexander continued to stare at her, feeling emotions he'd never felt before. It was so unexpected, but so incredibly beautiful. Usually an eloquent man, he was having difficulty finding the words.

"My life has always been one of duty," he finally said. "I was the eldest son, raised to take my father's place when the time came and raised to set an example for my brothers. They were twins – Adam and Andrew. Everything about my upbringing was so cold, so duty-driven. I fostered at six years of age and my master was a hard man. There was no warmth, no praise, only the message that there was always more to achieve. When I went with King Richard to The Levant, my brothers went with me. Like starry-eyed squires, they only thought of the greatness they would be achieving. They only wanted the glory. We departed with Richard in April, arrived in The Levant in September, and by June the following year, my brothers were both dead. Killed in the same battle. I have not been home since. I could not face my father."

Christin could hear the sorrow in his voice as he spoke of his brothers more in detail. The man had a tortured past that she could not have imagined.

"That was many years ago," she said. "Does your father know you survived?"

Alexander nodded. "He knows," he said. "I sent him word in the same missive I told him of Adam and Andrew's deaths. That's when… that's when I ended up serving Richard directly. If there was a dirty mission to be carried out, an assassination to accomplish, I was his man. Me and Maxton and Kress and Achilles, among others. Maxton and Kress and Achilles traveled in a trio, but me… I preferred to work alone. It is better that way."

Christin wasn't appalled by the talk. She'd heard it from her father, too, as he had been in The Levant. Unsavory things happened during war and she understood that. But in Alexander's case, she could see the agony behind his actions.

He had a deeper reason.

"Why are you telling me this?" she asked softly. "None of it matters to me."

"So you know the kind of man I am."

"I *know* the kind of man you are. My father and my brother would not respect you so if you were not a man of character."

He looked at her as if she'd just said something outlandish. Then, he shook his head. "Sometimes, I wonder if that is true," he said. "I am a man with a stained past."

"Are you trying to scare me away? It will not work, you know. I am not easily frightened."

One moment, Alexander was looking into her lovely face. In the next, she was in his arms. He didn't know how it happened, only that it had. She was warm and soft in his embrace, something he hadn't experienced in years, and certainly not like this. Never with someone he was coming to care about. It had been an impulsive move on his part, but not a surprising one. He looked at her, into those big, gray eyes, and knew there was nothing on this earth that could ever force him to let her go.

Ever.

"Cissy," he said softly, "look at me. *Really* look at me. You must decide if I am what you truly want, for I will not accept a whim. Mayhap you are infatuated with the rumors you have heard and not the man I truly am. Only you can decide. But if you decide I am the man you want, nothing will stand in my way to make you mine. Not even your father. Will you go against him if he does not approve?"

She was torn between the thrill of being held by him and the truth of his words. "Of course he will approve," she said. "He has no reason not to."

"You did not answer my question."

Her free hand was on his shoulder, moving to his neck. Her fingers brushed against his warm flesh. "Aye," she murmured. "You are the man I want. I do not make decisions based on whims. I cannot explain it, Sherry… from the moment we met, I felt something for you. Awe, respect, interest… all of those things. And you are devilishly handsome. When you look at me, I feel bolts of lightning course through my veins. But I never imagined you would feel the same way about me."

With a grin, his lips slanted over hers, kissing her as strongly and deeply as he had ever kissed a woman in his life. As he'd told her, his life had been one of cold duty, so to feel something warm and emotional had him reeling. His hands were in her hair, holding her mouth to his as he feasted on her. He was kissing her so passionately that he heard her gasp, as if he'd been smothering her, so he quickly pulled away, concerned he'd overwhelmed her with what he was feeling.

He was feeling everything.

"You have me," he whispered, his hands still in her glorious hair. "*All* of me. But at the moment, we must move you someplace safe until the king leaves Norwich. If he moves against you now… I cannot guarantee that I would not take my own advice."

She was licking her lips, dazed by the force of his kiss. "What do you mean?"

"I would kill him."

Christin believed him and it terrified her, perhaps more than the king actually making a move on her. She couldn't stand the thought of something happening to him because of her. Hand on his face, she kissed his bearded cheek.

"I know," she said softly. "I have heard there is a nice inn near the cathedral. I shall go there until this is over with."

He took her satchel from her and grasped her hand. "Come along, then," he said. "We must hurry."

He was starting to head out through the main gate and she dug her heels in. "Nay," she said. "Not that way. There is a gate that leads to the farmlands below. It will be easier to leave through the gate down there and we will not be seen by so many of John's soldiers."

Alexander shifted direction. He began to walk, still holding Christin's hand, passing into the small garden behind the keep. No sooner had he stepped foot into the garden than a massive shadow appeared in his way.

Sean de Lara emerged from the shadows.

Alexander came to a halt and dropped Christin's hand, facing off against a man that served William Marshal in the capacity of the king's bodyguard. But it was more than that; if the king ordered Sean to bring him a woman, Sean would do it without question. If the king ordered him to kill a rival, Sean would snap the man's neck and toss him in the nearest river. Much as Alexander had a terrible reputation for brutality,

Sean's could match it and then some. Alexander's reputation wasn't out in the open as much as Sean's was. Everyone in England feared the man known as Lord of the Shadows.

And here he was.

"Sean," Alexander greeted steadily. "What finds you out here? Isn't the king still inside?"

Sean nodded. "He is," he said, his gaze moving between Alexander and Christin. "Where are you taking the lady?"

Alexander quickly sized up the situation. Sean was a couple of inches taller than he was and built like a bull, but Alexander had the advantage of enormous strength and a sword hand that was better than most. Even though he and Sean were technically on the same side, Alexander was prepared to fight the man in order to remove Christin.

He was prepared to do what was necessary.

"I am taking her away until the king leaves," he said. "You were in the chamber when the king demanded to dine with her, Sean. Did you really think we would allow it?"

"Who is 'we'?"

"Me," Christin stepped forward. She didn't really know Sean well but she knew his mission. She knew he had to provide the illusion of being loyal to the king above all else. "I will not sup with the king because if he tries to molest me or, God forbid, succeeds, it will bring my father's wrath. Dealing with the French will be the least of your worries if my father declares war on the crown."

Sean's gaze settled on her for a moment before nodding. "I know," he said simply. "I have told the king the same thing but to no avail. But you should know that this runs deeper than his usual interest in a woman. I am afraid I may not have the opportunity to tell The Marshal when he arrives, so I must tell you, Sherry. All of this runs deeper than you think."

Alexander wasn't sure if he was still going to have to fight Sean off, but it didn't sound like it. At least, not at the moment. He cocked his head curiously.

"Deeper?" he repeated. "Sean, you should know that we had an incident at Ramsbury Castle a few days ago. Has anyone told you about it yet?"

Sean shook his head. "Nay," he said. "What happened?"

"We had information that Lord Prescombe was a double agent for the French crown," Alexander said. "We set a trap for him and as it turned out, he had a female French agent working with him. Christin cornered the woman and she told Christin that there is a threat against John under our noses. There is some manner of threat against him we are not aware of and The Marshal believes it may be one of the allies who will be in attendance at this celebration. That is why we are all here; to find out who, or what, this threat is."

Sean digested the information. "It is possible that it is one of the allies," he said. "It is equally possible it is not. It could be an assassin dressed as a soldier or a knight, someone who is able to get close to the king. I will have to shadow him closely to ensure he remains healthy."

Alexander nodded. "Indeed," he said. "It is important you know what we were told. But now with this added threat of the king being interested in Christin… if her father finds out, the king's days are numbered. It will tear the country apart."

Sean sighed heavily as the weight of the situation settled. "It is worse than that," he said. "If I do not have the opportunity, you must tell William that John has plans for Christin."

Alexander and Christin looked at one another, puzzled. "*What plans?*" Christin asked. "How could the man possibly know anything at all about me?"

Sean looked at her. "He knows that you are Christopher de Lohr's eldest daughter," he said. "He knows you are unmarried. He plans to marry you to his bastard son, Robert FitzRoy. The man is the son of a king, after all, with a great manse in Bishop's Lynn, and for ties to de Lohr, John is willing to take the risk. He is convinced that marrying you to his son will subdue your father."

Christin was genuinely trying not to look horrified. She was also genuinely trying not to run. She held her ground, looking at Sean as if he'd just given her a death sentence.

"Is this true?" she breathed. "There could be no misunderstanding on your part?"

Sean shook his head with genuine regret. "Nay," he said quietly. "There is no misunderstanding. I am sorry, Christin. I have tried to discourage him and I shall continue to try. But at some point, it will look suspicious if I do not support his wishes."

Christin understood that. She could see that Sean wasn't here to take her to John, at least not yet. He was keeping her informed of what was happening. She'd never felt so frightened in her life.

Alexander.

She looked at him to see what his reaction was to all of this. He was looking at Sean, staring at the man in disbelief. When he finally spoke, his voice sounded strangely weak.

"Then hiding her until the king departs Norwich will not matter," he said. "This is not a whim."

"Nay, it is not," Sean said. "If she escapes him here, there will be another time. John does not easily give up. But if we face it now, we can control it somewhat."

"How?" Alexander asked.

Sean looked at Christin. "I have an idea, my lady, if you would be willing."

Christin wasn't sure how to answer him. She wanted to leave. She wanted to hide out but Alexander and Sean seemed to think that wasn't a good idea. If John was on her scent, he would not relent until he found her. But she wasn't so convinced.

"Why must I face him?" she asked. "Why can I not simply hide away until he forgets about me. There are thousands of women in England. He will find someone else for his son, eventually."

Sean lifted his big shoulders. "It is possible," he said. "It is equally possible that by losing the opportunity to wed you to his son, he will go after one of your sisters. You have three, do you not? Brielle is the sister closest to your age. What if he takes her instead of you? Would that make you feel better?"

He sounded cold and Christin stiffened. "Of course it will not make me feel better," she hissed. "My father will go after him, anyway. I must send word to my father to hide all of my sisters until the king grows weary of us and moves on to another family."

"My lady, I have served John for years," Sean said patiently. "He does not forget. The more you elude his grasp, the more obsessed he will become. He went after your mother years ago. Did you know that? Your father saved her, but it took a massive war and great loss in order to regain your mother. John has had an obsession with the de Lohr women for a long time, so this is not something that will simply fade away. You must trust me on this."

Christin thought she had heard that at one point, how John and his henchmen had captured his mother. As she struggled with her reply, Alexander spoke quietly.

"What is your suggestion, Sean?" he asked. "Tell us and we shall do it."

Sean looked at him. Something in the way he'd said it made it sound as if he and Christin were a team. *We shall do it*. Given that he'd been lingering in the shadows when Alexander had kissed her, he could see that something was going on between them but, much to Alexander's credit, he wasn't acting like a crazed lover. He was acting like a man who knew his duty and Sean respected that.

It couldn't have been easy on him.

"John loathes ill-mannered women," he said. "That may seem foolish, but I assure you that it is true. Drinking, loud-mouthed, belching, farting… he cannot stand women who behave that way. He prefers his women young, quiet, sweet-smelling, and obedient. If Christin can behave like she was born in the slums of London, it could very well put him off her scent."

Alexander considered that seriously. "And you believe that is the best course of action?"

"Given what I know of the man, I do. Unless he feels her status as a de Lohr makes her a more worthy a prize over her bad behavior, we must gamble on her disgusting him."

It wasn't a foolproof plan, but strong enough that Alexander was willing to agree with him. He turned to Christin, who was standing there listening to all of it without much of an expression on her face. When she realized Alexander and Sean were looking at her, she simply shook her head in resignation.

"I can try," she said. "I have been called upon to charm men. I suppose I can make a good effort at un-charming one."

Alexander nodded in approval. "It will be difficult for you, but I have faith in you."

Christin smiled at him, making Sean feel as if he were intruding on something. But it brought up a valuable point.

"I would suggest no meaningful looks between you two in public," he said. "If John thinks you are fond of her, it will destroy her attempts in trying to disillusion him."

Both Alexander and Christin looked at him in surprise. "Meaningful looks?" Alexander repeated.

Sean cast him a knowing expression. "They do not call me the Lord of the Shadows for nothing," he said. "I have been watching you two for quite some time. You just did not see me."

When they realized what he meant, Christin hung her head, embarrassed, while Alexander merely smiled. "Is it that obvious?"

Sean's lips flickered with a smile. "When you kissed her, it was."

Alexander's smile lingered for a moment, but the light soon went out of his eyes. "Then you understand I will do whatever is necessary to ensure her safety, Sean."

The conversation took a somber, if not ominous, turn. "And I will do whatever is necessary to ensure the safety of the king," Sean said. "Sherry, I understand what is going on and I want to help, but not at the risk of my position. I know you understand that."

Alexander did. That was the trouble – he understood more than most. He knew what Sean would do to protect his position and, now, Alexander knew what he would do to protect Christin.

He could only hope it didn't come to that.

"I trust you, Sean," he finally said. "But I have a stake in this as much as she does. If your plan does not work…"

"If it does not work, then we will have to formulate another plan."

Alexander felt better about that, knowing Sean was willing to go above and beyond. But only to a certain point.

It was that point that had Alexander's concern.

"Then what do we do now?" Alexander asked.

Sean gestured to the apartments he had seen Christin emerge from. "She will change into her finest gown, come to the feasting hall, and make an absolute fool of herself," he said, looking to Christin. "You can do that, can you not?"

Christin sighed, knowing she had no choice. "I can."

"The worse you can behave, the better for us all."

"I will."

Alexander looked at her. "Pretend we are back at the wedding feast in the village and you are drunk on cheap ale."

Sean lifted his eyebrows. "Drunk on cheap ale? I am intrigued."

Christin shook her head. "Don't be," she said. "I made an absolute arse out of myself, and it seems that I shall be called upon to do it again."

Alexander grinned. "She vomited like a waterspout."

"Don't tell him that!" Christin said, appalled. She looked at Alexander and Sean, both of them grinning, and pursed her lips wryly. "I will change my clothing and wait for the summons."

Sean's smile faded. "I will come for you myself."

Christin nodded, her gaze moving to Alexander. Looking at him made her feel afraid again, fearful that this might not work. After everything they'd said between them, she didn't want this evening to be the last time she and Alexander spoke of their feelings for one another. She wanted to speak to the man every evening for the rest of her life.

But she had to get through tonight first.

"I will see you later," she murmured. "I will not fail. But if this does not go our way, promise me that you will not do anything foolish. Please, Sherry."

Alexander was struggling not to become emotional, an unusual state for him, indeed. "I will not do anything foolish," he said. "But I will do what is necessary."

She shook her head sadly, knowing what he meant. But she had to be clear. "You will not jeopardize yourself for me, do you hear? I can handle myself. But I could not live with myself if I knew you sacrificed yourself for me. Am I making myself clear?"

She was, but he wasn't going to give her the answer she was looking for. He couldn't. "You are the strongest woman I know," he said quietly. "We will prevail."

He said it to give her strength but also to make it clear that, in spite of her pleas, he would do what he felt necessary. Reaching out, he took her hand and kissed it, watching her as she headed back to her chamber, still carrying her satchel. He watched her until she disappeared inside before turning to Sean.

"I had better spread the word about what is to happen with her tonight," he said. "I am particularly concerned about Peter."

Sean knew that, but something caught his eye emerging from the keep. From where he was standing, he had a clear field of vision. He could see three men moving through the torch-lit darkness and as they moved over near the chapel, it occurred to him who they were.

"There he is," he said. "It looks as if he is with MacRohan and my brother."

Alexander could see them all, heading to the chapel for perhaps yet another private meeting. "I see him," he said. "I will go speak with him."

He started to move but a Sean stopped him. "How is my brother these days?" he asked.

Alexander knew that the relationship between the de Lara brothers was strained. More than strained, in fact. He could hear the concern in Sean's voice and he felt some pity for the man.

"Well," he said. "He serves flawlessly, as he always has. He's with de Lohr now, you know."

Sean nodded slowly. "With David," he said. "I know. Have you heard any news about my father?"

"You do not talk to him?"

Sean shook his head. "Nay," he said, his expression appearing almost vulnerable as he thought of his beloved father. "A few years ago, he was in London and came to the White Tower, where John happened to be in residence at the time. He begged to see me and when I agreed, he wept the entire time. I... I had to leave him at the gatehouse, sobbing over what I have become. It nearly destroyed me, Sherry. Therefore, I do not have any contact with him. I am trying to spare him the pain."

Alexander sighed faintly. "I have not seen my own father in over twenty years," he said. "Like you, it is my choice. I have my own reasons. But my father does not love me like yours does you. He would never show up and beg me to come home."

"How do you know?"

Alexander smiled thinly. "Because I killed two of his sons. I am sure he wishes me dead every day of his life."

Sean was too young to go to The Levant with Richard's Crusade, but he knew what men like Alexander and Maxton and Kress and Achilles had done there. He admired them greatly, but much like himself, they had built reputations for themselves that men feared and loathed. It was difficult to know that doing one's duty would ruin every other aspect of a man's life.

"I am sure to my father, I am dead," Sean said. "Even so... you have not heard any news of him?"

Alexander shook his head. "You might ask your brother."

"You know that Kevin will not speak to me."

Alexander's gaze lingered on the chapel. "He might if you happened to run into him," he said. "I will tell him that I am concerned with the security of the postern gate and that he must see to it. Mayhap you will be in the vicinity when he checks it. Meanwhile, I will go and tell Peter and Bric what is to happen tonight. We must all be prepared. Oh, and Sean?"

"Aye?"

"If John tries to bed Christin, I will kill him."

Sean didn't say anything for a moment. When he finally did, it was with a grunt. "Sherry…"

"I am telling you what will happen. It would therefore be in your best interest to prevent it any way you can."

"Sherry, if you make a move against the king, I will be forced to treat you like any other threat."

"I understand. You will do as you must."

"I will."

"So will I."

The rules were established, as hard as they were to acknowledge. There was no malice in the discussion, no hard feelings. Simply fact. As Alexander headed towards the chapel, Sean wondered if he'd find himself battling Alexander to the death before the night was out.

He liked Sherry. He didn't want to kill him.

He prayed it didn't come to that.

CHAPTER NINE

"KEVIN," ALEXANDER SAID as he entered the dark, dingy chapel. "Where have you been? I arrived earlier and was told you'd run off."

Kevin looked at him. "I did not run off," he said, offended by Alexander's statement. "I did my rounds of the keep and the king's encampment."

"Did you discover anything interesting?"

Kevin shook his head. "John is traveling lightly," he said. "He's brought no more than a hundred men with him, which must be giving my brother fits. I heard someone say something about a royal carriage, but I did not see one."

"And the keep?"

"Solid," he said. "I had the servants bolt the door that leads from the vault into the bailey. It could be an access point for any threats against the king, as they could enter from there, come up the stairs, and mingle in the great hall."

Alexander nodded. "Well done," he said. "But do one more thing for me and check the postern gate. I've heard it leads to the farm fields below. It could be another point of easy access we want to control."

Kevin nodded. "Where is it?"

Alexander gestured towards the east side of the keep. "Back behind the keep," he said. "Make sure it is secure."

Kevin would. Heading out into the cold night, this was the precursor work to the evening's feast and the main celebration that would take place tomorrow. Of course, Norwich had their own soldiers and knights, men who had also checked doors and access points into the castle, so what Kevin was doing was for The Marshal's peace of mind. He would want to know from his own men how secure the castle and keep were, especially if they were searching for a threat against the king.

Therefore, Kevin had made the rounds. He was still making them and would probably make them tomorrow as well. The garden was straight ahead; he could see the vines and bushes in the darkness. There was a pond in the middle of it, which blended in with its surroundings in the darkness, so he made sure to steer clear of it as he made his way to the postern gate.

The panel loomed before him. It was shorter than a man, but wide to allow the carts in from the farmlands below. It was secure this night, locked tight. Kevin tested the lock himself. Satisfied, he turned around to see a figure moving in the darkness.

His sword came out.

"Announce yourself," he said steadily.

The figure didn't say anything but as it drew closer, and Kevin could see the size of it, it began to occur to him who it was.

The very man he'd been trying to avoid.

Sean de Lara came close enough that Kevin could see his features in the weak light.

"Are you going to use that weapon on me?" Sean asked.

Kevin stared at his older brother a moment before lowering the sword. "Nay," he said. "You startled me."

Sean nodded briefly. "I know," he said. "I saw you coming this direction. I thought it might be the only way I would have a chance to speak with you if I surprised you."

Already, he was referencing the fact that Kevin would not talk to him under normal circumstances. Kevin sheathed his weapon.

"What did you want to speak of?" he asked.

Already, Sean could see that his brother was stiff and unfriendly. No warmth, no recognition of a brother. Not that he'd expected otherwise, but even after all of these years, it was difficult to stomach Kevin's reaction to him.

His reaction to the Lord of the Shadows.

That's what started it all. Kevin, as straight and pious and noble as he was, couldn't stomach what Sean had done to himself and to the de Lara name. He couldn't stomach that their elderly father still wept over the choices his eldest son and heir had made. While Kevin had lived his life as cleanly and as nobly as he could, Sean had killed and maimed for the king, the dirtiest and most horrible deeds imaginable. All in the name of keeping England, and a monarch, safe and controlled.

Sean had that power.

But it was a power Kevin loathed.

Therefore, Sean braced himself.

"There is nothing in particular I wish to speak of other than ask you how our father fares," he said after a moment. "If you would be kind enough to tell me, I would be grateful."

Kevin looked at him as if he'd gone mad. "What do *you* care?" he said. "You've kicked him aside and hurt him beyond repair, and now you want to know how he fares? I find that question extremely offensive."

"He's my father, too, Kevin."

"You gave up that privilege when you made the decision to lie with the dogs."

"Must we go through this every time we speak?"

"There is nothing for us to talk about, Sean. I have duties to attend to."

Sean was saddened. This was the way his conversations with his brother usually went. But this time, he wasn't so willing to let it go. He had something to say and he was damned well going to say it.

"There is plenty for us to talk about, but your arrogance will not allow it," he said. "I am sorry you do not understand the choices I have made. I am sorry you do not understand the sacrifices I have had to make in order to ensure a safer England. Safer for you and for Father, Kevin. But mostly, I am sorry you do not have the foresight nor the compassion to understand that I had to ruin my life to do this. Instead, you see it as some imagined insult against you and against the de Lara name. I have never asked for your approval, but the least you could do is not judge me for it. God knows, I don't judge you and I never have."

By the time he was finished, Kevin's jaw was flexing with emotion. Anger, hurt... so many emotions that he didn't keep bottled up very well when it came to his brother. Any confrontation with his brother like this had him off-kilter.

"Is that all you want to say?" Kevin said. "Because I don't have time for whatever soul baring you wish to do."

His words stung. Sean stared at him a moment, feeling sad and ashamed. "Then I am sorry to have troubled you," he said. "But I will say this – until now, I was always hopeful we could reconcile. I hoped that, someday, you would understand why I do what I do, but I can see that was too much to ask. I hope to God you are never faced with a difficult choice in your life, Kevin, because I do not think you have the character to make the right decision. I always hoped you did, but I can see that you do not. There is no need to be ashamed of me because I am far more ashamed of you and just how shallow you really are. In spite of that, I wish you a good life because I do not expect to ever talk to you again."

With that, he turned away, heading back into the shadows from whence he'd come. Kevin stood there a moment, watching him go, trying very hard not to feel any remorse or guilt. Sean *was* in the wrong, wasn't he? He was the one to choose to do the king's bidding, no matter what it was. He made the choice to prostitute himself to a monarch who wasn't worthy of Sean's greatness.

Wasn't worthy...

Sean was a great knight. One of the greatest, in fact. Kevin had always thought so, but he'd lost the respect for the man when he'd begun to serve John. It wasn't judgment.

It was a personal conviction.

But at the moment, his personal conviction didn't feel so triumphant.

It felt hollow.

With a heavy sigh, Kevin turned and headed back to the chapel.

CHAPTER TEN

S HE WAS READY.

Dressed in a gown that would be sacrificed this evening, an amber silk that had faded over the years, Christin presented a striking picture.

Wynter had styled her hair with beautiful and elaborate braids, with bows pinned to her hair, and all the while the two of them had plotted out the evening. Wynter was in on the scheme but sworn to secrecy, even to Lady de Winter or anyone else who should ask. It was critical that she deny all culpability. Christin didn't go so far as to tell Wynter about her conversation with Alexander and Sean, but rather made it seem like it was her own idea to turn the king's attraction off.

There was quite a litany of events to accomplish this.

With Wynter as her accomplice, Christin felt much more confident going into the situation. As Wynter scurried away to prepare for the coming feast, Christin sat on her bed and waited for Sean to make an appearance. But while she was waiting, she had several gulps of wine. Not enough to make her drunk or even tipsy, but enough that one could smell liquor on her breath. When she dabbed some in her dark hair, behind her ears, and down her cleavage, the warmth of her body gave the wine a rather stale smell. She'd even gone so far as to send Wynter to the kitchen yard and gather dung from the milk cow, which Christin promptly rubbed on her shift so that when her dress moved, the scent of cow dung was obvious.

She smelled like a drunken barnyard.

That was the plan.

Patiently, she waited for Sean, who came to the apartments right after the feast had commenced to collect her. A servant had summoned her and she'd gone down to greet Sean at the apartment entry. They didn't say a word to each other but when he got close enough to her, he smelled the cow dung and the wine. It was enough to wrinkle his nose.

"Well done, my lady," he muttered. "Are you ready?"

"Can't you tell?"

"Verily."

Sean escorted her into the great hall, which was alive with men and the allies who had arrived thus far for the king's celebration. Rather than allow Christin to grip his elbow in a polite gesture of escort, Sean had her by the arm instead, directing her into the hall and to the dais where the king awaited.

Not strangely, Christin felt a wave of fear wash through her at the sight of John. He was dressed quite well, in silks and furs, and his attention was riveted to her as she approached. Sean let go of her and she curtsied clumsily before the dais.

"Come sit next to me, my lady," John said. "I have eagerly been awaiting this meal."

Oh, but there was a lascivious expression on his face. Christin could see it; everyone else did, too, knowing that John was about to have another conquest for the night.

They couldn't have been more wrong.

Christin came around the side of the table, moving to the chair that John was indicating. He was smiling at her, a lazy predatory smile, but as she sat down and her dress billowed out, the first wave of cow smell washed over the table and the king.

It was a shocking first salvo in the war to discourage the king.

"It was so kind of you to invite me, your grace," Christin said, reaching for a full cup of wine in front of her. "I will admit, I was very nervous to join you. You are a great man, a king, and I am the daughter of a mere earl. But it seems to me that we are all part of God's family, so why should I be so nervous? I have been asking myself that all evening. I am sure you have had many ladies as guests at your table. Are they all so nervous?"

She was chattering a mad streak and John didn't have a chance to get a word in. Even after she asked the question, she took a very sloppy drink of wine and it spilled down the front of her. Using her sleeve, she wiped at her mouth and her chest where the wine had gone.

"Forgive me, your grace," she said. "I am ever so clumsy. Of course, the women you sup with must all be very graceful and gracious, but not me. I never had the grace that other women had and I surely am not a witty conversationalist, and all the time I have been here at Norwich, I have never had a suitor, so being asked to sup with you has made me giddy. But it is such an honor!"

Again with the sloppy drink. It washed back on her chin and she sputtered, spraying it everywhere as she coughed dramatically, as if the wine had choked her. It had sprayed onto John a little, and all over the food in front of her. She slammed the wine cup down and it sloshed over the sides.

"Oh!" she cried. "What a mess I have made! But it's not the first mess I have made, I assure you. My mother calls me Messy Chrissy. It's true! If something is broken, it's usually my fault because I break everything I touch. My father says I have the grace of a rutting bull. Can you imagine? A de Lohr who is not graceful?"

There was a leg of a swan that a servant had thoughtfully put before her, probably at the king's direction. As she talked, she picked it up and took a big bite out of it. Food was hanging out of her mouth as she smacked her lips.

"My family is going to be very surprised to learn that I have dined with you," she said, food spilling onto her dress as she chewed with her mouth open. "Honestly, it seems that I always dine with the same people so it is thrilling to see new faces, and of course, your grace is included. I bet I make a much more congenial dinner companion with you than my father ever has!"

She laughed loudly, dripping food out of her mouth, which she simply brushed off her skirts and kept eating. Meat was going everywhere at this point with very little of it actually going into her mouth.

Beside her, the king was watching her with confusion. When the food sprayed, his eyebrows lifted and a flicker of disgust crossed his expression. He watched her as she finished with the leg bone and tossed it, throwing it right into a man on the next table. As the man looked to her in shock and outrage, she laughed loudly at him.

"Sit down, you vile pig," she yelled at him, ripping off a wing on the peacock in front of her and throwing that at him, hitting him in the shoulder. "Oh, you don't like that, do you? Sit down before I come over there and shove that bird up your…"

"My lady, please," John interrupted, looking at her with a good deal of astonishment. "I appreciate civility in a lady. Please act accordingly."

Christin demurred unnaturally fast. "I see," she said, yanking more meat off of the swan. "I am sorry. I don't usually talk so much, but I want to be witty and entertaining. I do not want you to regret asking me to dine with you. But I will admit that I like wine. I developed the habit when I was young. My parents never could keep the wine away from me."

With that, she shoved the meat in her mouth and tried to take a drink of wine around it, but it was too much food and she ended up choking. All of the meat and wine came back out, spraying over the table. Some of it hit the king in the leg. Appalled, Christin used her sleeve to brush it from his knee.

"I am so sorry, your grace," she said. "I do not know what has come over me. I am just nervous, I suppose, and…"

She had mentioned her nerves more than once and John held out a hand to shut her up. "There is no need to be nervous, my lady," he said. "You must relax or there will be more food wasted than eaten. Lord de Winter has presented a lovely feast tonight for us to enjoy."

Christin's face screwed up as if she were going to cry. "It is beautiful, your grace," she said, her voice squeaky. "I am so ashamed. I will try to do better."

She grabbed the wine cup again, managing to spill most of it on her dress before the cup made it to her mouth. She drained the cup because there was very little left, tossing the cup onto the floor.

"More wine!" she bellowed.

She yelled so loud that John winced, sitting back in his chair and watching the woman behave as badly as she possibly could. It was astonishing, really. He'd never seen something so appalling in his entire life.

But that was only the first act.

More wine came, delivered by one of Lady de Winter's women who was, in fact, Wynter. And the wine wasn't wine as much as it was very little wine and boiled water, but there was enough wine to color it red. The king didn't know that. He watched as Christin drank half the cup, smacking her lips before delivering a belch that half the hall heard.

And that's when things got interesting.

"MY GOD," PETER breathed. "What is she doing?"

Alexander was at one of the tables with Peter, Bric, and Kevin. He had watched as Sean had directed Christin into the hall and when she took her seat with John. From that point on, all he could see was her animated conversation. She seemed to be talking up a storm to the king, who was watching her with increasing disbelief. Alexander couldn't hear the words and wondered what she was saying, but when she started eating the swan's leg and food began to fly, he suspected she was making herself out to be the epitome of an ill-bred woman.

Her brother was nearly beside himself.

"Just… wait," Alexander said to Peter. "Wait and watch. This is her show now, so let her perform. We told you that she is trying to disgust the king so he will turn his attentions elsewhere, so let her do what she must do."

"Has anyone told Old Daveigh?"

"I have," Bric said quietly. "He knows. Christ, she just dropped wine all down the front of her. She is called The Ghost, but this is not very ghostly."

"Nay, it's very obvious," Alexander said. "But oh, so brilliant."

The four of them were trying hard not to watch her because they didn't want the king or his men to catch on to what amounted to an act. They didn't want to blow Christin's efforts apart, so they focused on their food, on each other, only casting the occasional glance to the dais as the show continued.

But Alexander was coiled.

It was an unusual state for him. Usually, he was the calm one. He gave the commands and others followed because he was composed no matter what was going on, but at the moment, he felt as if his composure were hanging on by a thread.

Even if he couldn't hear her words, he definitely heard the wet, deep belch she emitted after she'd downed what looked to be a cup of wine. Half the hall heard it. As Alexander, Kevin, and Bric looked on with shock, Peter was having a difficult time holding back the laughter.

"I cannot believe she did that," Peter said, turning his head away so they couldn't see him laugh. "As a child, we used to have competitions on who could belch the loudest and Christin was always a force to be reckoned with. I cannot believe she has brought that talent to light."

As the others were trying not to look at the dais, open-mouthed, Christin let out another belch that was very wet and she ended up vomiting up some of the food she'd eaten. As she let it fall to the floor, spitting it out, Bric and Peter lost their struggle against the laughter. Heads turned away from the dais, they laughed so hard that Bric's face turned a deep shade of red. Peter couldn't catch his breath. All the while, Alexander was watching the entire event with a mixture of shock, amusement, and the utmost respect.

She was one hell of a woman.

He'd called Christin brave, but this went beyond what he thought she was capable of. It was the most barbaric behavior he'd ever seen coming from a woman, a performance carried out with the utmost skill. She wasn't afraid to get dirty, to make herself sick, or make a fool of herself, knowing it was all for an end result.

That elevated her tremendously in his eyes.

He could only hope her extreme efforts were working.

Little did he know she was about to take it to the next level.

"YOUR GRACE, FORGIVE me," Christin said as she moved her chair back, away from the vomit on the floor. "This has been a terrible evening. But most evenings go like this for me. It is the drink; it always does terrible things to me, yet I love it so. Life is very dull without wine, would you not say so? My favorite is from Spain. Do you have a favorite wine?"

John was absolutely appalled by what he'd seen. When she stopped belching, barfing, and chatting, he realized she'd asked him a question. He, too, scooted his chair away from the vomit and also from her, afraid she might belch and puke again.

"Gascony, I suppose," he said. "I find that I do not care where it comes from as long as it is fine."

Christin nodded vigorously. Her hair was starting to come undone, making her appear quite disheveled. "I agree completely, your grace," she said. Before she could comment further, Wynter came by with a pitcher of wine and Christin grabbed her arm. "I need more drink, wench. Fill my…"

She yanked too hard on Wynter's arm and the woman dumped half the contents of the pitcher on her shoulder and arm. A portion of it splashed onto John, who wasn't quite out of range. Outraged, and wet, Christin leapt to her feet.

"You foolish chit," she gasped. "Do you not realize who this is? You have offended the king with your sloppy behavior. Someone should teach you some manners!"

With that, she grabbed Wynter by the hair and pulled her down onto the king's table. Sean, who had been watching the fiasco so far and struggling not to laugh, stepped forward to pull the king out of the way as the two women began to fight on the table. Legs and hands were flying around. Gerard d'Athee was also there and Sean passed the king into the man's protective custody as those nearest the dais stood up, concerned to see two women fighting right on the king's table.

Unfortunately, the man Christin had hit on the shoulder with the bone from the swan was fairly close to the table where the women were brawling. He was a knight who served the House of de Mandeville, a de Winter ally. Christin, on top of Wynter at this point and smashing turnips into her face, caught sight of the man, who was looking at her with outrage. That was all it took for Christin to unleash on him. Picking up a bowl of stewed fruit, she hurled it at him.

"And that's for challenging me, you revolting dog!" she screamed. "You are an abomination!"

The knight was hit with the bowl on the jaw. As the fruit sprayed everywhere, he lost his balance and toppled back into the man next to him. That man didn't take kindly to it and soon the two of them were throwing punches. Because they were fighting, their colleagues began to push each other and, within very little time, a full-scale brawl had erupted at one of the tables. Food began to fly and dogs began to scatter.

But Christin wasn't paying attention to that. She wasn't hurting Wynter, nor was Wynter hurting her, but they were making a good show of pulling hair and smashing food into each other. This had been their plan all along and it was working splendidly. Christin grabbed a half a loaf of bread that had been artfully braided, with a hard crust, and began beating Wynter with it, who shoved her onto the floor.

Both women were on the floor now, rolling around in spilled food, wine, and Christin's vomit. Sean, who had been watching everything with great interest and even greater amusement, bent over Christin as she wrestled with Wynter.

"My lady," he said. "The king is..."

Whap! Sean was hit in the face by the crusty bread Christin was swinging around. With crumbs in his eyes, he staggered back to clear his vision as someone tossed a man onto the table on the dais. The man rolled into Sean, who immediately grabbed him, lifted him up over his head, and tossed him back where he came from.

It was an impressive move.

When he managed to clear his eyes, his attention moved back to Christin and Wynter, who had stopped fighting and were now hiding under the table, giggling uncontrollably. Sean wiped at his eyes again, shaking his head at the pair as he realized it was all an act. *All* of it.

He'd never seen anything so hilarious.

Or ruthless.

"Get out of my sight," he growled to Christin. "Back to your room. Bolt the door and I do not want to see you again while I am here at Norwich. Stay *away*. Do you understand me?"

Christin wasn't frightened nor offended. In fact, she completely understood. Giving the man a grin, she grabbed Wynter and bolted to her feet, both of them running from the hall, half of which was still in turmoil. Sean watched her go, trying to glare at her, but having the most awful time struggling not to laugh. Quickly, he departed because he was losing the battle.

But the fight in the hall was still going full bore. Men were brawling and food was still flying as Old Daveigh along with Alexander, Peter, Bric and Kevin tried to calm down the brawl. Alexander saw Christin flee the hall and he also saw Sean leave, departing quickly after the king, who had been hurriedly escorted out when the women started to fight.

For an evening that had started out with great trepidation, it could not have ended better as far as he was concerned. Christin had performed magnificently, something that he would be sure to tell William Marshal when the man arrived. She deserved a great deal of praise for what she had done. There would certainly be no concerns over the king trying to bed her this night.

Alexander had never been so proud of someone in all his life.

With a grin, he went back to work trying to help Old Daveigh calm his unruly guests.

CHAPTER ELEVEN

FROM THE UNPREDICTABLE rain that had set a precedent for the season, the day had dawned remarkably clear and strangely warm. There wasn't the usual chill to the air that there usually was, making it extremely pleasant for travel.

In fact, David had his helm off completely and the sun had turned his nose red as the de Lohr group headed into the outskirts of Norwich. There was a wedding feast still going on, but it looked as if it had been going on for a few days because some people were sleeping on tables, others were picking at food, while still others were haphazardly dancing with music played by exhausted musicians. There were drunkards passed out all around and tatters of flowers and garlands.

Christopher reined his horse to a halt, looking at the town square. It looked like a cluster of discarded poppets.

"It looks like one hell of a party," he said, tipping back his helm and wiping the sweat from his brow.

David looked around him, grinning. "I'm sorry I missed it," he said. "I cannot imagine de Winter's celebration is going to be any great cause for copious drinking like this event clearly was."

As the brothers were nodding, looking on ahead to Norwich Castle in the distance, they heard a voice behind them.

"It looks like one of the parties we used to participate in, long ago." It was a deep, loud voice. "Usually, it would be David passed out under the table as Chris and I arm wrestled to see who could throw whom to the ground first."

Christopher and David turned around, both of them grinning when they saw an enormous knight on a big, black warhorse coming up behind them. The man was wearing a tunic of William Marshal, as he was the garrison commander of the mighty Richmond Castle and probably the fiercest knight in the north of England.

"Cai," Christopher said with satisfaction. "Do my eyes deceive me? Is it really you?"

Sir Caius d'Avignon flipped up his visor, giving the brothers a full view of his smiling face. He was an enormous man, usually at least a head taller than everyone else around him, with hair and eyes as black as coal. His face was angular and strong, the brilliant smile displaying charmingly crooked teeth.

"It is me in the flesh, gentle knights," he said. "I should be asking *you* that question. Why in the hell would you attend a celebration in honor of John? He's not exactly your favorite person."

"For the same reason you would."

"The Marshal ordered you to?"

Christopher laughed softly. "He did not order us, but rather strongly encouraged," he said. "Besides, it is a chance for me to see my eldest children. They both serve at Norwich."

Caius nodded as he reined his horse next to Christopher. "I have seen Peter from time to time," he said. "An astonishingly good knight."

A prideful smile crossed Christopher's lips. "He comes from excellent stock and has had excellent training," he said. "His brothers are doing equally well. Curtis and Richard serve at Bowes Castle with Juston de Royans and they are both nearly as big as I am at sixteen and fourteen years, respectively. Myles is at Canterbury with David, still, and the younger children are at home with my wife and me. Rebecca has seen seven years, Douglas five years, Westley three years, and Olivia Charlotte is the baby."

"The baby has two names?"

"I liked one, Dustin liked the other, so she is called by two names."

Caius snorted. "How exhausting."

Christopher shrugged. "You get used to it," he said. "In any case, Dustin insists on keeping our children to her bosom. It is like extracting teeth with her to send a child to foster."

Caius chuckled. "That is quite a brood, my virile stud," he said. "Are you finished yet?"

Christopher cocked an eyebrow. "My wife says I am a dead man if she conceives a child again, so I would say that we are finished."

Both Caius and David laughed heartily at that statement, mostly because Christopher seemed rather fearful of the wrath of his wife in such a case.

"I cannot believe a man of your stature would be fearful of a woman," Caius said. "You are the husband. If you want more children, that is your right."

Christopher gave a loud, ironic snort. "When you marry, you shall understand," he said. "You're completely ignorant, d'Avignon. Give advice only for the things you're good for – slaying enemies and savages."

Caius grinned wolfishly. "The only thing I have been slaying as of late lies between a woman's legs."

That set Christopher and David off into laughter again. Caius was, if nothing else, quite entertaining. They had served with him in The Levant, part of the close circle of Richard's trusted men, and Caius had been jovial and witty at times. He was also one of the most brilliant, deadly tacticians around, so much so that the Muslims called him *Britania Faybr*, or The Britannia Viper.

He was big, fast, and deadly.

He was, therefore, a man that Christopher and David respected and liked. Christopher clapped the man on the arm.

"Come along, lad," he said. "Let us go and slay a few cups of wine and some of de Winter's fine food."

"No women?"

"Not for me, but be my guest if there are any eligible women in attendance."

Caius thought that sounded like a good idea. The three of them continued on through the village of half-drunk people, heading towards the enormous, square bastion in the distance. More people were arriving as well, groups of invited nobles, and they could see several houses that they knew, allies of de Winter and of William Marshal. There were several roads into Norwich, as it was the largest city in Norfolk, and parties were coming in from all over.

Christopher recognized all of them, in fact. Summerlin, de Leybourne, and Ashbourne were just a few groups of men he recognized. As the groups bottlenecked into the city gates, he found himself in conversation with Padraig Summerlin, the garrison commander of Castle Rising. He was a good man, married to one of Old Daveigh's daughters. It was quite a festive atmosphere as men arrived for days of drink and food in celebrations of the king's birthday the coming month. And just as they passed beneath the city gate, they began to hear a commotion behind them.

William Marshal was bringing up their rear with about a hundred solders and Maxton and Kress riding with him, armed to the teeth. Although Christopher and David had brought about the same number of men-at-arms with them, they were treating the ride a little more casually. David still had his helm off, enjoying the sun, and Christopher's shield wasn't even on his saddle. There was a small group from Thetford between them and The Marshal's party, one Lord Croxton, and Maxton and Kress scared the hell out of Lady Croxton as they pushed their group.

Christopher could hear Lady Croxton weeping loudly.

It was mostly Maxton, harassing people in order to make way for William Marshal, but Christopher didn't comment on the fact. That was typical Maxton; no tact, all business. He and Maxton had known each other for over twenty years and they had never particularly gotten along, mostly because they were so much alike in personality – forceful, commanding, demanding. But Maxton had a darker edge about him, something Christopher didn't have, nor did he like, and there had been times in the past when he and Maxton had butted heads.

But these days, they couldn't work up the energy to do so. They had accepted one another for who, and what, they were, and although they would never be the best of friends, they managed to get along for the most part. As Maxton pushed through the Croxton group to reach the de Lohrs and Caius, he ended up shoving the lone Croxton knight out of the way by kicking the man's horse in the flanks. As the animal bolted off, he turned his attention to the men he knew.

"Here we are, together again," he said, mostly focused on Caius. "Cai, God help you, you're uglier than I remember."

Caius snorted. "Thankfully, the women do not think that."

Maxton rolled his eyes, for it was true. They all knew that women flocked to Caius like a moth to the flame. His attention fell on David next.

"My lord," he greeted. "I see that you are still in the company of that one."

He nodded his head in Christopher's direction and David smiled thinly. "You mean the Earl of Hereford and Worcester?" he said. "Show some respect, Loxbeare."

Maxton turned to Christopher and the two of them gazed at each other, appraisingly. That was usual with them. "My lord," Maxton said. "All the way from the Marches, I see."

"And you," Christopher said evenly. "How is Gloucester?"

"Quiet. Just the way I like it. And Lioncross?"

"Quiet. Just the way I like it." Christopher looked at David and Caius, and now Kress as he joined them. "You would never guess that Maxton and I are allies along the Marches. He really loves me, but he will never admit it."

There was an ironic jest in that, and some humor. It wasn't true, but it wasn't entirely untrue, either. The relationship between the pair was complicated. As David and Caius shook their heads to the unspoken rivalry between Christopher and Maxton, Kress reined his horse next to the group.

"Greetings, my lords," he said, far more polite to Christopher and David than Maxton had been. "'Tis a fine day for much drinking and eating."

"You will keep the drinking to a minimum," William said as he rode up. "I do not need a bunch of drunken lords about with John on the prowl. Has he arrived yet?"

Everyone turned in the direction of the castle, the great square box on the hill that loomed over the town. There were banners flying, both de Winter and Plantagenet, snapping in the light breeze.

"I would guess he is here," Christopher said. "His feast begins today, after all."

William simply lifted his eyebrows, seemingly not too thrilled about the whole thing. He was here only because he had to be. The enormous de Lohr/Marshal group pushed through the village, as they were now on one of the wide avenues that headed for the castle. As they neared the first of several gatehouses that led to the keep, they could see a rider heading in their direction. A man in armor was thundering towards them. Christopher was the first to take notice.

"Look there," he said. "That looks like Peter."

It was. Everyone turned to see Peter galloping towards them on the heavy-boned warhorse his father had given him when he was knighted. Another expensive de Lohr animal that Peter was quite fond of. As the knight drew up alongside his father and uncle, the customary smile wasn't there.

In fact, he looked very serious.

"I thought it was you," he said to his father. "I had the men watch for your banner and they thought they saw it coming in through the city gate."

"They did," Christopher said to his eldest. "What has you riding out here like a madman?"

"John is here," Peter said, looking at the six knights before him. All powerful men, all of them knowing the stakes with John present at any gathering. "He arrived yesterday. Papa, we had an... incident last night with Christin."

Christopher stiffened. "*What* incident?" he demanded. "Be plain."

"She is well," Peter said quickly, seeing this father was immediately on the offensive. "She is not harmed, but there have been some developments. I rode out here to tell you because I am not entirely sure we will have any privacy once we enter the castle. John's men are everywhere. He brought a small army with him."

Christopher looked at William, who was trying not to show any great concern. "What developments have there been, Peter?" William asked calmly.

Peter wedged his big horse between his father and William. Even though they were in public, they were fairly isolated from prying ears with soldiers surrounding them and the noise of the city in general.

That was exactly what Peter had counted on.

"Papa, you must promise to remain calm," Peter said. "I am telling you this in the presence of Lord William on purpose. I will reiterate that Christin is well, but John invited her to sup with him last night. From what I was told, she tried to flee after the invitation was delivered but Sean de Lara caught her and told her not to run. He told her that John has confided in him that he wants Christin as a bride for his son, Robert FitzRoy."

Christopher, normally a neutral man, couldn't temper his reaction. His eyes bugged. "*FitzRoy?*" he hissed. "He has lost his damnable mind if he thinks I'll ever consent to a marriage between Christin and his bastard!"

Peter held up a hand. "I know," he said. "We all know. But Sean had a plan and we put it into action last night at the feast when Christin dined with John. Sean's plan was for Christin to behave horribly – he told her to drink, to belch, to behave like a base-born chit because John cannot stand women like that. He prefers his women well-bred and lovely and obedient, and Christin was anything *but*. Papa, you should have seen her – I have never seen anything like it in my life."

They were all hanging on Peter's every word. Christopher was close to exploding. "*What* happened?" he demanded.

Peter started to grin. "She pretended to be drunk," he said. "She chatted so much that John couldn't get a word in, she chewed like a common man, belched like a knight on a three-day drinking binge, ended up vomiting at one point, and then she got into a fight with a serving wench. It was brilliant, Papa, all of it. We've not yet seen John this morning and he has stayed far away from Cissy. If she wanted to discourage him, I think she did."

Christopher was still vastly upset but listening to his son tell the tale had him envisioning his beautiful, well-mannered daughter as she acted the part of a fool. He almost wished he'd been there to see it.

"Christ," he muttered, wiping a hand over his face. "She really did that?"

"She did," Peter said. "Sean thought it was better to discourage the king than to run from him. The more she would run, the more obsessed he would be. But if she proved herself undesirable…"

"Then John would put her out of his mind," Christopher finished for him, seeing the logic. Forcing himself to calm, he sighed heavily. "Cissy always was a bit of performer. Thank God she had the wherewithal to listen to Sean. Let us hope it throws John off her scent for good."

"I would not be too sure," William said quietly. When everyone turned to look at him, he simply lifted his shoulders. "John does not discourage so easily, especially if he believes the prize outweighs the negative aspects. To marry his son to a de Lohr… that would be a triumph for him and a defeat for you, Chris. I would not trust that your daughter's bad behavior has destroyed his aspirations."

Christopher pondered that for a moment. "I suppose not," he said. "I have been doing battle against John for over twenty years. I know what the man is capable of, better than most. But Christin won the first battle. Let us see if we can win the war because there is no possibility

John will ever have Cissy for his son. None at all."

William nodded faintly. "He would use your daughter against you," he said. "To ensure your neutrality in any movement against him, he would use her. Chris, you need to remove her from Norwich immediately. Take her back to Lioncross and keep her there. We cannot take the chance. Meanwhile, we are still dealing with a threat from within but it would seem that we have two fronts to this situation – John's interest in Christin de Lohr and an unnamed threat against John."

It was a portentous observation because it was entirely true. As the reality of the situation began to settle, the men looked to one another, understanding the irony of the circumstances they found themselves in. While they were trying to protect a king, he was trying to subvert one of their own.

The power struggle between John and William Marshal was real. Remove de Lohr and a good portion of The Marshal's power would be neutralized.

It was something that could not happen.

"What would you have Kress and I do, my lord?" Maxton asked. "Since we were the ones who interrogated Lord Prescombe, I feel as if we should focus on the unnamed threat. Would you agree?"

William nodded. "Indeed," he said. "Caius, you work with them. They will inform you of everything you need to know. Meanwhile, Christopher and David and Peter will work to remove Christin from Norwich."

"Sherry, Bric, and Kevin are at Norwich, too," Peter reminded him. "They are ready to do your bidding."

William's gaze trailed to the massive square keep before him. He found himself shielding his eyes from the sun as he looked at it. "Then find them," he told Peter. "Gather them. I would meet with all of my men when I arrive so we may make the appropriate plans."

Peter nodded, spurring his horse forward and thundering back towards the castle. Christopher watched him go, unable to fight off the powerful sense of trepidation he was feeling. John had always had an attraction to the de Lohr women; first Dustin, now Dustin's daughter.

It made Christopher ill simply to think on it.

Christin married to Robert FitzRoy...

Over his dead body.

"Cissy?" Wynter's head peeked in her chamber door. "Someone is here to see you this morning."

Christin was sitting by the hearth, drying out the hair she'd just washed because it had food and vomit it in from the previous night. In fact, she'd just finished a bath where she'd scrubbed herself from head to toe, washing away the wine stains and the cow dung. Combing the ends of her dark, nearly-dry hair, she glanced up at Wynter.

"Who is it?" she asked.

"He says to tell you that Sherry has come to speak to you."

That had Christin on her feet. Suddenly, she was quite eager to see who had come calling for her but she wasn't dressed for it. Quickly, she shirked her dressing robe, one made from heavy brocade, and dressed in a linen gown that was heavy in fabric, yet simple but lovely.

Wynter rushed into the chamber to help her, taking the comb and plaiting her hair into a braid that draped gracefully over one shoulder as Christin tied up the front of her bodice. She looked quite lovely and angelic in the simple linen that emphasized her curvy figure. She was petite and big-chested like her mother, which gave her a pleasingly round silhouette. Pulling on her slippers, she dashed from the chamber and headed down the stairs.

Alexander was standing in the doorway of the apartment building, smiling faintly at her as she came down the stairs far too quickly.

"Careful, my lady," he said, drinking in the sight of her. "It would not do to survive the king and then break your neck on the stairs."

Christin smiled at him, her face positively aglow. "I *did* survive the king," she said quietly. "I hope my performance did not change your mind about me."

He grinned, full-on, and began to clap his hands slowly. The applause echoed off the stone. "Brilliant," he said. "Positively one of the most brilliant things I have ever seen. If I was not already fond of you, last night's entertainment alone would have had me begging for a lock of your hair."

She smiled bashfully. "You would not have to beg, I assure you."

Alexander was quite certain he'd not smiled so much in years. "Truly?" he said. "If I ask you for a lock now, will you give me one?"

"Without hesitation."

He laughed softly. But all the while, his eyes were riveted to her as if he could look at nothing else. "Astonishing," he murmured. "You, dear lady, are astonishing. Will you walk with me this morn?"

Christin nodded eagerly, taking his elbow as they headed over to the garden. The day was bright, with puffy clouds overhead, and the castle garden looked much different in the daylight. There was a big yew tree, a pond, and many green and growing things that were starting to go dormant as autumn settled in.

Alexander walked her past the tree and over to the pond, all the while holding the fingers that were clutched around his elbow. Outside of the castle, he'd seen the groups of nobles coming into the castle and knew they would soon be inundated with people for the festivities, so his plan this morning was to have a few moments alone with Christin before William Marshal arrived. After that, there was no telling what he'd be called upon to do and he didn't want to take the chance that he might not see her.

Therefore, this was a precious moment.

And a nervous one. God help him, he was actually nervous. He'd spent all night staring up at the ceiling, reliving the events in the hall, wondering how such a beautiful, intelligent woman could actually notice a man like him. Certainly, he had prestige and a reputation, but a woman like Christin de Lohr should have far more than that. The attention of a fine woman wasn't something he'd ever really had to ponder, so this was quite new to him. He felt so inadequate.

But, oh... so lucky.

"I've not yet seen Lord de Winter this morning," Christin said, breaking into his thoughts. "I am not entirely sure how I am going to apologize for destroying his hall."

Alexander looked at her, grinning. "You did a splendid job of it," he said. "I've not seen that much chaos in quite some time. And that knight you kept threatening – the one you threw bones at – he's actually a good man so I hope you do not really think poorly of him."

She looked at him, mortified. "I do not know why I did that," she said. "It just came out. I should find him and apologize to him, too."

Alexander laughed softly. "He would run from you in terror," he said. "I will find him and make mention of the situation. I will ease things; have no fear."

Christin sighed heavily. "I was only concerned with the king's reaction, to be truthful," she said. "He seemed quite appalled, did he not?"

"He did, indeed."

"Do you think it was enough to discourage him."

"I think it certainly gave him pause, but I also think it would be wise for you to leave the castle and stay at that inn near the cathedral until he leaves. Just to stay out of his way."

She came to a halt, facing him. "If you think so," she said. "But I must confess all of this to The Marshal, too. It is possible he may not want me to leave. I had a task to perform at the celebration and that was to infiltrate the women. Remember?"

Alexander's smile faded. "I remember," he said. "But I do not think that will be wise after last night. I think it best to get you out of John's sight altogether. I think your presence will cause an added complication we do not need."

Christin could see his point. She averted her gaze, looking at her feet. "I've made a mess of things, I think."

He reached out, tipping her head up to look at him. His eyes glittered at her. "You have not," he said. "It is John who is to blame. But, then again, I cannot blame him when I look at you. You have stars in your eyes and the beauty of a clear night sky. There is no man in England who would not see that. But I have an advantage. I know that the quality of your character is equal to everything men see on the outside."

She was deeply flattered by his words. "Even after last night?"

"Especially after last night."

Reaching up, she stroked his cheek gently and he caught her hand, kissing it tenderly. They simply stood there a moment, gazing at each other, understanding that whatever was brewing between them had somehow solidified overnight. It was only yesterday that they were confessing their feelings. Today, they were free to speak of them and more.

Christin took him by the hand, pulling him over to a stone bench by the pond.

"Come and sit with me," she said. "Tell me how it will be between us from now on. I must remain here at Norwich because I serve Lady de Winter, but you… you will leave at some point."

Alexander nodded, politely helping her to sit before he sat beside her. "I will return to London with William Marshal," he said. "Where he goes, I go."

"When shall I see you again?"

That had been on Alexander's mind most of the night. "That is a good question," he said, holding her hand to his chest. "I told you that I have been a loner and a wanderer. I have friends, that is true, and very good friends. But I have never had a lady who I have been fond of, so this is all very new to me. All I know is that I do not want to leave when The Marshal returns to London. I want to remain here, with you."

Christin smiled at him, clutching the hand that was holding hers. "This is new to me, also," she said. "I do not want you to leave, either, but I know you must. I do not know when The Marshal will call upon me again and until he does, I will remain at Norwich."

Alexander sat there for a moment, staring down at her hands as they held his. He simply stared, clearly lost in thought.

"When Maxton and Kress and Achilles married for love, I thought it was weak of them," he said after a moment. "I did not know Maxton's wife very well, but I knew the women that Kress and Achilles wed. Although they were fine women, I still thought it was weak of them to make their careers secondary to their marriages. To these women, they surrendered. After all, we have served together for over twenty years, all of us. We have faced life and death together. We are a brotherhood like none other and I did not understand why they let their personal feelings interfere with that. But now... now, I do, because I find myself facing the same thing."

Christin was listening to him seriously. "And this disturbs you?"

He shook his head, slowly. "It does not. I thought it would, but it does not."

"Then what do you wish to do, Sherry? Do you wish to think about this? I do not want you to be confused and miserable over your feelings for me."

He looked at her, then. "There *is* no confusion," he murmured. "That is why this is all so baffling, but at the same time, all so wonderful. There is absolutely no confusion. I know what I want and I know what I feel, and both of those roads lead to you. Everything leads to you. And now I am trying to determine our future."

Christin could see that, in spite of his words, he was puzzled. As he'd said, this was new to him, so he was trying to plot a course. She scooted closer to him, gently laying her head on his shoulder.

"You do not have to decide anything today," she said softly. "We do not have to do anything right this very moment. We have time. But know this; no matter how long it takes for you to determine our future, I will wait for you. I will be right here, waiting for you."

Surprise washed over his features. "You would truly wait for me?"

She nodded. "Of course I would. I do not give my affections easily, Sherry. I do not give them at all, really. I assured you that this was not a whim and you told me that you would stop at nothing to make me yours. I will hold you to that, but I will not rush you."

He leaned his head so that it was resting on hers, a sweet and simple gesture that meant the world to him. "That is what's so strange about this," he said. "I do not want to leave you. I want to be with you every day for the rest of my life, so I want to determine the course of our future now. I will have to leave with The Marshal, but I will return for you as soon as I can."

She chuckled; he could feel her. "You must still speak with my father, you know."

"I know. And I will do that as soon as I can."

"What will you say to him?"

"That I wish to marry his daughter and ask for his blessing. That's to the point."

She lifted her head, forcing him to lift his. She stared at him for a moment. "Then… then you simply do not wish to court me? I have seen couples court only to have them move on to others when they realize that are not compatible. I have not seen it often, but I have seen it. I thought… I thought mayhap you meant we should know each other first before…"

She trailed off and he frowned. "What did you think I meant when I said I would stop at nothing to make you mine?"

She grinned, nervously. "I… I suppose marriage, but I did not wish to presume anything."

He grinned because she was. "Silly wench," he growled. "Of course I meant marriage. Why do you think I have been trying to figure out our future?"

She eyed him. "You are not going to be like Bric and lock me up in a castle somewhere, are you?"

He laughed. "Not you," he said. "You'd find a way to break out and then you'd come after me and throw bones at me."

Christin laughed right along with him, finding something so wonderful and giddy about laughing with a man she was quickly coming to adore.

"I would never throw bones at you, I promise," she said, sobering. "But it's as I told you before – I like serving with The Marshal. I feel as if I am making a difference as few women can claim."

He sobered also, reaching out to cup her face. "That is because you are young and beautiful, and he makes you do things that, as my wife, I would not permit you to do." He watched her as she reconciled herself to that. "If you wish to continue in that capacity, however, all you need do is tell me. I would not want you to be unhappy. But I will not marry a woman who wishes to continue her duty of flirting with men."

Now she looked wounded. "It is much more than that," she said. "I may not do important work like participating in battles or commanding men, but my work is important, too."

He immediately put his arms around her, his face finding delicious refuge in the side of her head. "I am sorry," he whispered into her hair. "I did not mean to suggest you were not valuable. You are; you are *very* valuable. But you are more valuable to me than anyone else on this earth. You will have to decide if that is more important than serving The Marshal."

Christin was all folded up in his massive arms, her chin on his shoulder. It was a moment that drained everything out of her until she was putty in his arms, for the man had an embrace like no other. She felt so very safe and adored, and it was something she never wanted to be without.

Certainly, serving The Marshal had been fulfilling. But being adored… even loved… by Alexander was more fulfilling than even that. For the first time in her life, she felt whole.

"There is no decision to make," she said, her arms around him, caressing him. "My choice is you. It will always be you."

"You are certain?"

She lifted her head to look at him, her features alive with all of the warmth and adoration she was feeling. "I've been waiting all of my life for you," she whispered. "I simply did not know it until now."

He pulled her close, looking into her eyes, seeing a life he never thought he'd have. Never did he imagine he'd fall for a woman, but Christin wasn't just any woman.

She was the most remarkable woman he'd ever known.

"I told you that I could only offer you me, that I had nothing more to give you," he said. "That is not entirely true. I have been thinking about my father… I will try to reconcile with him after all of these years. I am his heir, after all. You deserve your own home, Cissy. Mayhap… mayhap it is finally time to face my father. Every man must face his mistakes at some point, so mayhap it is my time to do that."

She smiled. "Do not do it for me," she said. "You must do this for you. But if I can be the catalyst to greater things for you, I am happy to be that."

A smile spread over his lips as he bent over her and kissed her gently on the cheek. "You are wise, indeed," he said. "I am looking forward to a lifetime of coming to know that wisdom. What a great privilege it will be."

With that, his lips claimed hers and he kissed her sweetly but with passion that quickly overwhelmed him. He had to fight the urge to ravage her, so the kiss was passionate but not lengthy. They were not in a private place, after all, and he'd probably shown her too much affection already. As he released her from his embrace and picked up both of her hands, kissing each one gently, they both heard a voice from over near the yew tree.

"I believe this is a good time to ask what I have been witnessing."

Christin gasped and stood up quickly, but Alexander didn't move. He remained on the bench with Christin's hands still in his grip as Christopher de Lohr moved from his position near the tree and began the slow, deliberate trek in their direction.

And he did not look pleased.

CHAPTER TWELVE

"YOU SUMMONED ME, your grace?"

Sean was standing in the doorway of John's chamber, the master's chamber that Old Daveigh and Lady de Winter had surrendered to the king upon his arrival. The chamber was spacious and comfortable, and afforded John a perfect view of the gatehouses that protected Norwich Castle. He could see the groups of nobles coming into the castle to attend his celebration.

So many groups, which John thought was rather impressive. He had no idea so many of them would have attended his feast. He wasn't well liked in Norfolk and was pleased to see he'd been wrong. The castle was filling up quickly and he could see encampments being set up in the baileys below.

But it wasn't today's feast on his mind.

It was last night's.

"Come in," he said to Sean as he remained by the window, feeling the cool breeze caress his face. "It seems that everyone in Norfolk has decided to come today. Free food and drink will bring them in, you know."

Sean entered the chamber, shutting the door behind him. "I believe they are coming to pay their respects to you, your grace."

John snorted as he came away from the window. Dressed in a silken robe, he was nude beneath it and the robe wasn't exactly covering him.

He'd had a somewhat fit body in his youth that, in his advancing years, was starting to shift and he was getting a belly on him. It was his belly poking through the opening of his robe and being that he was well-endowed, his flaccid member could also be seen. Sean found himself looking the man in the eyes because he didn't want to see anything else.

It was disturbing enough as it was.

"You are being kind because you know it is not true," John said. "They are here because Old Daveigh asked it of them. But that does not matter; that is not why I summoned you."

"How may I be of service, your grace?"

"Christin de Lohr."

"What about her?"

"You will take her north today."

Sean was greatly surprised. After the fiasco last night, that was the last thing he expected to hear. "If that is your wish, your grace."

"It is," John said. He wagged a finger at Sean as he moved to collect his cup of watered wine. "Last night was a disgrace. I would have believed the woman to have terrible manners for the fact that everything she did was exaggerated. Her manners were *too* terrible, if you know what I mean. Clearly, she was trying to dissuade me, but I am not easily deterred. I still want her for Robert and you will take her to him."

Sean's heart sank. "As you wish, your grace," Sean said. "But what about Christopher de Lohr? We have discussed how badly this could go for you if you abduct his daughter. Does this not concern you?"

John nodded. "It should, I know," he said. "But I do not believe Christopher will be a problem for one very good reason – he wants his daughter safe and whole. Control the daughter, you control the father. I know you are trying to protect me, Sean, but do not worry so. Christin de Lohr is the key to controlling the entire de Lohr war machine."

Sean had heard that before. He still couldn't believe that John was being so reckless, but the man seemed resolute. He'd already said what he needed to say when the idea was first brought about and he was afraid that any more conjecture on his part would cause John to be suspicious somehow, so he shut his mouth.

He had little choice.

The Lord of the Shadows was obedient in all things.

"As you say, your grace," he said. "When shall I go?"

"Quickly," John said, swilling the liquid in the cup. "Today, if you can. I am not sure who will be in attendance today but it is guaranteed that de Lohr allies will be here. Old Daveigh is a de Lohr ally, so whatever you do must not alert him. In fact... I believe I will send Gerard to take her north. You will remain here with me because I will need you to deter Old Daveigh if he becomes suspicious of what I have done. You are a much better persuader than Gerard is."

Sean nodded. "As you wish, your grace."

John stroked his chin. "I was tempted to taste her last night in spite of her behavior, but I decided to leave her a maiden," he said. "That will be my wedding gift to Robert."

"Does Robert know of your plans or should we send word ahead?"

"Gerard will tell him when he delivers her."

"Aye, your grace."

John turned back towards the window, wine in hand. "She thought she was quite clever last night," he said. "What Lady Christin does not know is that even if she looked like the hind end of a goat, I would still marry her to Robert. Nothing she can do will change my mind. Now, send Gerard to me. There is no time to waste."

Sean was already heading for the door. He quit the chamber, leaving the king to watch the arrival of the guests and drink his wine, but all the while he was thinking that he needed to find Christin and tell her to get the hell out of Norwich.

Their plan had not succeeded.

Worse still, he needed to find Alexander. The man had to know that Christin was in grave danger. He hadn't taken ten steps, however, when the chamber door opened again and John was calling for him.

"Sean!" he said. "Return to me. Send a soldier for Gerard. There is something more I need to discuss with you."

Sean sighed heavily, but he didn't let John see it. As one of the royal soldiers ran past him, going to find Gerard, Sean returned to the king's chamber, wondering when he was going to have the opportunity to tell Christin and Alexander of the king's directive. He was in a bind and he knew it, but nothing on earth was going to force him to show any measure of disloyalty to the king and his wants. He'd worked too hard to get here. For all John knew, Sean was the perfect knight, the perfect bodyguard, and the perfect killing machine.

As the minutes passed and Gerard eventually joined them, Sean could see that this was going to turn out to be a very big problem. He needed to break free of the king and couldn't seem to do it. When Gerard left with his orders, the king kept Sean with him, discussing a future journey to Nottingham.

But Sean could only think of one thing.

Run, Christin, run!

CHAPTER THIRTEEN

"WELL?" CHRISTOPHER SAID steadily. "Does anyone want to tell me what I have just seen?"

Alexander's heart sank. This wasn't how he'd planned to approach de Lohr about his daughter and, in truth, he was quite shocked to see Christopher in their midst. Releasing Christin's hands, he stood up to face the man.

In truth, it was all he could do.

"My lord," he said evenly. "It is good to see you. I was unaware you were attending today's festivities."

Christopher was focused on Alexander as if there were no one else around them. Not even Christin. But she saw the way her father was looking at Alexander and she hastened to break his concentration.

"Papa," she said, putting herself between Alexander and her father. "You did not tell me that you were coming to Norwich for the king's celebration."

Christopher's intense gaze shifted, now looking at his eldest daughter. "I will speak to you later," he said. "Go to your chamber and wait for me."

Christin could hear the tone of his voice and it wasn't a friendly one. She'd heard that tone before and it always struck terror into her. She'd never been one to disobey her father but, in this case, she was going to.

She was afraid of what would happen if she left.

"Papa, please," she said, trying to stay on an even keel. "What you saw… it was not what you think."

"How do you know what I think?"

Christin lifted her eyebrows in a gesture that looked very much like her mother. "You think we are out here being foolish and clandestine," she said. "You think that this is something meaningless and reckless. I tell you that it is not true; it is anything *but* meaningless and reckless. Sherry and I… he was going to speak to you but he did not know you would be here. If he had, he would have met you at the gate."

Christopher's gaze lingered on her before returning to Alexander. "I told you to leave us, Christin," he said. "Go to your chamber, please."

"Papa, I…"

"It's all right," Alexander interrupted her. "Go ahead."

Christin looked at Alexander, who was focused in on Christopher with the same intensity that Christopher was focused on him. Knowing she should obey at this point, since her father had every reason to be upset, she nodded in resignation. She was going to have to let Alexander address this since Christopher's anger was directed at him. But not before she spoke parting words to her father.

"Papa," she said. "I am going, but know this – I was a willing participant. He did not force himself on me. And… and I adore him. He makes me happier than you can imagine. Please do not ruin this for me."

With that, she walked away, heading towards the apartment building and her chamber, which happened to have a view of the garden. As she scurried away, Christopher maintained his eye contact with Alexander.

"She does not want me to ruin this for her," Christopher said. "What, exactly, would I be ruining?"

Alexander could feel the tension. It was like a fog, swirling between them. He'd known Christopher for so long, as they'd served together in The Levant and since, and he'd never once been on the man's angry side, so this was something new. He knew what Christopher de Lohr was capable of. Rather than become cagey or defensive, he reasoned that the best thing to do was to face it head-on.

He had to be honest.

"Up until yesterday, there was nothing to ruin," he said. "But yesterday... Chris, I have spent the past several days with Christin, along with Peter and Bric and Kevin, escorting her back to Norwich Castle after the visit at Ramsbury. I've known of your daughter for a few years but I've never spent any time around her. There was never any reason to. She is a de Lohr and the House of de Lohr is in a class all its own. I never presumed to attain a de Lohr bride, nor did I have any ambition for one. But you have raised a woman of astounding bravery, wit, and charm, and as we came to know one another, I found myself succumbing to her. I do not know how it happened, but it has. As a man who loves his wife, and I have heard rumor that you do, then surely you can understand how these things simply... happen."

Christopher was still staring at him. He was genuinely trying to decide how to react to all of this. He'd come on the hunt for his daughter and found her in the arms of Alexander de Sherrington.

Sherry.

An Executioner Knight.

"Do not bring my wife into it," he finally said. "Do not even breathe her name, for this has nothing to do with my wife and everything to do you with you and my daughter. Christ, Sherry, you're twice her age."

Alexander cleared his throat softly. "I know," he said, averting his gaze somewhat nervously. "I pointed that out to her."

Christopher scowled. "Was this *her* idea?"

Alexander shook his head quickly. "Nay," he said. "As I said, it just happened. We were speaking one moment about something completely neutral and in the next moment, we are declaring our feelings for one another. In fact, we discussed when I was planning on approaching you to ask for your daughter's hand and she was right. Had I known you were going to be here today, I would have met you at the gate. It would have been the first thing out of my mouth."

Christopher looked at him a few moments longer before finally looking away. He just couldn't look at Alexander any longer without wanting to wrap his hands around the man's throat. Turning away, he began to pace, digesting everything and trying not to become angry about it. Anger wouldn't solve the problem and there was most definitely a problem as he saw it.

"Sherry, you know I greatly admire you," he said. "You know that I like you personally. You are a fine knight and a loyal friend. But when it comes to my daughter, you must forgive me for being her father and not your friend. Do you understand that?"

"I do."

Christopher came to a halt and looked at him. "No offense intended, but I never considered you for my daughter," he said. "Not only are you twice her age, but the things you have done in your past, Sherry… my God, there are a half-dozen situations in The Levant alone that come to mind when you were less than noble when it came to the treatment of the enemy. I have *seen* what you are capable of. And I am supposed to allow you to marry my daughter?"

Alexander folded his enormous arms over his chest. "And I have seen what you are capable of," he said in a quiet but firm counter. "That does not make you any less a loving father and husband. It makes you a formidable soldier who will do anything to gain victory. One has nothing to do with the other."

"Explain."

"Just because I can kill a man and his child, both of whom have betrayed Christian knights, does not make me an undesirable husband."

Christopher cast him a long look. "It's not just that," he muttered. "I know what you did on your way home from The Levant. It took you eight years to return and I know what you did during that time. You spent some of it at the Lateran Palace as a guest of the Holy Father and you lived like a sultan with a harem. You did not think I knew that, did you?"

Alexander lifted his big shoulders in a dismissive gesture. "It was not as bad as all that."

His casual reply brought Christopher's anger around. "Then explain it to me so there is no misunderstanding," he growled. "You want to marry my daughter? Then tell me why I should consider a man who looks at a woman as no better than a pet."

Alexander's jaw flexed. "I was at the Lateran Palace as a guest of the Holy Father," he said evenly. "But the man used me as a personal attack dog and rewarded me handsomely. I was given a home of my own and twelve women, to be used by me at my discretion. Although I have great admiration and appreciation for women, I am not the kind of man who needs a different one in his bed every night and the women given to me grew fat and bored for lack of use. You did not hear that part, did you?"

Christopher frowned. "Are you telling me that you ignored twelve beautiful women?"

"I did not say that. But I did not have a different one in my bed every night, and there was not one of them that I was fond of or particularly interested in."

"Then they were whores."

"Aye."

Christopher threw up his hands. "And you expect me to allow you to marry my daughter?"

Alexander lifted a dark eyebrow. "Tell me truthfully that you never sought out the comfort of a whore before you married your wife," he said. "If the answer is no, then I will drop my pursuit of your daughter. I cannot undo the past; all I can do is make you a promise for the future. I will never disrespect Christin, I will always ensure she is safe and warm and happy, and I will be faithful to her for the rest of my life. Upon my oath, I swear this. Now, answer my question – did you ever seek the comfort of a whore before you married your wife?"

It was a clever question, one that had Christopher backed into a corner because he knew very well what the answer was. He couldn't even lie to Alexander because everyone knew of the escapades of the de Lohr brothers and Marcus Burton in their youths. He'd been a wild buck in those days, so denying he'd ever found comfort with a whore was stupid. It simply wasn't true.

Heavily, he sighed.

"Aye," he said. "But we are not talking about me. We are talking about you."

"And what I've done in my past is no worse than what you have done. Moreover, it will remain in my past."

He sounded sincere and given that Christopher had known him for so long, he knew that he meant it. Alexander de Sherrington did not go back on his word, in any case. It was true that he couldn't continue to throw stones at Alexander, knowing he shared much of the same past in certain aspects. He also couldn't attack the man's character, which was beyond reproach.

Therefore, he tried another tactic to see if he could shake the man loose.

"You say that these feelings for my daughter have happened within the past couple of days," he said.

Alexander nodded. "They have."

"Is it possible they are a whim?"

Alexander smiled humorlessly. "For me, nay," he said. "I never do anything on a whim. But I did ask Cissy that question."

"Cissy?"

"She gave me permission to call her by that name."

Christopher grunted, feeling like he was losing control as his daughter gave out permission for someone to use a family nickname. Even if it was Alexander. But the fact that he wanted to marry Christin made him something of an enemy at the moment.

"And when you asked her, what did she say?" he asked.

Alexander shook his head. "She assured me it was no whim," he said. "I believe her."

Christopher didn't have much to say after that. He'd said what he needed to say and now he needed to digest everything. Perhaps even talk it over with David. And then he needed to take his daughter home to Lioncross and lock her in a chamber and throw away the key.

Well, it sounded good in theory, anyway.

"I do not wish to discuss this any further at the moment," he finally said, turning away from Alexander. "You must give me time to deliberate on everything. I was not expecting this when I came to Norwich today, so you can imagine it is something of a surprise."

Alexander nodded, relieved that the man at least wasn't swearing at him or trying to kill him. "I understand," he said. "I wasn't expecting you, either, so I don't suppose I was too succinct in my presentation. I haven't had time to work up a truly good sweat about this."

Christopher smiled humorlessly. "You will do me a favor and stay away from Christin today, please," he said. "I do not want to have to worry about you two ending up in another amorous embrace while I am thinking this all over."

"As you wish."

"And The Marshal is here. He is gathering his men together and asks you to meet him in the lower bailey where his encampment is being set up."

"I will be there."

"If you see any other of The Marshal's men, tell them the same thing."

"I will."

Christopher simply walked away after that and Alexander stood there, letting himself feel some relief that the situation hadn't turned violent. Exhaling heavily, he happened to look at the women's apartment block to see Christin in one of the windows. When she saw that he was looking at her, she waved at him. He waved back, rather sorry he'd promised Christopher he'd stay away from her for the remainder of the day.

He suspected it was going to be more difficult that he imagined.

In fact, he knew it was a promise he couldn't keep.

CHAPTER FOURTEEN

DAVID SAW HIS brother coming.

Beneath crisp blue skies, the men had just finished setting up their encampment on the opposite side of the bailey from John's encampment, next to William Marshal's, when David saw Christopher coming through the big gatehouse that led to the keep. He could tell that his brother was upset simply by the way he walked.

He was stomping.

That was never a good sign.

David didn't go to greet him. He knew that Christopher would come to him soon enough, so he simply stood there, watching his brother's body language and suspecting he must have had a row with Christin. David couldn't imagine what it had been about, but he would soon find out.

As he stood there and watched, William emerged from a nearby tent. He had a dagger in his hand and was sharpening it on a pumice stone as he wandered over to where David was standing. He, too, could see Christopher stomping about and he paused in his sharpening to watch.

"Your brother appears upset," he finally commented. "Has he had a run-in with John already?"

David shook his head. "He went to find Christin," he said. "I cannot imagine what she might have said that would have upset him so."

William wasn't sure Christin had anything to do with it, but he kept his mouth shut. His money was on an encounter with the king. He spit on the stone and continued sharpening the dagger, one given to him by his wife and one he wouldn't let the squires tend to when they were maintaining the rest of his weapons. This little dagger had sentimental value, surprising for a man who usually gave little stock to emotion. Therefore, he carefully worked the blade as Christopher marched up on David.

In fact, his gaze was moving between David and William. His mouth was working as if he wanted to say something, but he finally hissed and threw his hands up, turning away and heading into the big de Lohr tent that was flying the bright blue and yellow standards on this day.

David and William looked at each other curiously before David finally turned for the tent. "I shall see what this is about," he said.

William was still grinding the blade against the stone. "Go ahead, but you and your brother will attend me in a few minutes when the other men gather."

"Aye."

As David headed into the tent, William started to turn away but thought better of it. Although he wasn't one for eavesdropping, he wanted to make sure Christopher's anger had nothing to do with the king. The two had historically shared a contentious relationship, so any flare in that dynamic was never a good thing.

Perhaps listening in might not be a bad idea.

Unaware that William was positioning himself outside, David entered the tent to find his brother gulping down a rather large cup of wine. Casually, he came around to collect his own cup.

"Did you find Christin?" he asked nonchalantly.

Christopher swallowed the gulp in his mouth. "I did," he said. "Do you want to know *where* I found her?"

"Where?"

"In the arms of Sherry."

David didn't quite get the meaning at first. He took a drink of his wine as the words settled and, puzzled, he looked to his brother.

"In the arms of...?" He frowned in confusion. "Sherry? I don't understand."

Christopher looked at him as if he were a fool. "They were embracing, David," he said, making a gesture indicating a hug. "You know – *embracing*."

Now, David understood. "Sherry?" he gasped.

Realizing his brother finally got the message, Christopher snorted. "Aye, Sherry," he said. "I found them in the garden and they made the perfect picture of two lovers."

David's mouth was hanging open. "*Sherry?*"

Christopher slammed his cup to the tabletop and poured himself more wine. "Alexander de Sherrington and my daughter are fond of one another," he said. "In fact, Christin told me that she adores him. He told me he wishes to speak to me about her, which I can only assume to mean that he wants to marry her."

David was astonished. "Sherry wants to *marry?*" he repeated. "That is the most outrageous thing I have ever heard. I never imagined him to be the type. And with *Christin?*"

"Aye."

"But he's twice her age!"

"I know," Christopher said in the same outraged tone that David had used. "But according to him, and her, their feelings for one another are real. Christin thinks I am going to ruin this for her."

David's expression screwed up. "Ruin what? Her affair with Sherry?" He shook his head. "He's an Executioner Knight, Chris. He lived at the Lateran Palace for years with a harem of women. Did you forget that?"

Christopher shook his head. "David, you are telling me something I already know," he said irritably. "I even reminded him of it, but he told me he hardly touched those women and they meant nothing to him. But he also made a good point."

"What is that?"

"He told me if I could deny ever touching a whore before I met my wife, then he would drop his pursuit of Christin. Given our reputations when we were younger, of course, I could not deny it."

David backed off a little because his brother was correct. They'd had their share of loose women, but they'd never had the harem that Alexander had possessed those years ago. With a grunt, he rolled his eyes and turned away, pondering the shocking situation of his niece and Alexander de Sherrington.

"But he's an Executioner Knight," he repeated. "He's a known assassin, Chris, the most ruthless kind."

"I know."

"The man is great to serve with and I respect him a great deal, but I cannot say I'd want him married to one of my daughters."

Christopher poured himself more wine. "Why not?"

David looked at him as if he'd gone mad. "I just told you. He's a ruthless assassin."

"You and I have been known to kill a man or two, and not always by the most noble or ethical of means."

"True, but Sherry serves William Marshal," David pointed out. "He will be away constantly in his service for the man and that is no life for Christin. She should have a husband who will remain with her. And what of his life as an agent for The Marshal? You've kept Christin well protected from the world at large. It will be a shock to her to be with such a man. She's an innocent."

"You're wrong."

It wasn't Christopher who replied, but William. He was standing in the tent opening, pushing the flap back as he entered. Christopher and David looked at him questioningly as he came into the tent, eyeing the two of them.

"Sorry," he said. "I was standing outside and overheard you. Am I to understand that Sherry and Christin have a romance?"

Christopher nodded. "Aye," he said, feeling some defeat now that his anger had worn thin. "Did you know about it?"

William shook his head. "I did not," he said, moving for the jug of wine on Christopher's table. "But that is a testament to Sherry's professionalism. Christin's, too."

Christopher's brow furrowed. "Christin? What do you mean by that?"

William glanced at him as he poured his wine. "Your daughter is not protected and sheltered, Chris," he said. "She is not innocent, either, as David has suggested. She has been an agent with me for two years and she is one of the best I have ever seen."

Christopher's eyes bugged. "*Christin?*"

"Christin."

"My daughter?"

"Your daughter. If you did not know that, then she is, indeed, good at what she does."

Christopher's jaw dropped. "It's not possible."

"I'm afraid it is." William brought the cup of wine to his lips and took a sip before continuing. "She's a de Lohr, Chris. She is young, that is true, but she is courageous, bright, and fearless. Had she been born male, she would have made a superb knight. I have used her on many a task and she has performed flawlessly."

Christopher stared at him. After a moment, he hunted down a chair and sat heavily. He found that he had to sit down or fall down. Shocked didn't even begin to cover what he was feeling at the moment.

"Christin is an agent?" he muttered as if trying to convince himself of the truth. He sat there for a moment, dazed, before his focus moved to William. "We knew Peter was, but Christin?"

"Peter recruited her," William said, watching Christopher wrestle with the news. "Chris, I tell you this because your daughter is not the fragile little girl you seem to think she is. She is one of the strongest women I have ever seen."

Christopher put up a hand. "She is my daughter," he said. "She is not some ruthless Marshal assassin."

"You would be wrong."

His eyebrows lifted. "*What?*"

William was genuinely trying to be gentle about the situation because he could see that Christopher was reeling, but the man had to know. His daughter was no weakling.

"Do you remember back at Ramsbury, Chris?" he asked. "Peter and Bric and Sherry and even Christin, all of them, were in the great hall and then everyone disappeared. I do not know if you remember that, but…"

Christopher cut him off. "I remember it well," he said. "I even commented about it to David. But we were only assuming Peter was involved."

William shook his head. "I want to explain something to you," he said. "I am telling you this not to cause you shock or even pain, but because I have an end motive in mind. At Ramsbury, we were chasing a French double agent, Lord Prescombe. We caught him, but we caught his companion, too. Or, I should say, your daughter caught her. When the woman attacked Christin, your daughter killed her. No fear, no hesitation. She killed because she had to, because she had no choice. But she is a true de Lohr to the bone. Do you know why she returned to the hall in a different gown from the one she had been wearing earlier in the evening? It was because there was blood all over it and she did not want you to see it. She covered her tracks, even from you."

Christopher sat there and stared at him, his expression growing darker and darker. "Christ, William," he hissed. "Are you telling me that my daughter is risking her life for your political games?"

"It was her choice, Chris," William said quietly. "She is truly gifted, so much so that the men call her The Ghost."

"*She's* The Ghost?" Christopher was on his feet now. "We thought it was Peter!"

William smiled wryly. "Nay, man, it is your daughter," he said. "They call her The Ghost because she is the last person one would suspect. She is quiet and efficient in everything she does, moves swiftly, and leaves no trace if she can help it. Trust me, Chris; your daughter is a rare female."

That didn't help Christopher's outrage. "To hell with that," he growled. "I am taking her back to Lioncross and putting her under lock and key. How dare you risk my daughter's life!"

William held up a soothing hand. "That is the nature of this business we are all in," he said. "Tell me something; if she was male, would you be so outraged? Is it simply because she's a woman?"

"A woman should be protected!" Christopher was so angry that he was shaking. "And this is no ordinary woman; this is *my* daughter. She is playing dangerous games with men far more trained than she is – and you are letting her."

"Have a little faith in me," William said. "She does not go into a situation that may overwhelm her. Everything she does is with great thought. I hope you realize I would not intentionally or recklessly put her in danger."

But Christopher would not be eased. "I know you," he said. "I know what you are capable of, now with two of my children to do your bidding. Do you think this makes me happy?"

"You do my bidding."

"But I have been doing this kind of work for thirty years!" Christopher boomed. "My children have not! You are calling upon them to do the work of seasoned men who have been doing this kind of thing all of their lives. Neither Peter nor Christin have that kind of experience."

William was calm in the face of an irate parent. "You give your children no credit at all, do you?" he said. "Peter is a great knight and Christin is great in her own right. But I will admit that I am concerned with a romance between Sherry and Christin. I have watched Maxton and Kress and Achilles succumb to women and it has dampened their devotion to me. Not intentionally, but because their focus is on their wives and families. They acknowledge that and we all accept it, and still they answer my summons when they can. But for two of my active agents to be engaging in a love affair is dangerous for all concerned."

"It is dangerous, anyway," Christopher said unhappily.

William held up a finger to emphasize a point. "It is dangerous because emotion is involved now," he said. "I need Sherry focused on his duties and I need Christin focused on hers – I do not need the added burden of them being focused on each other as well. Emotion can cause mistakes and poor judgment."

Christopher could see that the man was leading to something. "What do you intend to do?"

"Speak with Sherry, at the very least," William said. "Chris, I will say one thing to you about this situation and then I will say no more. You raised intelligent children who can think and act for themselves. Now, when they are doing so and have found something they have a passion for, the same thing *you* have a passion for, you are considering shaming at least one of them by taking her back to Lioncross. How do you think such an action is going to affect your relationship with your daughter, who has acted autonomously as an agent for two years? She is going to resent you. She may even run away from you and continue doing what she was born to do. Would you really treat your daughter like a foolish child when you have raised her to be a fine, strong adult? At some point, your children have to lead their own lives. They want to be a tribute to the de Lohr name. *Let* them."

With that, he set his cup down and quit the tent, leaving Christopher and David in tense silence. Christopher found his chair again, rubbing his forehead as the stress of the situation settled.

"Christ, David," he muttered. "Is he right about this?"

David shrugged. "He sees the situation from a different perspective," he said. "You see it from a parent's point of view."

Christopher looked at him, his features twisting with disbelief. "Has Cissy really been a spy for two years and we did not suspect?"

David snorted, but it was an ironic gesture. "I think we started to back at Ramsbury," he said. "But hearing William's confirmation… that is shocking."

"Without a doubt. That means he recruited her when she had seen sixteen years."

"What do you intend to do?"

Christopher leaned back in the chair. "I do not know," he said honestly. "I am not thrilled with any of this, but William has a point – I raised my children to be strong and fearless, and when they are, it frightens me."

David could see the turmoil in his brother's face. "I think the first thing I would do is speak with Christin," he said. "Tell her you know that she serves The Marshal. Mayhap you can gain perspective on how she really feels about it."

Christopher nodded. "I suppose," he said. "She's my little girl, my firstborn with Dustin. I cannot think of her as anything else."

David smiled ironically. "I know who can."

"Who?"

"Sherry."

Christopher put his hands over his face. "You had to remind me."

David's smile turned genuine. "William has a meeting with his men in a few minutes," he said. "Let us be part of it. You cannot fight this, Chris. As difficult as it is for me to say this, I think William makes sense. Your children are a tribute to you – let them be."

Perhaps he was right. Christopher wasn't sure yet. But one thing was for certain – he had a situation with Christin and Alexander, and Marshal or no Marshal, he was going to deal with it as a father would.

CHAPTER FIFTEEN

HE HADN'T BEEN able to leave John for hours.

Sean was usually composed and collected in all situations, but the fact that John had kept him close for the past several hours and he'd not been able to break away to warn Christin or Alexander about the king's intentions had him edgy. More and more guests were arriving for the celebration, but John had restricted himself to his chambers, watching everything from his perch high above.

For several hours, he watched the incoming banners, identifying each one, pointing them out to Sean, who was preoccupied with the fact that Gerard had been gone for some time. He knew Gerard and how the man worked, and to say he was underhanded and sly didn't begin to cover it. Gerard was as dirty as they came and it greatly concerned Sean that the man was now in charge of taking Christin north to Robert FitzRoy.

In fact, the whole situation had him concerned, but not as concerned as John was when he saw the de Lohr standards raised in the encampment village below. Then, the man realized Christopher de Lohr had, indeed, come for his celebration and that drove John into a rage fairly early on. If the man was present at Norwich, then undoubtedly, he would be in the company of his daughter most of the time. That made their task far more difficult and John was furious about it.

Already, the situation was not going as planned.

"Did you hear me, Sean?"

Sean had been lost to his own thoughts and the question came from the king. He'd been staring from the window but not really seeing or hearing, so he quickly shook his head.

"Alas, I did not, your grace," he said. "My apologies. I was thinking of the best route to Bishop's Lynn for de Lohr's daughter. We want to ensure she makes it to your son before de Lohr can get to her and, as you have noted, the man is here."

John came away from the window he was looking out of. "My dear Sean," he said. "Always planning ahead. The fact that Christopher is at Norwich is unexpected, but I suppose in hindsight, I should have guessed. He and de Winter are allies."

"Technically, he is your ally, too, your grace."

John lifted his shoulders. "We have never been allies," he said. "Mayhap he has fought for me, but he's never truly been my ally."

"It will be even less so if you take his daughter," Sean said quietly. "Since he is here at Norwich, will you not reconsider speaking to him about a betrothal? It will go much better for you if you do. It might even heal any rifts, perceived or otherwise. But if you simply take the man's daughter, it will irrevocably damage any chance of creating a solid ally out of de Lohr."

John nodded his head as if he were truly thinking about the suggestion. "I know," he said. "You have told me that before and I've had others tell me, also."

Sean lifted an eyebrow. "Who else have you told about your scheme, your grace?"

John snorted. "Gerard said the same thing as you did," he said. "Gerard hates everyone and even he was concerned. I have also told Monnington. It was his idea, after all."

Sean didn't even look at the spoiled young lord in the corner. He'd been in the chamber for the better part of an hour, ever since he awoke with a horribly aching head from the night before and wandered into the chamber as if it were his right. Given that he'd provided a grand idea to the king, at the moment, he had that freedom. But too much wine and too many women, the privilege of John's courtiers, had made young Evan a bit difficult to take. Although he'd been in the chamber for a time, he blissfully hadn't said a word.

"I hope young Lord Dorè knows to keep his mouth shut, your grace," Sean finally muttered.

John looked over at the hungover young nobleman. "He does," he said confidently. "He is trustworthy. Oh, and Mandeville is here, you know. He believes it to be a terrible idea, also."

He was referring to one of his long-time courtiers, William Mandeville. Sean hadn't seen the man yet, as he tended to float in and out of John's circle as he went about his own business, but he was relieved to hear that the king hadn't spread his plans further.

"There are at least three of us telling you not to risk this, your grace," Sean said. "Yet you still intend to?"

John nodded. "If I ask for a betrothal, de Lohr will deny me," he said frankly. "I know he will. I must therefore take the lady. I consider the rewards of this action greater than the consequences, for de Lohr will not dare act against me if he values his daughter's life."

"And you have the control," Sean muttered softly.

"Indeed, I do."

"I, for one, do *not* think it is a terrible idea," Evan suddenly piped up. "I think it is a brilliant idea and you should be ashamed of yourself, de Lara, for thinking otherwise."

Sean turned to the young lord. "Cease your prattle, boy," he growled. "You know nothing in the grand scheme of things."

A threat from Sean de Lara was not taken lightly and Evan visibly blanched. He'd been brave until the massive de Lara turned on him. He knew the man and he knew his terrifying reputation.

Now, he wasn't so brave.

"What I meant to say was that the king's wish is obeyed in all things," he said, making sure he was well away from Sean should the man decide to lash out at him. "It is our duty, all of us, to obey."

Sean looked at the king. "Must I really speak with this piece of filth, your grace?"

John chuckled, enjoying the moment. "You do not have to, of course," he said. "But he is a lord on the Marches. When you inherit the Trilateral castles from your father, you will be a lord on the Marches, too. Mayhap it is good if you establish a rapport with young Evan. You will need allies when you are the Lord of the Trilaterals."

Lords of the Trilaterals was the de Lara hereditary title, something that Sean would indeed inherit from his father someday. Hyssington, Trelystan, and Caradoc Castles along the Welsh Marches would all be his.

"I do not need an ally who would go behind my back and betray me as he is betraying de Lohr," he rumbled, looking at Evan still cowering back in the corner. "I hope de Lohr finds out what you have done and wipes you from this earth. A quarter of his army could destroy you most completely, so I hope you are prepared to deal with that when the time comes."

Evan stiffened. "Is that a threat?" he demanded. "Are you going to tell him?"

Sean rolled his eyes, exasperated. "I will push aside my policy not to speak with rubbish just this once and tell you that I do not speak of anything the king says with anyone other than the king," he said. "I do not speak to de Lohr and if you impugn my honor just once more, I will forget you are a lord and make it so your body will never be found. Is this in any way unclear?"

Evan audibly gasped and inched his way towards the chamber door as John held up a calming hand.

"Evan, listen to him," he said. "Know your place and you shall remain in one piece. Cross my Lord of the Shadows and you will cease to exist. Sean is beyond reproach and you would do well to remember that."

As Evan settled down, rebuked, John turned to Sean. "Gerard already has a plan to steal Lady Christin away," he said. "Since de Lohr is here, you will have to help us by making sure de Lohr is none the wiser to his daughter's abduction."

Sean nodded. "I will do all I can, your grace," he said. "What is the plan?"

"She seems to stay to the apartments next to the keep," John said. "Gerard says there is a postern gate there that leads to the farm fields below. He can remove her from her apartment and take her through the postern gate where horses will be waiting, along with about a hundred of my men, and he must do it sometime during the day when her father is occupied and less likely to look for her. When she does not show up at the evening's feast, Gerard and the escort will be several hours away by that time."

Sean could see the logic in that plan because it took Christin out of Norwich the easiest way, bypassing the gatehouse guards who would undoubtedly question a man carrying a screaming woman.

"Where would you have me, your grace?" Sean asked.

"Go with Gerard," he said. "Stay with him. Help him remove Christin if you must, but cover his retreat to ensure no one follows."

Sean nodded, but it was clear that he wasn't happy. "I will ensure the mission is a success, your grace," he said. "But may I make a suggestion?"

"Of course."

"Let me go instead of Gerard. He has no self-control and it is very possible that Lady Christin will not reach your son a maiden. You do not want her sullied by one of your guards."

John scratched his chin. "Nay, I do not, but I want you with me, so I have little choice but to send her with Gerard," he said. "I will make it clear to him that he is not to touch her. If he does, it will be at the risk of his life."

"I hope that is enough, your grace."

John did, too. He had other things to worry about, like Christopher de Lohr at Norwich, so his attention was stretched.

"Go and find Gerard now," he said. "He should already be moving the escort down to the gate in the farm fields below, where the postern gate leads. Make sure your plans are coordinated with him. Meanwhile, I will bathe and dress for the feast this evening. And take Monnington with you."

Sean immediately headed out of the chamber, crooking a finger at Evan as he went. The young lord was too terrified to refuse, so he moved slowly as Sean held the door open for him. Once they were through the door, however, the situation changed dramatically.

The master's chamber had a narrow staircase that led down to the floor below, steeply pitched and curved in a half-spiral. The second the door to the king's chamber was closed, Sean grabbed Evan by the neck and slapped a hand over his mouth so the young lord couldn't scream. Taking him to the top of the stairs, he hurled Evan so fast and so powerfully down the stairs that the man ended up hitting the ceiling of the stairwell before plunging to his death to the floor below.

Sean stood at the top of the steps, hearing him hit. He swore he could hear the bones crunch.

"That is for Christin, you little bastard," he whispered through clenched teeth.

Almost immediately, Sean could hear people gasping as they found the dead man at the base of the stairs and he quickly went down the steps, telling everyone the young lord had slipped and fallen. He was convincing enough that he was believed, a terrible tragedy on the day of the king's celebration.

But then again, no one was foolish enough to contest the Lord of the Shadows.

When John heard what had happened, he didn't contest him, either. But he didn't believe him. Still, it didn't matter; Evan Monnington had served his purpose.

There was a young woman to abduct.

CHAPTER SIXTEEN

JUST BECAUSE HER father had chased her away so he could speak to Alexander didn't mean she was going to *stay* away.

Christin was on the hunt.

She ran into Kevin near the keep and he mentioned that The Marshal was calling his men together to discuss the feast that night. But when she headed down to The Marshal's encampment, she happened to see her father entering The Marshal's tent along with Bric, her Uncle David, and Alexander. Knowing her father was in that meeting meant she would stay away unless she wanted to blow her cover.

Therefore, she hid.

The meeting went on for about an hour and she'd managed to work her way behind his tent, listening to everything that was being said. She never heard her father speak, but she heard Alexander speak up on several occasions and it set her heart to fluttering. Even the sound of his voice made her sigh. She hadn't seen her father since he'd sent her away so she didn't know what was said between him and Alexander, but she intended to find out. She knew her father was very protective, and caught off guard, which made for a bad combination. The idea that he might have ruined her budding relationship with Alexander gave her a sick feeling in the pit of her stomach.

So, she waited.

She knew the meeting couldn't last forever and, in truth, she'd only been to a few of these all-gathered meetings. If Susanna was there, then she was usually there, but The Marshal still had ideas about women and them participating in men's games. He needed women like Susanna and Christin, but he still didn't fully pull them into his fold. But Christin wasn't offended by it because she was grateful for as far as she had come.

Towards the end of the meeting, the conversations drifted and men began to leave. Mostly, Christin had heard everything she already knew about John, and about the alleged threat from within, so it really wasn't anything she hadn't heard before. When the meeting started breaking up, however, she peered around the side of the tent and watched her father and uncle head back to their encampment.

She saw Bric, Peter, Caius, and Kevin depart also. It occurred to her that her father must know Peter to be part of The Marshal's spy ring considering they were both in on the very same meeting. That thought didn't give her much hope about the man's mood considering it was probably the second dose of important news he'd received that day – first her romance with Alexander and then the confirmation that Peter was an agent for The Marshal.

The poor man had already had a hell of a day and it wasn't even time for the feast yet.

With men drifting out of The Marshal's tent, Christin waited for Alexander to appear. Maxton and Kress were still inside the tent, along with Alexander, so she went back to the spot where she'd had the best luck eavesdropping only to hear that William knew of Alexander's romantic interest in her. Christin sighed faintly, knowing her father must have told The Marshal. She wondered what kind of trouble she'd be in for now, but part of her was glad that it was out. Perhaps a little sooner than she would have liked, but at least it was out in the open now.

She hoped Alexander wasn't in too much trouble for it.

Unfortunately, William kept his voice quite as he spoke to Alexander, so she could only catch bits of the conversation. Maxton and Kress never said a word; it all seemed to be William and, on occasion, Alexander, but he wasn't speaking very loudly either. It all seemed to be calm and quiet, which was good. Or, so she thought. Finally, she heard the tent flap move and she peeked around the corner of the tent to see Alexander heading towards the gatehouse that led up to the keep.

Swiftly, she followed.

Since she didn't want her father or William to see her, she had to dart through The Marshal's encampment, essentially running to catch up with Alexander. He was just crossing the bridge into the keep when she came up behind him.

"Sherry?"

Startled, he came to a halt and whirled around. "Where did you come from?"

Christin threw her thumb over her shoulder, a vague answer. "That way," she said. "I saw you come out of William's tent."

"You did? Where were you?"

She wasn't going to lie to him. She was, if nothing else, an honest person, so lying to people she cared about didn't come naturally.

"I was behind William's tent, listening to everything he said," she confessed. "I heard him say that he knows about… us."

Alexander nodded slowly. "He does," he said. "Is that all you heard?"

She gazed up at him, the breeze whipping her dark hair across her face. "I did not hear any details, if that is what you mean," she said. "What else did he say?"

He regarded her for a moment. "Your father asked that I not speak to you for the rest of the day, you know."

"Are you going to listen to him?"

Alexander glanced around to see if he saw Christopher or David, or any other Marshal man. When he didn't note any familiar faces, he took her by the elbow.

"Nay," he said quietly. "Come with me."

She went with him, gladly. He was walking rather quickly and led her straight back to her apartment block. Before proceeding inside, however, he paused.

"Who is in the building?" he asked.

Christin instinctively glanced up at the gray-stoned building. "At this time of day, it is difficult to tell," she said. "Since there is a great feast tonight, it is possible that Lady de Winter has the women in the kitchens to oversee the preparations. Why?"

"Because I must speak with you privately and this may be the only place that I can do it."

Christin didn't say another word. In fact, he sounded rather ominous so she was eager to get on with it. Opening the door, she led him inside, calling a few times to see if anyone was about, including Wynter. Receiving no reply, she bolted the entry door.

"My chamber is upstairs," she said quietly.

He stopped her before she could head up the stairs. "Won't they question the fact that you have locked the entry door?"

She shook her head. "Not when I explain that I was afraid of the king," she said. "They will not question that. Just make sure you are not discovered. I may have to push you out the window to escape."

He gave her a wry smirk and let her lead him up to her chamber on the second floor, the one with the view of both the keep and the garden. Admitting him inside, she closed the door quietly and bolted that one, too. Then, she faced him expectantly.

"Well?" she said. "What do you wish to speak of?"

They were quite alone, behind two locked doors, and Alexander found that he was having trouble focusing on anything else but her. Not The Marshal or her father or the king filled his mind. It had only been a few hours since he'd last seen her, but he felt as if it had been a million.

There was something about the woman that grew more beautiful each time he saw her. Her dark hair, long and curling, her dark brows arched over eyes of a pale gray… there was nothing about her that was unspectacular and he wanted this relationship to work so very badly. He never knew how badly until this very moment.

He took a deep breath.

"Your father and I had a serious discussion when you left," he said. "He was not happy, Cissy. Surely you know that."

"I know," she said, sobering. "Did he ruin things for me, Sherry?"

He looked at her, grinning. "Hardly," he said. "But he did bring up a few things about me that you must be aware of. I thought we would have time to discover one another, not give you an entire accounting of my life for the past twenty years all at once, but it seems that might not be the case. Before you and I proceed, there is something you must know about me."

"Continue."

"I used to have a harem."

She cocked her head curiously. "A harem?"

"That means I had a group of women at my disposal," he said. "To fulfill my needs. When I returned home from The Levant, I took my time. I ended up at the Lateran Palace in Rome with the Holy Father. Whilst there, I provided a service for him. If he had an enemy, I would deal with them. If he wanted me to do something sly and deadly, I would do it. In return for this service, he provided me with a house of my own and twelve women."

She scratched her head curiously. "They took care of your home?"

He tried not to grin at her surprising innocence in the matter. "Nay, sweetheart," he said, putting his hands on her arms. "I am trying to tell you that these women were provided to me to take care of my *needs*. As a wife would take care of husband."

Her eyes widened as she realized what he meant. "Like a brothel?"

Quickly, he shook his head. "Nay, because they belonged only to me," he said. Then, he sighed heavily. "I was unmarried. I was not betrothed. There was no one woman who had my loyalty. I took a few of these women to my bed because, sometimes, men have physical needs. Now do you understand?"

"Oh," she said, an expression of hurt crossing her features even though she pretended otherwise. "They were… special to you?"

He shook his head. "Nay," he said quietly. "I did not feel anything for them. They were simply possessions."

"Is that what a woman is to you? A possession?"

"God, no," he waved her off. "I am trying to be completely honest with you about my past by telling you something unsavory that your father brought up. But I will tell you what I told him – although I cannot undo the past, I can make a promise for the future. I will never disrespect you, I will always ensure you are safe and warm and happy, and I will be faithful to you for the rest of my life if you decide that I am the man you want. Upon my oath, I swear this."

Christin believed him without hesitation. He was a knight of the highest order and men such as Alexander did not take a vow upon their oath lightly.

They meant it for life.

"I believe you," she said, her eyes glimmering warmly at him. "Did my father?"

Alexander chuckled, a nervous gesture because he honestly wasn't sure if she would have accepted his vow so easily. "I think so," he said. "Your father and I have known each other a very long time. He was concerned about my past, as he should be. He is a father protecting his daughter. But men have pasts; most do not live like priests until they marry. I want you to know that you can ask me anything about my past and I will answer you honestly. I say this because I am certain your father will tell you things he knows about me and I do not want you to be surprised. I want you to hear the truth from me."

She appreciated that he was being forthright. "You are an Executioner Knight, a legend," she said. "I am sure you did not gain that reputation by living in a monastery for the past twenty years."

He laughed softly. "I did not," he said. "And your father knows that."

Her smile faded. "Do you think he will try to dissuade me?"

Alexander shrugged. "It is possible," he said. "He tried to chase me away but I would not go. I have found the woman I wish to spend my life with and I will not leave her, no matter what."

It was a sweet thing to say and Christin's smile returned. "He cannot say anything that will shake me, either," she said. "I am sure he wishes I would marry a stalwart young knight with no past and a bright future. I am sure every father wishes that for his daughter. But there is no young, stalwart knight in England that could turn my head from you, Sherry. I have made my choice."

Alexander looked at her, fortified by her declaration but knowing they more than likely had a difficult road ahead of them. In fact, he knew of one right away.

It might change everything.

"You did not hear what William said to me?" he asked.

She shook her head. "Nay."

Alexander averted his gaze, thoughtfully, trying to find the best way to tell her what he must. It was difficult for him to spit it out, but he had to.

Better now than later.

"He is not happy about our association, either," he said quietly. "He fears that it will impact any tasks we are assigned together, and he is not wrong. He has the same concerns with Achilles and Susanna, although so far, they have proven him wrong. Still, he is afraid our emotions will get in the way of our judgment."

"What does that mean?"

"It means that he wants to separate us," he said softly. "It means that he wants to put space between us to either kill what we are feeling for each other or, if that is not the case, at least give us time to think. We are not to serve together unless absolutely necessary."

Christin's brow furrowed as she listened, genuinely trying not to become upset. She was struggling to be pragmatic, to see things from The Marshal's perspective, but it was becoming increasingly difficult.

"He is siding with my father," she said after a moment. "Surely, my father must have spoken to him and told him what happened. There is no other way he would have known."

Alexander knew that. "I am sure he did speak with him."

"Then you lied to me."

"When did I do this disgraceful thing?"

"You told me that my father wasn't trying to ruin this for me. Clearly, he is."

He could see that she was becoming upset no matter how hard she was trying not to. He admired her strength in the matter; a lesser woman would have been in tears by now. Christin was stronger than that.

But she wasn't unbreakable.

"Come with me," he said, reaching out and taking her by the hand. He led her over to the bed. "Sit down, please."

She did, gripping his hand tightly. He could feel the tension, the fear, in her grip so he sat down beside her and took both of her hands in his, holding them against his thigh. Looking her in the eyes, he could see how much she was struggling with the situation.

Truth be told, he was struggling, too.

"I have had time to think about everything since this morning, so I want to discuss it with you," he said quietly, seriously. "Only yesterday, we were declaring our feelings and, today, we have already had to face serious opposition. Would you agree with that statement?"

She nodded. "I would."

"But that does not mean it is ruined. Nothing is ruined, Cissy. Do you understand?"

She took a deep breath, forcing herself to calm. "I do," she said. "I am sorry if I sounded snappish and weak."

He smiled at her. "You are dealing with the stress of this situation far better than any woman I know of," he said. "Ever since we reached Norwich, this has been a tribulation for you. You've had to deal with an amorous king, an angry father, and an unsympathetic commander. But you have dealt with it all beautifully and you will continue to do so. Every moment shows me how strong and capable you are, and that simply makes me adore you all the more. So, I swear to you, nothing is ruined. But we do have to think of a few things about our future. It sounds ridiculously premature to say that, but it's necessary. I have no intention of letting you go, so if we have a plan in place, we'll both feel better. Agreed?"

She was visibly calming in the wake of his logic. "Agreed," she said, smiling weakly. "And thank you."

"For what?"

"For not letting me go."

He shook his head, reaching up to gently touch her cheek. "Never," he whispered. "For now, I think we must adhere to the plan we set earlier – that you must leave the castle until the king departs. That will keep you away from him. If your father does not know about last night, he soon will, so I am sure he will agree. The fastest and safest thing to do is take you to the inn near the cathedral, as we discussed. I will escort you there myself, so you should pack a satchel and be ready to leave as soon as I can secure the horses."

She nodded. "What about my father? Will you tell him?"

He nodded. "Of course," he said. "As soon as you are safely away, I will tell him everything. I suspect he may even come to you at the inn and I further suspect he will want to take you back to Lioncross Abbey with him."

Her brow furrowed. "I am not entirely sure I want to go there."

"Why not?"

"Because it is a massive fortress and once I am there, it would be a simple thing to keep me locked away from you."

Alexander chuckled. "Do you seriously think those old walls would keep me away? You do not know me very well."

She grinned. "That is something I hope to change," she said, squeezing his hands. "I was so hoping we would have more time to talk and come to know one another. But if my father takes me back to Lioncross…"

He cut her off gently. "It will be the safest place for you right now," he said. "You will be far away from John and he can focus his attention somewhere else."

Christin thought on John and his determination, and of a future where she and Alexander were separated for an unknown amount of time. "And then what?"

He shrugged. "The Marshal and I must have a serious discussion about the situation," he said. "It may be that you will stay at Lioncross for some time and I will come to you when I can. It may be that you must give up your life of spying altogether, which I hesitate to say because I know you love it. I do not want to see you unhappy, but I will say this... as my wife, I would prefer you not continue to serve The Marshal."

She cocked her head thoughtfully, looking at him in such a way that told him she was considering everything quite carefully. Perhaps that wasn't what she wanted to hear, but at least she wasn't outright denying him.

"I do love serving The Marshal," she finally said. "Susanna continues to serve him even though she and Achilles are married."

"That is true."

"May I serve as she does?" she asked. "As time and the situation allows? It's simply that I feel it is important work, Sherry. I have told you this. I would not do anything you did not approve of."

She said it in such a way that he didn't immediately flare. Not that he would have, and he didn't expect her to give up so easily, but what she said made sense. Moreover, she was willing to give him the control, even this early on in their budding relationship. That spoke of her willingness to compromise. Regardless of what he wanted, however, he couldn't have denied her.

She was gifted.

He understood that.

"We do not have to decide anything today," he said. "I suppose that I do not see any issue with you continuing to serve in some capacity, but that is far in the future, sweetheart. Let us get through the immediate situation and we'll address the rest. But I think, for now, getting you to the inn and then on to Lioncross is the best course of action. You will be safe with your father, in any case. The king cannot touch you."

Reaching up, she gently touched his hair and he closed his eyes, savoring the sweetness of her touch. It was such a gentle moment of discovery, having the freedom to touch one another in a setting that allowed them complete privacy. At the moment, there was nothing lustful about it, simply the excitement of something new and wonderful at hand.

"You are worried about the king, still," she said. "You do not think that last night truly discouraged him?"

Alexander opened his eyes. "With John, we have no way of knowing," he said. "All I know is that we should not take any chances when it comes to you. I want you safe and away from Norwich."

"Today?"

"Today. Right away."

"Will you do something for me, then?"

"If I can."

She smiled, embarrassed, and he could see her cheeks flushing. "I am not sure how to say this," she said. "I fear we may spend a good deal of time apart and I was wondering… you see, I've never been kissed by someone other than my father or mother or uncle. It would give me a memory to take with me if you would…"

Alexander was on her in a flash, his hands cupping her head as his lips slanted over hers. Instead of stiffening with surprise, she was immediately soft and compliant, and he pulled her into his arms, kissing her deeply. Everything about her was warm and honeyed and the more he tasted, the more he wanted.

She was exhilarating.

He lost himself. While one hand held her against him, the other began to roam. He touched her hair, feeling the long and silken strands, before he gently stroked her arm, her back, the curve of her torso. Everything about her was so soft and beautiful, and his mouth left hers to nibble on her jaw.

Her neck...

Her shoulder.

He wanted to move lower on her. God knows, he did, but it wasn't the right time. At least, he didn't think so until Christin untied the front of her garment and yanked it down. Suddenly, both shoulders were fully exposed as was the rise of her full breasts. She'd pulled it down just short of her nipples and he didn't ask questions. He didn't chastise her or pull the front of her dress up.

He feasted.

He suckled on the top of her breasts, gently kissing, gently tugging at the tender flesh. Christin gasped at his intimate touch. As he bent lower to plant his face in the valley between her breasts, her small hands snaked into the neckline of his tunic, her bare hands against his bare shoulders, caressing him.

Touching him.

Now, he was on fire.

Never in his life had he ever known a woman to be so immediately and insistently intoxicating. There was something about Christin that drove him mad the minute he touched her, as if he'd always meant to have her, as if they'd always been meant to be.

Nothing had ever felt more natural.

The front of her gown came down to her waist.

Now, his mouth was on her nipples, suckling her furiously as he laid her back on the bed. Christin didn't put up a fight. She lay down, with him on top of her, arms around his neck as he nursed her breasts, first one and then the other. All the while, she was gasping with pleasure, her hands in his hair, until her fingers tightened around the strands and she yanked him up. This time, her mouth claimed his and, somehow, in all of the kissing and fondling, he ended up on his back with her straddling him.

He was more aroused than he'd ever been in his life. His hands found their way under her skirts, which were merely a shift and a surcoat, so there wasn't much resistance. His hands gripped her hips at first before sliding to her buttocks, tender and soft. Christin didn't flinch, allowing his hands to roam as she continued her role as aggressor, suckling his lower lip, responding when his tongue probed her mouth. Everything he was doing to her, she was responding and then some.

In fact, Alexander could hardly believe how responsive she was. He pulled his mouth away from hers and resumed suckling her breasts, partially sitting up as she sat upon his lap as a man would sit upon a horse, with her legs parted. The harder he suckled her, the more she bucked and gasped until his hand moved down her belly to the thatch of dark curls between her legs.

Since she was straddling him, the jewel between her legs was an easy target and he stroked her gently. His touch in a very intimate place caused her to start, unfamiliar with someone touching her in such a place, but she didn't try to pull away. She let him stoke her as he suckled her breasts, one hand her holding against him while the other went to work between her legs.

God, he knew he should stop. He should stop at that very moment but he couldn't bring himself to do it. She was alluring beyond measure, unafraid of his touch, brave as he'd never see a maiden in this situation. Visions of Christopher de Lohr running his sword through his gut had occurred to him, but they were fleeting because some things were worth dying for.

Christin de Lohr was one of them.

She was already very wet and hot, and he carefully inserted a finger into her. Christin gasped at the tender intrusion but didn't try to shake him or pull away. In fact, her head rolled back and she closed her eyes, experiencing the tender trials of his touch. One finger went into her, thrusting gently, before he inserted two.

Christin shuddered.

"Cissy," he murmured against her breast. "I should not go on. You know I should not go on."

Her response was to roll her pelvis forward, awkwardly, but the message was obvious. "Please don't stop," she breathed. "Please, Sherry... I am yours. I will always *be* yours. Give me all of you to remember during the time we shall be separated. Will you not continue?"

He sighed raggedly. Her nipples were in front of his face and he leaned over, taking one between his teeth and gently tugging at it.

"You already have all of me, Cissy," he whispered. "But what you are asking... are you certain this is what you want?"

She thrust her pelvis against his hand again and Alexander had his answer. Therefore, he untied his breeches and freed his engorged manhood. Grasping her hips, he pulled her forward so she could feel the long, hard length of him.

He thought it might give her pause, but it didn't. She had simply found something to rub her wet heat against and Alexander moved his member so the tip of it came to bear against her virginal passage. Christin was so highly aroused, but so inexperienced, that she thrust her hips forward again to capture him and he ended up sliding nearly his full, long length into her.

The sting of possession brought a yelp from Christin. All of the fondling and suckling had been pleasurable, but the actual act of mating had been something different. She came to a halt in her wriggling, her head dropping to his shoulder to bite off her gasp of pain, and Alexander grasped her hips again and held them steady as he thrust hard, all the way into her.

With a groan, torn between pain and pleasure, Christin wrapped her arms around his neck and buried her face in the side of his head. He could hear her breathing heavily in his ear and he wrapped his arms around her, holding her close.

"You are more courageous than any woman I know," he whispered. "Relax, sweetheart. I promise you will like this."

He nursed at her breasts to distract her as he recoiled and thrust again, moving in and out of her gently at first but with increasing power. Christin remained straddled on his lap, her legs spread wide as she welcomed him into her body for the first time. He was skilled and he was gentle, and he succeeded in building a heat within her loins that had bursts of lightning surging through her. The lightning grew stronger with each successive thrust.

In very little time, Christin was experiencing her first release. Her body was young and highly sensitive, and Alexander held her tightly as wave after wave of ecstasy rolled over her. Just as she was catching her breath, another climax hit her and she cried out, loudly enough that Alexander had to put his hand over her mouth so others would not hear her groans of pleasure. But her pleasure fed his own and after one great and powerful thrust, he quickly removed himself from her body and spent himself on her coverlet.

Even when he was spent, he didn't want it to be over. It had been such a soul-baring experienced that he thrust into her again, gently, and continued to stroke in and out of her, feeling her warm wetness surround him, feeling her climax yet again as her body bucked and shuddered involuntarily. He had to smile, thinking that it was quite miraculous, all of it. Amazing, even.

She was amazing.

And he was marked for life.

"Are you well?" he asked huskily. "Did I hurt you?"

Her arms were still around his neck, her face in the side of his head. She mumbled something but she was so muffled that he didn't hear what she said. He shifted so she had to loosen her grip on him and lift her head.

"What did you say?" he asked, amused.

Her hair was hanging in her face. She even had a piece of it in her mouth, which he pulled out. When he pushed her hair away from her face, he could see that her eyes were still closed. He started to laugh.

"Cissy?" he said. "Say something."

She grinned, peeping her eyes open. "I said that all is well," she said. "And I think I love you."

Her arms tightened and she kissed him again, deeply, and he responded instantly. It was a kiss of desire, of emotion, and most of all, of joy.

Of two people who had finally found one another.

"Am I truly so fortunate, sweetheart?" he breathed against her mouth. "Do you truly?"

She pulled her lips away long enough to look him in the eye. "I think I have loved you since before I met you," she said softly. "My father and uncle would speak so highly of Alexander de Sherrington and when we met, I knew I already loved you. I admired you so much that the admiration became something else once we came to know each other. I cannot explain it better than that. I have been yours since the beginning, Sherry, only you did not know it."

He grinned, holding her head between his two enormous hands. "I know it now."

"You do."

He kissed her again, gently this time. "Now," he said. "It is time for you to pack a satchel and prepare to depart. I will return for you once I've finished preparing the horses."

"Shall I meet you below, in the farm fields?"

"Nay."

She looked at him, surprised. "Why not?"

"Because there are enough men around now that we can lose ourselves leaving through the main gate," he said. "I am confident that there is so much activity, and everyone is focused on the evening's feast, that we will be able to slip by unnoticed. Also, I do not want you out of my sight, so you will remain here until I return for you. I do not want you wandering alone with all of the soldiers around and with the king's men lurking. Therefore, pack your bag and I will return for you shortly."

He seemed determined. Christin simply nodded, trusting him and his plans. He kissed her once more, twice more, before moving to help her pull the top of her dress up. Realizing their time alone was ended, she made an unhappy face and begrudgingly climbed off him, refitting her dress, which was bunched up around her waist. The bodice went back up and the skirts went back down, and she looked at her coverlet to see the evidence of their activities.

Alexander was on his feet, tying off his breeches, as she went to the bed and noted a wet, slightly pink stain on it. He turned to see what had her attention and, noticing the evidence of their activities, reached down and flipped the coverlet over without a word. Now, the stain was on the underside with the clean coverlet above. When she looked at him, rather embarrassed, he smiled as he bent over and kissed her forehead.

"It is not that I am ashamed of what we did," he said quietly. "But I do not want others to know of it, for obvious reasons. What we shared, Cissy… that is for us alone and no one else."

She nodded. "Agreed."

He put a big hand on her face, cupping her cheek and forcing her to look at him. "Are you sure you're well?"

"I am fine."

"No discomfort or regrets?"

She shook her head, throwing her arms around his neck and squeezing him tightly. "Never," she murmured. "But already, I miss you. Please hurry back to me, Sherry. Every day of this separation will be torture."

He enveloped her in his enormous arms, memorizing the feel of her against him to recall on the days to come. He honestly didn't know what the future would bring them, or how long they would truly be separated, but he didn't want to frighten her with his speculation. He wanted this moment to be as warm and without angst as it could possibly be.

"It will be torture, indeed," he said after a moment. "But I carry your love and that will give me the strength of the archangels for what is to come."

Kissing her on the side of the head, he let her go, heading for the door. He was about to lift the latch when a word from her stopped him.

"Will I carry your love, also?" she asked quietly.

He paused, turning to her. The twinkle in his dark eyes told her everything even before he spoke. "You do," he murmured. "It does not seem possible that I am capable of saying this so soon, but it is what I feel. My love was only meant for you."

With that, he slipped from the door, out into the dark landing beyond. Christin went to the door, hearing his boot falls as he descended the stairs and headed out into the day beyond.

With a smile playing on her lips, she closed her door and bolted it. She simply stood there for a moment, reliving the past several minutes, feeling as if her heart had wings. She never knew that she could be so completely and utterly happy, as if she were walking on clouds. It didn't seem possible.

But possible, it was.

He loved her.

Pushing her silly daydreams aside, she went on the hunt for her satchel.

CHAPTER SEVENTEEN

THANK GOD HE'D been able to break free.

Sean was free and clear now that Monnington's body had been cleaned up off the stones where he landed. As far as everyone was concerned, it was a terrible accident.

Now, he was on the hunt.

He had no idea where Christin was, but he needed to get to The Marshal or Christopher to tell them what was afoot. Unfortunately, that meant going to the encampment area where there were dozens of lords set up for a nice, long stay in honor of the king's birthday celebration.

Sean wasn't so certain he wanted to head down there because there would literally be hundreds of witnesses to his presence in the de Lohr encampment and that wasn't something he wanted to explain to the king should word get back to him. The same could be said for entering The Marshal's encampment, so he realized as he came to the main gatehouse that led down into the baileys that he wouldn't be able to go to them.

They would have to come to him.

But that didn't stop him from heading out into the encampments, however. He was hoping to catch the eye of anyone – Maxton, Kress, Alexander, even his brother – *anyone* – and perhaps he could convey to them that he needed to speak. For all the witnesses to his presence would know, however, he was simply perusing those who had come to the celebration, information he would relay to the king. As long as he wasn't seen specifically speaking with de Lohr or The Marshal, his behavior would be perfectly normal.

The de Lohr and Marshal camps were right next to each other and the first person he happened to see was his good friend, Caius d'Avignon. Tall, black-haired Caius spied him almost immediately as he stood speaking to Maxton, who turned around casually to notice Sean standing back on the roadway that led to the gatehouse. When Sean tightened his gloves, or at least pretended to, and used his right hand to point discreetly to the keep, they realized it was a signal.

Caius followed, leaving Maxton to inform The Marshal of Sean's appearance.

Sean wandered back inside the walls that enclosed the keep with Caius strolling casually several yards behind him. There were a few of the king's soldiers lingering in this area, near the stairs that led into the keep, but he ignored them. He went around behind the chapel, watching as Caius entered the area.

When Caius saw him back behind the chapel, he continued forward, winding his way among the outbuildings before doubling back and ending up behind the chapel where Sean was. Or, at least where he thought Sean was. When he didn't see the man immediately, he grew frustrated and started to walk to the front of the chapel when a big hand shot out and grabbed him from the doorway at the rear of the chapel.

Sean yanked him into the dark, empty church.

"Jesus, Sean," Caius grunted. "You scared the hell out of me."

Knowing that was an impossible task, Sean fought off a grin. "I doubt that," he said. "No one frightens The Britannia Viper and lives to tell the tale."

Caius looked at the man, smiling. "That is true," he said, his gaze lingering on Sean a moment. "I am the very model of an unflappable man. It has been a long time, my friend."

"It has."

"I would ask how you have been, but I suspect that is not a fair question."

Sean shrugged. "I am well, if that is what you mean," he said. "But doing what I do… it is every bit the hell you thought it would be, Cai. I would say that you should be glad you are not in my shoes, but there are days when I wish you were with all my heart."

Caius' smile faded. "I know," he said, feeling both guilt and sympathy. "Were it not for you, it would be me known as Lord of the Shadows. The Marshal offered the position to us both but you were the one who volunteered. I know it was to spare me the horrors of it, Sean. I've always known."

Sean sighed faintly. "It does not matter now," he said. "It is my task and has been for years. But know that, physically, I am well. I have more money than I know what to do with, courtesy of the king, and he speaks of giving me a lordship, although that has not happened yet. I will emerge from this rich, if nothing else."

Caius grunted. "It is small compensation for serving the bastard."

"Agreed."

"I told Kevin what happened, you know," Caius said. "I told him that I had an equal chance of becoming the Lord of the Shadows but that you volunteered before I could make my decision. It did not seem to matter to your brother at all. He is still quite angry at you."

Sean's mood darkened. "I know," he said. "I tried to speak with him yesterday but he does not want to see reason. He does not want to understand why I did what I did. He sees the hurt I have caused and that is all he sees."

Caius lifted his eyebrows in resignation. "He is a little brother who's much-adored big brother has turned to the wicked side of politics, for all the world to see," he said. "Kevin must grow up, Sean. When he does, he will understand."

"Possibly," Sean said. "But I do not hold out hope. And I have little time, so I do not wish to waste it speaking of Kevin. There is a situation you must relay to The Marshal immediately. More than that, you must relay it to Christopher de Lohr."

"What about?"

"John informed me yesterday that he wants Christin de Lohr to marry his son, Robert FitzRoy," he said. "Because of this, a plan was put into action last night in that Christin behaved horribly at supper to discourage the king from having any ambitions on her. She did a magnificent job of presenting a wretched, ill-behaved woman, but it did not deter John. He and Gerard d'Athee have concocted a scheme to abduct Christin from Norwich and take her north to FitzRoy to be married."

Caius' brow was furrowed with concern. "When?"

"Today."

"What's the plan?"

"To remove her from the postern gate and take her to the farm fields below. Less resistance than passing through four gatehouses if they take her from the keep."

Caius exhaled sharply. "Christ," he muttered. "Where is Christin?"

Sean shook his head. "I do not know," he said. "I would assume in her chamber, which is in the apartment block to the east of this chapel, but I just saw Sherry heading down to the lower baileys."

"What does Sherry have to do with Christin?"

"They are lovers."

Caius' eyebrows lifted in surprise. "They are? I'd not heard."

"I believe they have been trying to keep quiet on the matter," Sean said. "In any case, she is not with Sherry, but I shall try to locate her. Hopefully, she is in her chamber behind a locked door."

"If they are lovers, then Sherry will want to know about this, too."

"Indeed. And you must tell him after you tell The Marshal and Christopher."

Caius nodded, already moving for the door. "What will you do when you find Christin?"

Sean was right behind him. "Hide her," he said. "John cannot abduct what he cannot find, and it will give de Lohr a chance to get her out of Norwich."

Just as they reached the door, they both heard screaming.

HE'D TOLD HER to wait in her chamber, but restless, she couldn't seem to do it.

Dressed in a dark blue wool traveling dress with a matching cloak and her dark hair braided, Christin wanted to leave immediately. Her bag was packed just a few minutes after Alexander had left her to go down to the stables. He'd told her to wait for him, but she was confident that it would be an easy walk to the stables to meet him there. There were gangs of men around, all going about their business, shielding her in case royal eyes happened to be watching.

Certainly, nothing could happen with a crowd all around.

She saw no reason to wait.

Impatience got the better of her. So did nerves. She was afraid to stay in her chamber, knowing that was the obvious place to look should the king's men come on the hunt. Somehow, she felt more vulnerable in her chamber. Or perhaps she felt vulnerable because she was without Alexander. When she was with him, she felt safe.

It wasn't the brightest decision to leave her chamber, but she did.

She wanted to find Alexander.

The encounter with him that afternoon had done something to her. She'd always been singularly focused, strangely so, on her tasks for William Marshal. As she'd told Alexander on more than one occasion, it made her feel as if she were part of something. As if she were making a difference as few women could claim, and that was still very true, but now… now, all she could seem to focus on was Alexander.

She could see their children, strong sons with de Lohr and de Sherrington blood, lads that would grow up to be great knights and tributes to both their father and grandsire. For the first time in her life, she was thinking of marriage and children, not of missions for William Marshal.

She was thinking of love.

It was like a dream, all of it.

Just as she was coming off the stairs, the entry door opened and Wynter stepped through. She looked at Christin in surprise.

"There you are," she said. "Where have you been? Lady de Winter has been asking about you."

Christin's cheeks threatened to turn bright red then and there, but she fought it. "I… my father is here," she said, walking that fine line between a lie and the truth. "I have not seen him in some time, you know."

The implication was that she'd been with her father and Wynter believed her. She had no reason not to.

"I know," Wynter said. "I would like to greet him, also. How is he faring these days?"

"Fine. My Uncle David is here also."

"Lovely," Wynter said, smiling. But her smile quickly faded. "Did you tell your father what happened last night? With the king, I mean?"

Christin shook her head. "Nay," she said truthfully. "It will greatly upset him. You know that he and John have never had a good relationship and I fear upsetting the entire celebration if I tell my father that the king invited me to sup."

"But you were brilliant in the way you handled him," Wynter insisted. "You can tell your father what you did to discourage the king and he should have a good laugh over it."

Christin grinned. "We were brilliant, weren't we?" she said. "You were astonishingly smart, Wynnie. For a moment there, I thought we were truly fighting."

Wynter laughed. "Are you sore this morning? My arse hurts a bit where I fell onto the floor."

Christin giggled, rubbing her bum. "A little," she said. "But it was worth it. The king fled in disgust and that is exactly what we wanted."

"True," Wynter said. Then, she pointed to Christin's satchel. "Where are you going with that?"

Christin looked at the bag. "I am going to the village, to the inn we discussed yesterday," she said. "It is best that I stay out of the king's way, at least until he departs Norwich. I do not want to give him the chance to change his mind and decide he wants to dine with me again."

"He would do so at his peril, but I think it is wise if you leave, too. Does your father know?"

"I am going to find him right now and tell him."

Wynter hugged her. "Then Godspeed," she said. "Be safe, Cissy. I will see you soon."

Christin headed for the door. "Remember," she said. "You do not know where I have gone."

"My lips are sealed."

"Even if they torture you and throw you in a fiery pit."

Wynter laughed. "I will let them roast me before I tell."

Christin blew her a kiss as she headed out the door, out into the bright day beyond.

It was after the nooning meal and the sky was the most brilliant shade of blue. At least, Christin thought so. She stood there a moment, looking at the sky, wondering if it had always been that color. Somehow, everything looked brighter to her, lovelier than she'd ever seen it. That's what Alexander had done for her – he made her see things through different eyes.

Life was beautiful.

She didn't even realize she had a smile on her face as she stood there, looking at the sky. Then, her gaze moved towards the gatehouse with the bridge that led down into the lower baileys. There were guards there, men wearing the crimson and gold tunic of the king, but there were also guards with the de Winter standard. She was confident that she could walk past them all. Summoning her courage, she headed towards the gatehouse.

But the king's soldiers, who were lingering by the stairs that led into the keep more than they were actually by the gatehouse, suddenly turned in her direction. When she saw that they were walking towards her, and looking at her, she got panicky and she turned around, heading back to the apartment block.

Unfortunately, there were royal soldiers there that she hadn't seen before. She knew for a fact there was no one there as she'd just left the building because she'd looked around. She'd been aware of her surroundings.

... *hadn't she?*

Or was she looking up at the sky, thinking of its beauty?

Her heart began to race and her breathing quickened. Where were all of these royal guards coming from? They were roaming around Norwich as if they belonged here, but then she was sadly reminded that Norwich Castle was, indeed, a royal holding. The de Winters were the stewards. With the king here, the royal guards had every right to be about the property.

She was beginning to sorely regret leaving the apartment.

She wanted to go back inside, but the royal guards were near the entry now and she was afraid to move past them. When she turned around to try and go back towards the gatehouse, to the stables where Alexander was, the guards that had been near the keep entry were much closer now, heading right for her.

She bolted.

Racing towards the garden, she ran between buildings, trying to lose the guards who were following her. She thought that running off might pull them away from the entry to her apartment, so she dashed around the side of the building, running in a circle. But the moment she turned the corner that would give her a clear shot to the building entry, she ran straight into a big, warm body.

He grabbed her and the fight was on.

Christin may not have been a trained warrior, but she knew how to fight. She immediately lifted her knee, ramming it as hard as she could into the groin area but coming into contact with mail and other protection that prevented her from hitting her mark. The big man tightened his grip as she fought.

"Easy, lady, easy," he said. "No need to fight. It will not do any good."

Christin dropped her satchel so she could get to the dagger she always had tucked into a sheath on her leg. She was fearless as she grabbed for it, bringing it up into the man's gut. It made contact because she heard him grunt, but as he loosened his grip, more hands grabbed her.

Unable to escape, she started screaming at the top of her lungs.

A hand slapped over her mouth and someone yanked the dagger from her grip. Kicking and twisting, she was fighting for her very life as a group of royal soldiers ganged up on her, surrounding her, but they weren't stealing her away. They were mostly standing there, holding her as they looked at the man she'd stabbed.

The man was down on one knee, his hand to his lower gut as bright red blood poured. The guards, holding on to a wildcat, were confused as to what to do.

"Where do we take her, d'Athee?" one of them demanded.

Gerard was crippled with a fairly serious stab to the lower abdomen. He grunted in pain. "Find de Lara," he rasped. "Find the man and..."

"Get your hands off of her."

Sean was suddenly in their midst, grabbing Christin away from the soldiers who were smothering her. He pulled her into his grasp, slapping a trencher-sized hand over her mouth so she couldn't make any noise.

"What in the hell happened to you?" he asked Gerard.

But Gerard was in too much pain to respond civilly. "That bitch stabbed me," he said, groaning as he stood up. Suddenly, a big hand lashed out and caught Christin on the side of the head, hard enough to knock her cold. "That's for goring me!"

As Christin went limp, Sean picked her up. "Touch her again and you will answer to me," he growled. "The king wants her to reach Robert in one piece, not damaged goods. Where are the horses you intended to take?"

Gerard was nearly doubled over, trying to stanch the flow of blood in his side. "Down below," he said. "At the farm gate. Get out from the postern gate and the path will take you right to them. I cannot ride like this, Sean. You must take her to Bishop's Lynn."

Sean didn't even question him. He was on the move with the soldiers in tow, all of them heading quickly to the postern gate. One of the soldiers opened the gate for Sean and he ducked through it, taking the slippery footpath down to the fields below where an abundance of neat rows of cultivated crops were being harvested in sections.

The area was surrounded by a big wall, like the one that surrounded the castle, and the farmers paused to watch as an enormous knight and about ten soldiers escorted an unconscious lady down to a larger group of royal soldiers waiting at the gatehouse that protected the farming fields.

Sean handed Christin over to another soldier as he mounted a horse meant for Gerard. The soldier returned Christin to him and Sean took a moment cover her face up with the cloak she was wearing, at least as much as he could. He didn't want it announced that Christin de Lohr was being whisked out of Norwich because he didn't want a battle on his hands from anyone who recognized her. Battles resulted in injuries and he didn't want to see her inadvertently hurt.

But the responsibility of her was something of a surprise, but not an unwelcome one. Unlike Gerard and the king, he didn't think in a two-dimensional fashion. Sean thought beyond the obvious to the improbable, to the obscure, and to the logical. He wasn't thinking a day ahead or even a week ahead; he was thinking far ahead of that. It meant he wasn't going to return Christin to her father because he had a plan, but he needed her cooperation to accomplish it.

He had an idea on how to end this once and for all.

Making sure Christin was covered up, Sean spurred the horse onward, followed by about a hundred royal troops, all of them thundering their way out of Norwich and heading for Bishop's Lynn.

CHAPTER EIGHTEEN

CAIUS COULD HARDLY believe what he'd just seen.
He'd been out of sight when Sean had approached a group of royal soldiers holding Christin hostage and he'd seen, clearly, when one burly bastard had hit Christin on the side of the head, rendering her unconscious. Greatly concerned, he continued to watch while Sean carried Christin out through the postern gate, followed by a collection of soldiers.

All of it had happened so quickly.

Now, they were gone.

The man who had struck Christin was still standing there, holding his bloodied gut, and when he turned around, Caius recognized him. *Gerard d'Athee.* The king's bodyguard, a man that didn't have Sean's intelligence, but he had his strength. He was purely an animal.

Caius sank back against the wall of the chapel, watching as Gerard headed back to the keep, holding his bloodied wound. When the man disappeared into the keep, Caius came out of hiding, coming to realize what had just happened – *the king and Gerard d'Athee have concocted a scheme to abduct Christin from Norwich and take her north to FitzRoy to be married.*

That's what Sean had told him.

Apparently, in the wake of the wounded Gerard, Sean had been tasked with carrying out the man's duties.

But Caius knew he couldn't let him get far, even if it was Sean. Turning for the gatehouse, he began to run. He was a very tall man, taller than everyone around him, and he was also big and strong, which meant men naturally moved out of his way. Those who didn't were shoved aside as he raced towards The Marshal's encampment.

"Cai!"

The shout came from behind him and he slowed to see Kevin running up behind him.

"Cai, what's wrong?" Kevin demanded. "Why are you running."

Caius stopped long enough to grab Kevin by the shoulder. "Christin has been abducted," he said. "The king's men, including your brother, have taken her out of the castle through the postern gate."

"*What?*" Kevin hissed. "How do you know this?"

"Because I saw it," Caius snapped. "I want you to go to the stables and find Sherry. He should be there. Tell him to get to The Marshal's tent immediately because, clearly, something must be done to help her. And if you see Maxton or Kress or anyone else, tell them to get over to The Marshal's tent as well."

Kevin appeared a bit shocked, but he didn't ask any further questions. He did as he was told, dashing off towards the stables as Caius picked up speed again and charged into The Marshal's tent.

William wasn't there.

Frustrated and apprehensive, he rushed over to the de Lohr tent only to find Christopher and David sitting, quite calmly, over some cold beef and wine. They both looked at Caius in surprise but before they could speak, Caius stated his business.

"My lord, we have a problem," Caius said to Christopher. "The king has abducted your daughter. Even now, she is being taken out of Norwich."

Christopher was on his feet, an expression of disbelief on his face. "What's this?" he demanded. "How do you know?"

"I saw it happen," Caius said. "I'm not sure how the situation evolved, but Gerard d'Athee and about a dozen royal soldiers had your daughter captured by the keep. I was speaking to Sean at the time and we heard screaming. Sean approached Gerard while I stayed to the shadows and it was clear that Gerard was wounded. As I watched, Sean took your daughter and spirited her out of the castle through the postern gate."

That didn't clear up the situation much for Christopher. "Sean?" he repeated. "And royal troops?"

Caius nodded, frustrated because it was clear that Christopher had no idea what he was talking about. "My lord, listen to me," Caius said. "Clearly, you have not been told that John has set his sights on your daughter. He wants her for his bastard son, Robert Fitzroy."

Christopher's eyes widened. "I know that," he snapped. "Christ, are you telling me... oh, my God... then she didn't discourage him last night, after all."

"My lord?"

Christopher waved him off. "No time to explain," he said. "I must go after her immediately."

He and David were already running for the tent flap, bursting through only to see William, Maxton, Kress, and Peter heading in his direction. William saw them, and the panic on their faces, and he pointed to their tent.

"Inside," he commanded. "*Now.*"

"Like hell," Christopher growled. "I must go and..."

William cut him off, physically putting his hands on the man and shoving him back into the tent. "Chris, inside," he said again. "*Go.*"

With little choice, Christopher and David fell back into the tent, with William following. Caius, Peter, Maxton, and Kress were behind them, all of them crowding in.

"William, he has my daughter," Christopher raged. "I must go after her."

William shook his head. "Nay," he said evenly. "You will remain here, with me, and we shall confront John about this immediately. I will send Caius and Maxton after her along with fifty of my men, but you...

you stay with me, Chris. We must deal with John on his level."

"I do not want to deal with John!" Christopher boomed. "Sean took her, for Christ's sake. Why doesn't he just bring her back?"

William gazed at him steadily. "You know why."

Christopher's jaw began to work but he didn't explode, saying things that others should not hear. He knew Sean was an agent for The Marshal and he knew how hard the man had worked to gain the monarch's trust, meaning he had to carry out the king's wishes no matter what the cost to his friends or comrades. Christin would be considered collateral damage to the greater scheme of things.

But Christopher wasn't going to let that happen.

"I want my daughter back," he growled. "I'll kill Sean if he gets in my way."

William sighed heavily. "Chris…"

But Christopher waved him off sharply. "I have every right to regain her," he said. "If Sean wants to fight me, that is his choice, but I will show no mercy. We are talking about my daughter, William. My child, my blood."

"I know."

"I am going to get her back and then I shall make John sorry he ever considered her for this outrageous scheme. I am going to make him pay."

William knew he had a wildfire on his hands. An angry Christopher, with thousands of men at his disposal, was never a good thing. He looked over his shoulder to Caius. "You and Maxton get mounted," he said quickly. "Kress, you go with them. You will get the soldiers mounted while Caius and Maxton prepare their mounts. Hurry, now; there is no time to waste. And for pity's sake, find Sherry and Peter and Kevin. I have need of them."

As Caius, Maxton, and Kress headed for the tent flap, Kevin burst in.

"Sherry has gone after Christin," he said. "I tried to stop him, but he would not listen."

Everybody was scattering. William was trying to keep Christopher and David calm while the tent cleared out of everyone else, all of them racing to their mounts to follow Alexander. Not one man was going to let him face this alone, for the brotherhood of William Marshal's agents was strong.

The Executioner Knights' brotherhood was even stronger.

Especially since they were dealing with the Lord of the Shadows, who would not give up his prize easily.

God, William prayed silently as he realized how badly the situation was veering out of control, *Sean, please keep that woman safe!*

Anything else guaranteed that half of England would go to war against the king.

ASHDOWN.

It had been a long time since Alexander had thought of his home, the place where he'd been born. As he prepared his horse for the ride into the village, he found himself thinking of Ashdown and of his father, Phillip. Truth be told, he hadn't thought of either in years, but that had mostly been because he'd spent the first several years after his brothers' deaths torturing himself over what happened, what could have been, and what he should have done differently.

As he'd told Christin, his younger brothers had been his responsibility.

Andrew and Adam had been so full of life. That's what they called it, anyway, but the reality was that they were full of arrogance, bravery, and recklessness. Alexander couldn't even count the times he'd had to rein that pair in, like a pair of wild horses. Usually, it was Adam who would lead and Andrew who would follow, and they had been so very excited to go on the great quest with Richard. They had only been two years younger than Alexander, but their maturity had been far more lacking than his.

But it was a maturity that quickly developed once the hardships of the journey to The Levant began to take their toll. The travel, the lack of food, of water, and the harsh elements had forced the twins to quickly grow up. It had been a rude awakening for all of them, and once they'd actually reached The Levant, they might as well have traveled to the moon. Nothing was as they had expected and the pair had difficulty adjusting. Alexander had helped them as best he could, but he was having his own difficulties.

He blamed himself for not paying more attention to them.

Odd how his feelings towards Christin had brought back so many memories of his brothers and his father, or perhaps not so odd considering that's the last time he really allowed himself to feel love. He loved his friends, of course, but love for family was something different.

Or love for a woman.

Alexander never thought he would ever return to Ashdown, but now that he was planning on taking a wife, he would have to reconsider. He was his father's heir, after all, and Christin deserved a home of her own. She was a great lady who deserved everything he could provide for her. It seemed strange to him to even think that considering he was the one who always wandered, the one who was the loner. He worked alone, he traveled alone, because he liked it.

But he was alone no more, soon to be domesticated.

And it didn't bother him one bit.

But first, he had some obstacles to overcome, not the least of which was a very powerful warlord by the name of Christopher de Lohr. After he took Christin to the inn by the cathedral, his next move would be to tell Christopher what had happened, and why. He snorted softly, leaning on the horse as he realized he felt like a giddy young squire with his first love, terrified of the girl's father.

He didn't think he had it in him.

"Sherry?"

Alexander was tucked back in a stall, but his head came up when he heard his name. "I am here."

Kevin appeared. Alexander was about to turn back to the horse when he caught a glimpse of the expression on the man's face. He took a second look at the strained countenance.

"What's the matter with you?" he asked.

"You must come," Kevin said. "Caius said that the king has abducted Lady Christin and you must come to The Marshal's encampment immediately."

Alexander blinked as if he didn't understand the statement. "Abducted her?" he repeated. "But I was just with her. Not fifteen minutes ago."

Kevin shook his head. "Caius saw the entire event," he said. "He said my brother spirited her out from the postern gate. Please, Sherry, you must come."

Alexander suddenly rushed him, grabbing him by the arms. It was clear that whatever confusion he had was instantly cleared up, like the sun bursting through the clouds.

"Sean took her?" he demanded. "Caius saw Sean?"

Kevin could see the panic and rage in the man's eyes, unusual for Alexander, who was always the consummately controlled knight.

"Aye," he said. "He saw my brother taking her from the postern gate along with several of the king's men. That is all I know, I swear it. You must go to William, Sherry."

Going to William wasn't what Alexander had in mind. The singular thought he had was the fact that Sean had taken Christin out of Norwich. Sean had warned them of the king's plan and they'd concocted their own counter-plan because of it, but it was clear that either their plan hadn't worked or Sean had been planning on taking Christin out of Norwich all along. Perhaps he'd only pretended to work with them to lower their guard.

But Alexander didn't truly believe that. At least, he hoped it wasn't the case. When it came to Sean de Lara, nothing was for certain. Yet he knew one thing; he wasn't going to William. He wasn't going to take the chance that The Marshal would somehow prevent him from going after

Christin.

He was going after her and he'd kill anyone who tried to stop him, de Lara included.

Bishop's Lynn, Sean had said. FitzRoy had a manse in Bishop's Lynn.

That's where he was going.

Without another word, Alexander turned to his horse, who was fully prepared at that point. Alexander had his sword on the animal, sheathed, as well as his saddlebags. He was ready to go.

And go, he would.

As Kevin called after him, trying to stop him, Alexander thundered out of the stable, heading out of Norwich Castle.

CHAPTER NINETEEN

WILLIAM HAD MANAGED to talk Christopher out of riding after his daughter immediately, but things weren't well with him.

Not in the least.

Caius, Kevin, Maxton, Kress, and Bric had mounted up and taken off after Alexander, who had less than an hour's head start on them. Sending five heavily-armed and seasoned knights after Alexander, and Sean and Christin, was the only way to keep Christopher and David from starting an all-out war, at least at the moment. With Peter surprisingly siding with The Marshal and begging his father to be calm, they managed to convince Christopher to remain at Norwich and confront the king. Retrieving Christin was only part of the problem.

The larger issue was, in fact, John.

He had to be stopped.

Therefore, Christopher agreed to confront the king on his actions, but it was going to be on his terms. While William went into the keep to arrange the meeting with the monarch, Christopher had roused his entire contingent of one hundred heavily-armed de Lohr men into the keep of Norwich, prompting the king's soldiers who happened to be in the keep to confront them. The great hall of Norwich saw bloody action as Christopher's men easily dispatched the royal guard.

Unfortunately, that hadn't been part of the plan.

William had sought out Old Daveigh before seeing the king, and they had been in Old Daveigh's solar when they heard the clash. Shocked, they emerged into the great hall as the de Lohr men were trampling the king's guard.

Old Daveigh's first reaction was to summon his own men to beat back the de Lohr troops, but William prevented him from doing so because he knew it would be a bloodbath. William didn't want allies going after each other even though what Christopher did could be considered quite hostile. Truth be told, Old Daveigh understood. He backed off and let William deal with it.

Fortunately, William wasn't too late. By the time he got up to the king's chamber, the door was open and Christopher was standing a few feet away from John with his enormous broadsword in his hand. The king's personal guard were poised and ready to strike, and David and Peter were poised also. It threatened to be one hell of a battle as William rushed into the room, hoping he could prevent regicide.

"De Lohr, back away," William commanded, moving to put himself between John and Christopher. "Do it now before this turns into chaos."

Christopher was singularly focused on John. He didn't even move when William commanded him to. He only moved when William put himself in front of John and then Christopher was forced to look at him. Even then, he didn't step back until David tugged him.

The look in his eyes was positively deadly.

When William was certain Christopher wasn't going to charge, he turned to John.

"Your grace, we are aware of your plans for Christin de Lohr," he said evenly. "We are also aware that you have put those plans into action. I can only deter de Lohr for so long before he will overwhelm me and snap your neck, so now would be a very good time to tell him why you did this and assure him that his daughter will not be harmed in any way. I would also suggest you send a messenger to catch up to de Lara to tell him to release Christin to my men, who happen to be following. Do these things and there will be no bloodshed. Fail to comply and I cannot protect you. I am not sure I want to."

John was sitting in a comfortable chair, looking at William quite casually. There was no sense of urgency in his features, as if he didn't have a dozen armed men around him.

He was arrogant, and confident, that way.

"I will not send a messenger after de Lara," he said frankly. "This is a great opportunity for Lady Christin. Surely de Lohr can see that. My son is a titled lord and when he marries Christin, he shall be the Duke of Dersingham. His daughter will be a duchess. All you had to do was ask me calmly and I would have told you the truth."

Behind William, Christopher's features twisted with disgust. "The Duchess of Dersingham?" he repeated as if it were the most distasteful thing he'd ever heard. "I would rather see her married to a pauper than titled and married to your bastard. But you knew that; otherwise, you would not have abducted her."

John's focus was on Christopher. "Is it so bad to be related to the crown, de Lohr?" he asked. "You served my brother flawlessly. You have always been faithful to England. Why not consider this a reward?"

Christopher's jaw was ticking dangerously. "It is a curse," he growled. "It is a burden and a shame. I do not want to be related to you or anything about you, so send a man to head off de Lara or this will not go well for you."

"This will not go well for *you*," John snarled, all of the casual nature abruptly out of his manner. "Do you think to threaten me, de Lohr? I could have you arrested for that."

Christopher snorted. "I would like to see you try," he said. "You and I have been doing battle for more than twenty years and I would think, by now, you would realize there is nothing you can do to me. I, however, can do a good deal to you."

John was on his feet. "You will not do anything as long as my son is married to your precious daughter."

"What is that supposed to mean?"

John laughed, but there was no humor to it. "Let us be plain," he said. "If you wish to see your daughter in continued good health, then you will behave yourself. Behave poorly and Christin shall pay the price. Is that clear enough?"

Surprisingly, Christopher didn't explode with rage. He stood there, eyeing John, calculating his options. He'd been in a position like this with the man more than once and he knew what would work on him. He knew what kind of threat would make a difference.

And he didn't doubt for one moment that John meant what he said.

Christin would pay the price if he stepped out of line.

But he wasn't finished with this, not at all.

"It is as clear as rain," Christopher said. "But allow me to be clear, also – although you and I have never been close allies, I have never rebelled against you. When you needed military might, the de Lohr army always answered the call. Is this not true?"

John nodded slowly. "It is."

"At any given time, I can raise ten thousand men between Lioncross Abbey, Canterbury Castle, and my various garrisons," Christopher said. "I can raise twice that by summoning my allies. Twenty thousand men are at my disposal."

John lifted an eyebrow. "What is your meaning?"

Christopher's jaw ticked as he spoke, indicative of the rage in his chest. It was enough to cause beads of sweat to pop out on his brow.

"I mean, quite plainly, that this action will change how I serve the crown," he said. "It means that the crown is now my enemy. *You* are my enemy. It means that I shall ally myself with Philip of France and allow his troops into Lioncross and every other property I possess. It means that when I have gathered tens of thousands of men, I shall march on you and I shall destroy you. I would rather see Philip sitting on the throne of England than you. I would rather see England become part of France than have to swear fealty to a piece of human wreckage. When you took my daughter, you destroyed the last thread of loyalty I had to you. I will gladly see you and your family destroyed and I will not shed a tear. Is this in any way unclear?"

When he was finished, it was John who was sweating. Twitching, sweating anger because of all of the warlords in England, Christopher de Lohr was the one who could truly carry out the threat and he knew it.

"Do it and your daughter dies."

Christopher smiled thinly. "If she dies, so do you and everyone you care for. I will wipe through the House of Plantagenet like the plague."

He hissed the last words, emphasizing the fact that he meant what he said. Through it all, William watched the entire exchange, watching each threat become more severe than the last, like watching a chess match where the end game was only death.

Nothing else.

William was a diplomat but above all else, he was a fighting man. Some called him the greatest knight England had ever seen. Therefore, he understood the gravity of this situation better than most.

He took a deep breath.

"John," he said quietly, and quite informally, "send a messenger to de Lara. Have him bring Christin back to Norwich, unharmed. If you do this, Christopher will forget about this… incident. He will forget his threats, which he is perfectly capable of carrying out, as you are well aware."

John was glaring at Christopher, incapable of tearing his eyes away. When one is faced with an enemy, it does not do well to take one's eyes from him.

John knew that.

"Nay," he said through clenched teeth. "I will not. She marries my son."

"Then I will kill your son," Christopher said. "There are not enough guards in the civilized world to protect him. If I want him dead, he shall be dead. And then I shall go to work on you."

William held up a hand. "Gentlemen, *please*," he said, trying desperately to steer the conversation back to something productive. "Let us sit and discuss this calmly. But John, I would strongly suggest you send a messenger to de Lara now. The situation will not improve until you do. Do you not understand that?"

But John wouldn't do it. "I told you I would not."

"Then you are exchanging de Lohr's fealty for his daughter's marriage to your son," William said. "Instead of creating an alliance, you are destroying one. Is the price worth it?"

John's twitching was growing worse. He'd been known to fall into fits if enraged enough. He started to back away, keeping his eyes on Christopher, as Gerard suddenly stepped from the shadows.

Big, ugly, nasty Gerard was John's attack dog. It was true that Christin had wounded him, but he'd had a physic dress the wound and little else. It had stopped bleeding, anyway, and that meant he resumed his duties even if he was feeling weak. He had a particular message for de Lohr, anyway, and would not be stopped.

"Your daughter stabbed me," he said to Christopher. "She rammed a dagger into my gut. Did you raise such a ruthless bitch?"

Christopher looked Gerard over. "You do not look any worse for the wear," he said. "And if call my daughter a bitch again, you shall pay the price."

Gerard didn't have the sense that most men had. He only knew violence and all of the things that went along with it. That was his world, his life, his vocation. In his mind, there was nothing else.

"Who is going to make me?" he said. "You? I am not afraid you, de Lohr. Everyone else is, but I am not. You cannot harm me."

Christopher's gaze lingered on the man for a moment before returning his attention to the king. "I will not speak with filth," he said. "Call back your dog before he makes the situation worse."

John was indecisive, which was usual when Sean wasn't around. Sean would whisper in his ear, telling him what to do or what to think, and that was what he would do. Or other courtiers would do the same, as John was not without an abundance of people around him to make suggestions or give advice. But there was no Sean in the room at the moment, or other courtiers, so his hesitation emboldened Gerard.

"Out, de Lohr," the man snarled, unsheathing his weapon. "Get out or I will make you regret your refusal."

Christopher's sword came out, but David was faster. Even in his youth, there was no one faster with a sword, and David charged Gerard with lightning speed. Gerard barely had time to lift his sword before David was on top of him, shoving him back with a staggering blow and causing him to lose his balance. The armed guards in the room began to move to help Gerard, but Peter and Christopher turned on them, holding them off as William drew his sword to protect the king.

Startled and afraid, John began screaming as William put himself in front of the king, backing the man up, away from the fighting.

"Cease!" John cried. "Gerard, do you hear me? Cease! David, stop your attack!"

But David wasn't listening. He'd had enough of his brother being insulted by the king and then by Gerard, who was unworthy to even be in the same room as his brother as far as he was concerned. Gerard gave David a good fight for a minute or so before the wound to his side began bleeding again, and paining him greatly, and he found himself on one knee as David beat him down, finally knocking the sword from his hand. As David grabbed his hair and went in for the kill, William barked.

"David!" he boomed. "You will not kill him, do you hear? Leave him be and back away."

David was poised to ram his sword right down Gerard's throat. It would have been so easy to do it. But he listened to William, knowing any refusal would not be well met, so he let Gerard go and backed away. As he moved off, he kicked Gerard's sword all the way across the chamber, far away so Gerard couldn't rise up and attack him again. He returned to Christopher and Peter, who had eight of the king's guard cornered. As the de Lohr men decided what to do with a collection of soldiers, William turned to John.

"For God's sake, John," he hissed. "If you do not want to see England destroyed, then send word to Sean and have him return Christin to

Norwich. You have no choice."

John was torn between fear and defiance. "You are only now back in my good graces, William, or have you forgotten?"

William shook his head. Considering that John spoke the truth, and William had spent the past couple of years abroad because of his contentious relationship with John, he was well aware that his presence in England now was fragile. He was home and he wanted to remain.

"I have not."

"Then you do not give the commands, William."

"In this case, I do. Do as I say or I will let de Lohr destroy you."

John was beginning to twitch again from anger. "Do your duty and control him," he said. "If you do not and he rises against me, the loss of England will be *your* fault."

William lifted his eyebrows. "Unfortunately, you probably believe that," he said. "But the truth is that your cruelty and pettiness is what will destroy it. I have recently come from Ramsbury Castle where a French spy foretold of a threat against you. She called it a threat from within. I am starting to think that you are the only true threat to England, John. Mayhap it is you who will finally destroy this country."

John pulled away from him, glancing at Gerard, who was just starting to get to his feet. The man was pale, his lower abdomen bloody. John looked around the chamber, at what was happening, and took a defiant stance.

"Get out and take the de Lohrs with you," he said to William. "I am going back to London. I will not stay where I feel as if my life is threatened."

William watched him as he backed away, heading for a doorway that led to the bedchamber.

"Your life is threatened by your own doing," William said. "Save England, John. Recall de Lara. The fate of your country is in your hands."

John didn't reply. He retreated into the bedchamber with Gerard stumbling after him, and that was the end of it. With a heavy sigh,

William turned to Christopher and David and Peter, who still had the royal guards cornered. Sword still in his hand, William came up behind them.

"Chris," he said quietly. "Get out. Take your son and your brother with you. And get your men out of the keep. Old Daveigh does not deserve the turmoil we have brought him, so be quick about it. We are departing this place."

Christopher didn't even look at him, nor did he sheathe his sword. But he left, which was about all William could hope for at the moment as he watched David and, finally, Peter follow him. William remained, however, covering their retreat before quitting the chamber after them.

God help him, he had such a mess on his hands that he didn't even know where to start. William knew he had to get Christopher and Peter and David out of Norwich and he had to make apologies to Old Daveigh. But he found himself praying that his agents following Sean and Christin would catch up and wrangle Christin away from Sean. And given there was some emotion involved now with Alexander and Christin, he seriously wondered if Sean was going to survive.

So many unknowns.

The danger, for England, is already here. It is right under your nose.

That's what the spy had told Christin. William hadn't been wrong when he told the king that he was his own worst enemy.

The danger, for England, was John.

CHAPTER TWENTY

The Cock and Bull Inn
Dereham

CHRISTIN HAD BEEN conscious since nearly the moment they'd left the town of Norfolk.

She'd started to fight as she became aware, thinking it was Gerard who held her, but Sean had whispered in her ear and she'd calmed down immediately. He'd begged her to be still and cooperate and he promised to get her out of this alive, but that was all he would say. Christin knew exactly what was going on and she could see that she was surrounded by at least twenty or more of the king's soldiers, so fighting and trying to flee would not have been in her best interest.

Therefore, she would have to trust Sean.

The party had ridden very hard and fast until sunset when the horses needed to be rested, so they'd stopped at the village of Dereham where Sean had paid for a room at The Cock and Bull, a large and crowded establishment in the center of town. Sean had pulled her off of his horse, heaving her over his shoulder as he headed inside and took her straight to a chamber at the top of the stairs.

All of the manhandling was all for show because the king's men were spreading out in the common room below and Sean didn't want them to think he was showing Christin any mercy. The fearsome Lord of the Shadows wasn't capable of mercy or kindness, and Sean had to project that image. For all the king's men knew, the woman meant for Robert FitzRoy was being closely, if not cruelly, guarded by de Lara.

That's exactly what Sean wanted them to think. As soon as they entered the chamber and he shut the door, Christin turned to him with big eyes.

"What now?" she hissed. "Sean, what is going on?"

Sean held up a hand to silence her. "We need to make a show for the guard," he said quietly. "Remember the night of the feast and the rather awesome act you put on?"

She sighed sharply. "Clearly, it did not work if I am still being taken to FitzRoy."

Sean nodded. "It worked," he said. "But John decided your breeding and name was worth your horrific manners. Now, I want you to scream and cry when I tell you to. Understand?"

She nodded, lifting her shoulders in a gesture suggesting she really didn't know what he meant, but she soon would. Suddenly, he tossed a chair into the door, rattling it, and smacked his hands together several times, loudly. It sounded like slaps against flesh.

"Scream," he murmured.

Christin did. Loudly. She cried and screamed, pleading for mercy as Sean grinned at her antics. She picked up the chamber pot, empty, and tossed it to the floor for good measure, crying loudly.

It was the performance of a lifetime.

All the while, Sean stood back by the door and laughed silently until he finally held up his hand for her to cease. She did in an instant and they both stood there a moment, listening to see if any of John's soldiers had come up to the chamber to listen to the ruckus. With no sounds on the landing outside of the door, Sean moved to the other side of the chamber, pulling Christin with him.

"If I know Sherry, and I believe I do, he is not far behind us," he whispered. "Cai saw everything that happened and undoubtedly told him, so I will find Sherry and anyone else who happened to come with him."

Christin frowned. "If you are going to find him, why can you not take me to him? We can slip out without being seen, can't we?"

Sean shook his head. "Above all else, my position with the king must remain solid," he said. "There must be no hint in the minds of anyone that I am anything other than the king's most loyal subject, so I cannot take you to Sherry and I cannot allow you to escape. In fact, we are going to go to Bishop's Lynn for a reason."

"What could that possibly be?"

"Because you are going to meet Robert Fitzroy."

She stiffened. "I will not meet him and I will not marry him. Have you lost your mind?"

Sean shook his head. "I have been thinking about the situation in detail and of the only possible solution to it."

Christin threw up her hands. "The solution is to return me to Norwich," she said, trying to keep her voice a whisper so no one would overhear. "I must return!"

"So the king can abduct you again?" he said. "So you can return to Lioncross and spend the next several years fearful of being abducted by the king, or of your sister possibly being abducted? *Think*, Christin. Running does not solve the problem."

She was trying not to become upset or panicked. "We *did* try to solve the problem," she murmured. "I made a fool of myself at the feast last night because you said I should and it did not work. It did not deter him."

Sean was quite for a moment. "How long have you been an agent for The Marshal?"

"For nearly two years."

"And in that time, you have accomplished some fairly unsavory tasks."

"Aye," she said honestly. "It was my duty."

"I know," he said. "Scream again, by the way."

"What?"

"Scream again so they still think I'm brutalizing you."

Christin did, howling and begging for mercy, enough to make Sean chuckle again, until she quieted down. He nodded in approval.

"Now," he said. "On to my point. Have you ever been tasked with killing a man?"

She nodded, somewhat solemnly. "I was, once."

"Did you accomplish it?"

"Aye. Why do you ask?"

Sean's dark blue eyes glimmered. "Because the problem in this entire situation is Robert FitzRoy," he said. "Think about it – he's the crux of this issue. If you eliminate him, John will no longer need a wife for his son."

Her eyes widened. "Eliminate him?" she said. "You mean kill him?"

He nodded slowly, seeing that she understood what he was getting at. "Treat him like any other mission," he said. "Get close to the man and make sure he does not live to see the morning. Break his neck, suffocate him with a pillow, or push him down the stairs. If you do not, you will never be free of him or his father."

Christin could see exactly what he meant and it was actually quite brilliant. Sean saw something to the situation that she did not – how to end it for good. "Why didn't I think of that?" she muttered, mostly to herself. "This time, the mission will be my future."

"Exactly. It is in your hands. Are you brave enough?"

Brave? Of course she was. Christin had been born brave. But something was troubling her. "Is FitzRoy an active participant in all of this?" she asked. "What I mean is, did he ask to marry me?"

Sean shook his head. "He does not even know you are coming."

Her brow furrowed. "And I am to kill this man who is essentially innocent of his father's plans?"

Sean could see, in that moment, that she wasn't hardened like the rest of The Marshal's agents. Like he was. He would kill and not ask any questions, but she still had a conscience. That was the blessing of her youth and her sex. She still had emotions that hadn't been driven out of her by age and hardship and duty. He envied that, but it was a bad quality to have for a spy who was expected to do things that were, at times, unconscionable.

"Robert FitzRoy has never been innocent of anything in his life," Sean said. "He was born from a rape when the king forced himself on the daughter of his tutor. He has lived in the finest houses and he has done things that you would expect from a man with no soul, much like his father. Christin, if you do not kill him, you will be forced to marry him. You must choose between him and you. What will your choice be?"

When he put it that way, there was no other choice she could make. "Me," she said quietly. "I choose me. I will do what is necessary."

Sean's eyes glittered at her. "Good," he said. "I will remain at Bishop's Lynn as long as I can if you need assistance. But whatever you do, you must do it as soon as you arrive. The longer you wait, the more your courage will wane and the more FitzRoy may simply overwhelm you. It is a difficult task and I understand that, but you must show no mercy because, surely, if the marriage goes through, none will be shown to you. The king wants this marriage because he wants to control your father and the moment you become Lady FitzRoy, your life is only worth the degree of your father's good behavior. Therefore, it is kill or be killed."

She was looking at him with some fear, but she tempered it well. She had to. She'd known from the start that this was a political move by the king against her beloved father. She would not be the instrument to Christopher de Lohr's caging.

She had to protect her father most of all.

"I will not fail."

Sean believed her. "Now," he said. "I am going out to find Sherry before he burns this village to the ground in his rage. You will stay here and bolt that door. Do not open it for anyone but me. Is that clear?"

Christin nodded. "It is," she said. "And… Sean?"

"Aye?"

"Thank you. For all of the help you have given me… thank you."

He simply nodded, faintly, and quit the chamber, leaving Christin to rush forward and bolt the door. She stood there a moment as her last vestiges of bravery fled, allowing herself to feel her fear for the first time.

The prospects were utterly terrifying.

It was enough to drive her to her knees.

IT WAS AFTER dusk, with a cold evening settling over the land, and Alexander knew that Sean and John's men hadn't gone any further than Dereham because the night was only lit by a sliver moon and to ride out in the darkness would be foolish.

Especially with valuable cargo.

Therefore, he entered the village in the dark and from the outskirts, leaving his horse tethered in a copse of trees to shield the animal as he slithered in. Through gardens and alleys, beneath windows as families shared their evening meal. He was stealthy in his movements, hunting for John's men, heading for the center of town and any liveries there might be. He was fairly certain John's men would stash their horses in a livery but he was quickly surprised to realize they were camping on the other side of town, out in the open.

Alexander ducked down low, watching the camp in the distance. There were at least two big fires and men gathered all around. He found it rather surprising that there were so many men; he'd had no idea that so many had accompanied de Lara when they'd taken Christin out of Norwich. He would have thought it might have been another army except for the fact that he could plainly see the crimson royal tunics on some of the men closest to the fire.

He seriously wondered if Christin was somewhere in their midst. He couldn't imagine they'd keep her out in the open, in the elements, and he didn't see de Lara anywhere, which led him to believe that Sean and Christin were somewhere in the town. That had him looking around the center of the village, which was several buildings surrounding the town well in the center. There was an inn across the square. He could see the light coming from the windows and hear the soft roar of men from a door that was partially propped open. Just as he headed in the direction of the inn, he saw a very big figure emerge onto the street.

Sean.

Where there was Sean, there was Christin. Alexander's heart began to race. He sank back into the shadows, watching as the man went across the alley to the livery. Not wanting to be seen, Alexander waited as a wagon lumbered by him, using it for cover as he darted across the street, taking position next to the entry of the livery and peeking inside.

He could see Sean over by the rear of the livery as the man was fussing with his horse; Alexander couldn't quite see what it was. But Sean's back was to him and that was all he needed to sneak up behind him and throw the blade of a dagger across his neck.

Sean froze.

"I am not going to ask you why you did what you did, for I already know," Alexander hissed in his ear. "But you will take me to Christin and if you do not, I will kill you and find her myself."

Realizing who it was, Sean put up his hands to show he was not a threat. "You do not need to kill me," he said steadily. "Christin is unharmed and she is comfortable and safe. But you and I must speak."

Alexander didn't move. The dagger remained at Sean's throat. "I want to see Christin."

"You are not going to see her until you and I have had a chance to speak. But if you'd rather kill me, then get on with it."

Alexander's dagger remained at his throat a moment longer before just as swiftly dropping it. He stepped well back, away from Sean so the man couldn't lunge at him with any ease. He faced Sean in the dim light, feeling many different emotions, not the least of which was anger.

Pure, naked anger.

"What in the hell did you do?" he finally demanded. "I thought that whole performance last night was to deter the king from wanting Cissy for his son? Did you lie to us just to put us off our guard?"

Sean shook his head. "I am sure it looks like that, but I would not do that, nor did I," he said. "I spoke with the king this morning and he was not deterred by Christin's performance. He considers her breeding and name more important than bad manners, only I could not get away from the man to tell you that. By the time I got away from him and went to find The Marshal, the wheels were already in motion."

Alexander stared at him a moment before shaking his head. "Christ," he muttered, visibly relaxing. "I did not want to believe you had betrayed us, but this looks bad, Sean."

"I know," Sean said quietly. "The only reason I was the one in a position to take her was because she stabbed Gerard with a dagger. The man was bleeding and in no position to ride."

Alexander looked at him. "D'Athée?"

"Aye."

"The man is an animal.'"

"He is, which is why we are all most fortunate that I am at the head of this and not him."

Alexander put his dagger away, leaning against the stall for support. "She always carries that dagger with her," he muttered. "Where is she?"

Sean gestured in the direction of the inn. "In The Cock and Bull," he said. "As I said, she's very well. And she and I have had a discussion that I must have with you. In fact, I was just going out to find you now. I knew you would be in pursuit and I suspect de Lohr is, too."

"I am sure he is," Alexander agreed. "But I left before he did. He cannot be too far behind."

"Then you are going to have to tell him what I am about to tell you," Sean said, "because I have over one hundred of the king's soldiers with me and every one of them is a witness to my behavior, so I cannot linger or delay. I must get Christin to Bishop's Lynn as quickly as possible."

Alexander sighed heavily. "Then you are going to take her," he said. "I will not let you. You know that."

Sean put up a hand. "Listen to what I am going to tell you and you can decide if this plan will work. I believe it will. But you will have to be brave, Sherry. Brave as you've never been in your life."

"I already do not like this."

Sean went over to the stall where Alexander was leaning. He, too, leaned against the wall next to him, keeping his voice low.

"Christin is a trained agent," he said quietly. "She is trained to kill, among other things. Sherry, the king is not the center of this issue – FitzRoy is. I can give Christin over to you now and you can run with her, but that will not stop John from seeking a wife for FitzRoy. If he loses Christin, she has a sister. Three of them, in fact. If John wants FitzRoy to be married to a de Lohr daughter badly enough, he will do everything in his power to make it happen."

Alexander knew that. "Brielle is a year younger than Christin, I believe, but Rebecca is very young. Eight or nine years, I think."

"That will not matter to John. He will abduct an eight-year-old girl and marry her to his son."

Alexander sighed heavily. "Then what do you suggest?"

"Eliminate FitzRoy and the problem is over."

Alexander looked at him. "Kill the man?"

"Aye, but Christin will have to do it. She will be the only one able to get close enough to him."

Alexander stared at him for a moment before shaking his head. "She *is* capable."

"Aye, she is. Let her kill FitzRoy and send the body back to de Lohr to do with it as he pleases."

Alexander fell silent, pondering the plan. It was actually quite feasible and made a good deal of sense, only he didn't like putting Christin in such danger. She was going to have to get close enough to the man to kill him, which meant she would have to be close, indeed.

Nay, he didn't like that in the least.

"And what if she fails?" he finally asked. "I am not saying that it will not work, or that it is not a good plan, because it is. Eliminating FitzRoy would solve the entire issue. But she may need help, Sean."

"What do you suggest?"

Alexander was forming his own plan at the moment. "If I know de Lohr, he is not far behind," he said. "He probably has his entire army with him, and David's, too. If you can delay the journey enough for de Lohr to catch up, he can engage John's soldiers while you continue on to Bishop's Lynn with Christin."

"Alone?"

"Nay," Alexander said, his dark eyes glimmering. "With me posing as a royal knight. With both of us at Bishop's Lynn, and any witnesses to our actions tied up with de Lohr's army, we can make short work of FitzRoy and no one will know you were in on it."

Sean lifted an eyebrow. "John will know I delivered Christin to Bishop's Lynn."

"But he will not know you were part of the man's death," Alexander said. "De Lohr can claim responsibility for it, as I'm sure he would like to. You can simply tell John that it happened after you left."

It seemed sound enough. As they sat there and mulled over what was to come, they caught sight of two very big bodies entering the livery from the rear. Ducking low, they watched, coiled and prepared to strike, until they realized that one of the men was Bric.

Alexander was on his feet.

"Bric?" he hissed. "What in the hell are you doing here?"

Along with Bric, Kevin came into the light, both of them heading straight to Alexander and Sean. But as they did so, they unsheathed their swords, thinking that Alexander might need help against Sean. Not knowing what was happening, they had little choice.

"We followed you," Bric said, looking between Alexander and Sean and realizing that Alexander wasn't armed. "Sherry, what is happening here?"

Alexander put up a hand. "You can sheathe the sword," he said. "There is no trouble. In fact, we were just discussing a plan to end this situation once and for all."

Bric stared at him for a moment before emitting a heavy sigh, both relieved and confused, as he put his sword back into the leather scabbard at his side.

"Thank God," he said. "I thought I was going to have to do battle with the Lord of the Shadows and it was something I was not looking forward to."

"You and me both."

"Where's the lady?"

"In the inn across the way," Sean answered the question. "Who else is here with you?"

Bric turned to the front entry of the livery, straining to see in the darkness. "Cai, Maxton, and Kress," he said. "We all followed, thinking it would be a titanic battle between you and Sherry. The others are scouting the royal soldiers across the way, looking for the lady and for you."

"Go and retrieve them," Sean said. "We do not want the royal soldiers to see them."

Bric eyed Alexander, looking for approval considering this was a very odd situation. When Alexander nodded faintly, Bric took off and headed out in the darkness, leaving Kevin standing there alone.

Kevin's gaze was on his brother.

"You've created a mess, Sean," he said. "You cannot imagine all of the men now riding to stop you."

Sean simply looked at him, casting Alexander a long look before turning away. After his conversation with his brother in the garden of Norwich, he wasn't apt to give the man any more of his time.

He was finished.

Alexander, however, wasn't finished and he resented Kevin for speaking on something which wasn't his right to comment on. He was a follower, not a leader, and Alexander suspected he'd said it simply to dig at his brother.

"Your brother has probably saved Christin's life," he said. "He is here to help, not to turn against us."

Kevin was looking at Alexander but he could see Sean moving away in his periphery. "But he took her from Norwich," he said. "We all had to go running after him, and you. Why did he take her?"

"Have you not been told?"

"Only that the king wants to marry her to his bastard son."

"He does. And when Bric and the others get here, we will tell you of Sean's plan to ensure this situation ends once and for all."

Kevin's gaze lingered on him a moment before glancing at Sean, who was over by the livery entry, watching for the other knights to return.

"Then I will wait to hear what scheme we are to put into play," he said. "You do know that de Lohr is behind us with his army."

"I assumed as much."

"His men were breaking down their encampment as we were leaving," he said. "I also saw Christopher, David, and Peter head to the keep of Norwich with about fifty soldiers. I am sure they were going to confront John. Without Sean to defend the man, we could very well have a dead king by now."

There was contempt in that statement. He couldn't even say "my brother", only "Sean" as if that put distance between him and his brother. As if there were no familial relations.

It was so… cold.

Alexander had known Kevin for a few years. He never served with him in The Levant, but they'd worked together several times since he'd returned. He was strong, faithful, and skilled. But he was also very rigid when it came to Sean and everyone knew it.

Alexander had never interfered or commented on Kevin and Sean's relationship, but given that he'd had brothers once, Kevin's attitude rubbed him the wrong way. Considering they would soon be fighting for Christin's life and his future with her, he didn't need or want any complications.

Like feuding brothers.

"Sean does his duty and he does it well, Kevin," he said quietly. "I don't give a damn how you feel about it, however. So for this mission, you will treat him with respect. I don't care what you do when your time is your own, but this is *my* time. Sean de Lara is risking more than you can ever imagine to control an uncontrollable king and you would do well to remember that. Whatever your personal feelings are, bury them. I don't want to see them."

Kevin looked at him with some surprise, perhaps some indignance. "When have I ever not been professional, Sherry?"

But Alexander shook his head. "Whenever you speak of your brother, it is with such scorn," he said. "Just now, you did it. You speak about him as if he were dirt and you will not do that again in my presence. It is beneath you and it is incredibly disrespectful to your brother."

Standing at the livery entry, Sean heard him and turned around. "Sherry…"

But Alexander cut him off. "Nay, Sean. If he is going to display such contempt in my presence, then I have something to say about it." He returned his focus to Kevin, who was starting to stiffen. "Kevin, I had two brothers who went with me to The Levant. They were younger than I was and they were full of arrogance and foolishness and talent and delusions of grandeur. They were both thorns in my side, but they were also my dearest loves. No matter what I did, they loved me. They worshipped me. Once, I was forced to kill two young boys because they were scouting for the Muslim army. Had I let them go, they would have given away our position, so I did what had to be done. Instead of hating me for it or telling me I had shamed the de Sherrington name by murdering children, they helped me bury the bodies and they showed me great compassion, even at their young ages because they understood the torment I went through for the greater good. I did it to save my men and they knew that."

Kevin was looking at him most guardedly, taking a step back as if to turn away from him, but Alexander stopped him.

"Is that what you do when you don't like to hear something?" he asked. "Do you turn away from things that are unpleasant because you do not have the capacity to understand or show compassion? Because if that is truly the case, then you are not the knight I thought you were. *You* are the one shaming the de Lara name; not your brother. Do you know why? Because part of being a great knight is showing mercy and understanding, both of which you seem to have trouble with when it comes to your brother. My brothers died in the Battle of Acre, right before my eyes, and there isn't a day that passes that I don't hate myself for not being able to help them. There isn't a day that goes by that I don't miss them and weep for them. You still have your brother, yet you shun him, and that makes me sick. You could show him compassion and understanding, yet you choose not to. And I think that is pathetic."

By this time, Kevin was standing there, looking at him as if he either wanted to shout at him or throw a punch. Alexander took a sharp, deep breath and turned away, heading out into the rear yard to cool off so he wouldn't wrap his hands around Kevin's throat. The things he'd told the man were things he'd kept buried, so to speak of them shook him up. But he couldn't help himself. He couldn't stand seeing Kevin treat Sean the way he did.

It simply wasn't right.

As Alexander took to the rear yard, Sean remained by the door, watching the figures of Caius and Bric in the distance. But his mind was on what Alexander had just said. He'd never defended himself against Kevin and to hear Alexander speak so harshly to his brother deeply touched him. He'd known Alexander for a few years, but it wasn't as if they'd been close friends or had served side by side. Still… Alexander understood Sean's position and he'd just hammered that into Kevin.

Not that Sean believed it would do any good, but he was still grateful.

As he stood there and pondered the situation, he could see Caius, Bric, Maxton, and Kress heading back in his direction. He ducked back into the livery, moving towards the rear of it to summon Alexander, who saw Sean motioning to him. He entered the livery about the same time everyone else did and when they realized that Sean really was on their side, both Sean and Alexander repeated Sean's plan.

Have de Lohr's army engage John's men.

Sean and the group will ride to Bishop's Lynn, pretending to be the escort and deliver Christin to FitzRoy.

Kevin volunteered to rendezvous with Christopher's army to deliver the news, perhaps simply to get away from Alexander's disapproval and his brother's presence. Or perhaps it was to prove that he *was* a good knight, dutiful and diligent. In any case, he separated himself from the rest and headed back the way he'd come.

At that point, everyone knew what was expected.

The rest was up to Christin.

CHAPTER TWENTY-ONE

"**H**OW FAR AHEAD of us do you think they are?"

The question came from David. It was just after dusk on a cold, damp night. The de Lohr army of one hundred men, plus William Marshal's troops, totaled about two hundred and twenty men and given that they were out in the middle of nowhere between towns, they were going to have to stop for the night and sleep in the nearby field.

William had headed back to London with John when the king hastily departed Norwich Castle before his celebration feast, leaving Old Daveigh with piles of food and many confused guests to eat it, confused because the king had departed without warning. Or perhaps there had been some warning, considering rumors of de Lohr storming the keep with his men had spread like wildfire. The de Lohr brothers had departed, the king and William Marshal had departed, and all that was left was hundreds of soldiers, dozens of lords, and Old Daveigh trying to convince everyone that nothing was amiss.

But it had been clear that something was.

But Christopher couldn't worry about that. He was only concerned with getting to his daughter before Robert FitzRoy got his hands on her. Several of William's agents had ridden ahead to prevent this while Christopher and David and Peter moved slowly with the army, but it couldn't be helped.

And that was frustrating.

"They were not too far ahead of us when we started out, but that gap is growing because two hundred men move much slower than just a few," Christopher said. "We are going to have to trust Sherry and the others to prevent a travesty from happening."

"I can ride ahead and see where they are, Papa," Peter said. "Would you like me to?"

Christopher looked up into the night sky. There was a half-moon, meaning it wasn't too bright, but it wasn't pitch-dark, either. There was enough of a glow to travel by.

"It might make you feel better, Chris," David said quietly. "Let him go."

Christopher simply nodded and Peter took off, spurring that expensive warhorse down the dark and rocky road. Christopher and David watched that big, white butt fade off in the darkness.

"David," Christopher ventured.

"Aye?"

"I have come to a decision."

"What is that?"

"I am going to kill FitzRoy."

"I know."

"I am going to kill him and send his head back to John with a message. I am finished tolerating our king. I was content to ignore him so long as he did not touch me or my family, but he has destroyed that stance."

David looked at him. "I agree," he said. "He could easily turn on me, too. I have three daughters, Chris. I would kill the man if he turned his attention to one of them."

"We are protecting our family."

"We are, indeed."

They left it at that because neither one found it necessary to voice what would happen when FitzRoy's head was sent back to John. It was quite possible that John would seek to punish them by trying to take their lands or essentially declaring war on them. Christopher and David were large enough, combined, that they could hold off quite an onslaught and even though they would not ask their friends or allies to help them, they knew they would. Even William Marshal would.

And John knew it, too.

It was quite a future that was shaping up for them all. Not wanting to linger on it, at least for the moment because the mood was becoming quite heady, David changed the subject slightly.

"And once she comes home, what are you going to do about Sherry?" he asked. "He went on ahead of everyone to save her, Chris. Clearly, he thinks a great deal of her and, after this, I do not think he will fade away, even if you want him to. Especially if Christin is fond of him as well."

That took Christopher's attention off of John and FitzRoy and on to Christin and Alexander, a much less volatile subject.

Sort of.

"He is *twice* her age," Christopher said.

"You already said that," David said. "We know that. Is that your only complaint against him?"

Christopher gave him an exasperated look. "I am not against him," he said. "But he's so... old and seasoned compared to her."

David shorted. "You mean compared to your daughter who was recruited by William Marshal as a spy at the age of sixteen years? Jesus, Chris, show some fairness. Your daughter is not the innocent child you seem to think she is."

"She's not a hardened battle warrior, either."

"You are giving her absolutely no credit. If she has been serving The Marshal for the past two years, then you *know* what kind of things she has been doing."

Christopher made a face at him and turned away. He didn't want to think of his daughter as a spy, doing things that only tough, seasoned men should be doing. His sweet little girl who, as a child, would take charge of all of her siblings and would order them to her will as well as any battle commander.

She was just like her mother in that respect.

His wife, Dustin, was the Grand Dame of Bossy Women. She looked like a delicate, beautiful flower with her gray eyes and long, blonde hair, but much like her daughter, looks were deceiving. She was no shrinking violet and, clearly, Christin had taken after her in that respect.

But it was still difficult for Christopher to accept.

"Mayhap she has been doing things I would rather not have her do," he finally said. "But she is still my daughter and, like it or not, I still view her as a child. And in answer to your question, I am not sure what I am going to do about Sherry. I had always hoped that Christin would marry a man closer to her age, a strong and reputable knight with an inheritance. As far as I know, Sherry does not have that."

"You married Dustin without an inheritance," David reminded him. "You had nothing until you married her and then you had everything. The same could be said for me. In any case, you'll have to do better than that if you want to find fault with Sherry. I believe he will make her a good husband."

Christopher looked at David. "You do?"

"Aye."

"Why?"

David grinned. "Because there is no finer knight I know of," he said. "Sherry is loyal and brave, strong and intelligent. And if he is fond of Christin and wants to marry her… I can find no fault with that. He would make an excellent addition to the family."

If David was in support of Alexander, Christopher was going to have trouble denying him. Perhaps David was seeing something he wasn't. Moody and weary, he finally called a halt to the army and moved them off the road and into the smattering of trees to the west. It was some shelter, and not directly on the road, and the men began to set up camp.

David was in the middle of the men, issuing orders, but Christopher stood on the periphery, simply watching. His mind was too occupied for him to be effective in something like this, so he let David and a few senior sergeants take charge. He kept looking down the road, thinking of his daughter, wondering where she was and if she was safe, praying that Alexander and the others had reached her. He knew for a fact that Sean would not give up his prize easily and that, most of all, concerned him. He didn't want Christin injured when Alexander and Maxton and Kress, as well as Bric and Kevin and Caius, went after Sean to try and separate him from Christin.

Indeed, that had him greatly worried.

And then, he heard something.

Hooves, he thought. Someone was riding swiftly. As he focused on the dark road ahead, he began to see horse's legs coming into view. But it wasn't simply one horse; it was two. Two knights were riding towards him and he immediately recognized Peter, but there was a second knight with him he couldn't make out.

"David!" he shouted.

As he headed for the road, David broke away from the men and ran over to him, standing alongside him as Peter and the other knight approached. The horses kicked up rocks as they brought them to a halt and Christopher realized he was looking at Kevin, also.

Kevin had ridden ahead with the group of The Marshal's agents.

His heart was suddenly in his throat.

"Kevin," Christopher said, trying not to panic. "Why are you here? Has something happened?"

Kevin and Peter dismounted their horses. "If you mean Christin, she is well, my lord," Kevin said as he pulled off his helm, wiping the sweat from his brow. "We have located both her and Sean and the king's men, and Christin is well. Sean took her but only because he was forced to. Above all, he must present the illusion that he is loyal to the king."

Christopher breathed a heavy sigh of relief. "Thank God," he said. "Where is she?"

"Up ahead in the village of Dereham," Kevin said. "My lord, I have come on behalf of Sean and Sherry, who have come up with a plan to end this situation once and for all. But we need your help in this matter."

"Help?" Christopher repeated as if the very suggested insulted him. "I will not only help, I will lead the charge to regain my daughter. What is this about, Kevin?"

Kevin took a step closer to them, lowering his voice so the soldiers milling about could not hear.

"Sean is taking your daughter to FitzRoy because he must," he said quietly. "As I said, he must maintain the illusion that he is loyal to the king. But he also believes that he should take her to FitzRoy for one very important reason."

Christopher's eyebrows flew up. "I would like to hear that reason."

Kevin glanced at Peter somewhat nervously before continuing. "My lord, I am sorry to have to be the one to tell you this," he said. "I did not think this would ever be my duty to disclose, but it is a well-known fact that you are unaware that your daughter serves The Marshal as a…"

"Spy," Christopher cut him off. "I know. William told me."

As Kevin looked surprised, Peter's eyes widened. "You *know*?" he demanded. "How long have you known, Papa?"

Christopher shrugged. "Only a few hours," he said wryly. Then, he pointed at Peter. "And I shall deal with you later for it. I understand it was you who recruited her. For shame, Peter. Pulling your little sister into a man's game."

As Peter tried not to look sheepish, or afraid of fatherly retribution, Kevin spoke up. "Then if you already know of her service, you must know that she is good at what she does," he said. "*Very* good. Sherry and Sean believe that Christin can kill FitzRoy and end this situation once and for all."

Christopher's jaw dropped in astonishment. "What?" he hissed. "They are putting the burden on her for this?"

Kevin continued quickly. "It is not as it sounds," he said. "But the truth is that she can get the closest to FitzRoy where the rest of us cannot. Eliminate the reason for the king's fixation, and you eliminate the problem. If FitzRoy is out of the way, then Lady Christin is safe. So are any other daughters the king wishes to pledge to his bastard son should a de Lohr betrothal fall through."

Christopher shut his mouth, mostly because the solution made perfect sense. Eliminating FitzRoy was something he'd already told David he was going to do, but he believed his only chance to accomplish it would be after the marriage took place. He never thought he would make it in time to stop the wedding. Now, Alexander and Sean had come up with a solution.

Whether or not he liked it.

Christin would be the assassin.

He stood there a moment, mulling it over, as Kevin, Peter, and, most of all, David watched him carefully. Christopher could be their biggest ally or their biggest obstacle. If he didn't like the plan, then they were back to the beginning, so they could only pray he agreed with it.

Letting his daughter do the dirty work she was apparently born to do. She was, after all, a de Lohr.

Finally, he sighed.

"I suppose that it is logical that she should be the one to do it since she will be able to get close to him," he said. "I cannot say I like the idea of my daughter carrying out such a brutal task. That is man's work. Considering she has been serving The Marshal for two years now, however, I suppose I must try and look at her as one of his agents and less like my daughter."

Both Kevin and Peter nodded their heads, with Peter speaking first. "Papa, you've not seen her in action," he said. "Her hands are steady and her mind is strong. Back at Ramsbury while you and Uncle David were feasting, Christin was attacked by a French spy. She killed the woman without hesitation. She can do the same thing to FitzRoy and this nightmare will be over."

Christopher sighed heavily, trying to digest what he was being told about petite, pretty Christin. Was it true she was a killer in disguise? If he believed Peter, then she was. What was it that William had said to him? *Your children want to be a tribute to the de Lohr name. Let them.*

Perhaps it was time to do that.

It wasn't as if he had a choice.

"Very well," he finally said, though it was clear he wasn't completely supportive. "You said you wanted my help. What would you have me do?"

They were all breathing a sigh of relief to varying degrees and Kevin spoke quickly. "You and your army must engage the king's soldiers," he said. "Sean has about one hundred men with him, men that Gerard had originally planned as the escort. When Sean took Christin, he had no choice but to let those men go along. They must be engaged by you and your army while Sean and the rest of us, disguised as royal knights, take Christin to FitzRoy. Sean says that the royal soldiers must not be witness to any interaction he has with FitzRoy, especially because Christin will kill him. Sean must disavow all knowledge of Christin's actions to keep himself separated from the incident."

Christopher could see the logic. "That is true," he said. "He essentially brought one hundred witnesses with him."

"That is what he said."

"How far is Dereham?"

Both Kevin and Peter looked up the dark road. "Mayhap six or eight miles up the road," Kevin said. "The king's men are camped outside of the village."

Christopher thought on that before looking to David. "If we leave in the morning, we shall not be able to catch up to them fast enough," he said. "But if we go tonight and catch them by surprise before sunrise…"

"Then we will most certainly keep them busy," David finished for them.

Christopher nodded. "We must gather the senior sergeants and tell them that we are marching through the night and why," he said. "Then we will inform the men. But for now, let them have a hot meal. We can make it to Dereham well before dawn. Kevin, return to Sherry and your brother and tell them that we will be there come sunrise to keep John's army busy while they head on to Bishop's Lynn."

"Aye, my lord."

Kevin fled. They watched him go, but Christopher found his attention settling on his son, who was looking after Kevin most wistfully. He could tell that the man wanted to be off on a great adventure, not stuck with his father and uncle. Even if they would be engaging in battle on the morrow.

"Well?" he said to Peter. "What do you want to do? Ride with your sister and Sherry and the rest of them, or face battle with me and your uncle."

Peter looked at him. "I would face battle with you," he said. "You need me more than Christin does. She has Sherry and the rest of them. You only have Uncle David."

David scowled. "What is that supposed to mean, you foolish whelp?"

Peter, who had a bit of a wicked streak in him, put his hand on his uncle's shoulder. "I saw you back at Norwich," he said. "When we faced the king and his guard? I saw how weak and pitiful you were, Uncle David. I was afraid I was going to have to save you."

David knew he was jesting but his pride would not let him walk away from it. He looked at Christopher. "You had the opportunity to drown him when he was young," he said. "I told you that you should have done it."

Christopher started to laugh. "There is time yet still."

"Is there?" David said as if surprised. "Good. I plan to tie him in a sack and throw him in the river."

"I am too big for a sack," Peter said.

David shook his head, heading off towards the camping army. "Never underestimate my determination to shove you into a sack. If you don't fit the first time, I shall figure out a way."

Peter was grinning, receiving a gentle slap to the head from his father as they followed David towards the army. Already, the smells of food and bread were in the air, but Christopher wasn't much thinking on that. He was thinking of the daughter he was going to have to trust to men he'd known, loved, and served with for years, only somehow it was different now.

It was Christin.

And Alexander.

He was going to have to trust that Alexander would keep her safe.

He could only pray.

CHAPTER TWENTY-TWO

The Cock and Bull Inn

WHEN CHRISTIN HAD departed Norwich, she'd had the satchel she'd packed for her escape into the town with Alexander, which someone had managed to pick up when she had dropped it in the fight against Gerard and Sean. It must have been one of the royal soldiers, who had carried it with him and then given it to one of the servants at the inn, who delivered it to her. Suddenly, she found herself with a sleeping shift along with clean clothing, a comb, pins for her hair, soap, and other necessities.

She considered herself very fortunate.

Sean had disappeared and although she'd waited for him, patiently she thought, it became clear that he wasn't returning any time soon, so she sent for a bath and food, which were brought to her in that order. The bath was nothing more than a big pot and a stool, which she sat upon while she washed with several inches of hot water in the bottom of the pot, but it had been heavenly and she'd put on her sleeping shift by the time the food arrived.

The meal was a stew with great hunks of cream-colored bread with a dark crust and butter on the side. The stew had beans and cabbage and barley in it, and it was quite delicious. She ate two big bowls of the stuff along with most of the bread, stuffing herself while she waited for Sean to return.

But still, he didn't come back.

With all of the food gone and the bath water cold, Christin decided to stop waiting for Sean and simply go to bed. She was exhausted. Crawling into the rather small bed that had a surprisingly clean, if not slightly stiff from being boiled, coverlet, she fell asleep quickly, only to be awakened by someone whispering in her ear.

"Cissy?"

Startled by the heated whisper, she threw up a balled fist just as she caught a glimpse of Alexander's face. His catlike reflexes prevented her from making contact with his nose as he caught her fist in one of his big hands. She looked astonished and he simply grinned.

"That could have been disastrous," he teased. "I rather like my face the way it is."

"Sherry!" she gasped. "How in the world did you get in here?"

He sat on the edge of the bed, still holding her hand, only now he was kissing it. "You have a window that is shockingly easy to climb through," he said. "All I had to do was shimmy up the tree outside and grab hold."

She sat up, looking to the open window. The shutters and oil cloth had been pushed back, letting the cold night air in. A little more alert now, she realized what he'd done.

"Then I am glad you were the one who discovered that," she said, yawning. "It would not do for some cutthroat to crash into my chamber."

He was still grinning, still kissing her hand. "I *am* a cutthroat and I *did* crash into your chamber, but at least I mean you no harm," he said, watching her smile. "At least, not in the literal sense. Are you well after your adventure today? I saw Sean in the livery. He told me everything."

She nodded. "I am fine," she said. "But I have a confession to make. I was outside of my apartment when they set upon me. I was going to meet you in the stable, but they were waiting for me. I tried to get away and that is how they were able to catch me. There were just too many of them."

His smile faded. "I told you to stay in your chamber. Did you think I did that just to hear the sound of my own voice?"

She was properly contrite. "Nay," she said. "I am sorry. I suppose I was simply eager to see you. I could not wait."

Of course, he couldn't become cross with her when she put it like that. He sighed heavily, eyeing her appropriately so she would know he was not pleased with her behavior, but she smiled sweetly at him and he surrendered without a fight. He put his arms around her, hugging her tightly.

"You are forgiven," he murmured. "Truth be told, I could not wait to see you, either. That's why I climbed in your window."

Christin clung to him, drawing strength from him in a way she never knew possible. When he held her in his arms, it was as if nothing in the world could touch her. She felt safe and warm and deliriously happy. But she knew it was only temporary, at least until they resumed their trek to Bishop's Lynn.

She relaxed her hold.

"Did Sean tell you about his plan for FitzRoy?" she asked softly.

Alexander loosened his grip so he could look her in the eye. "Aye," he said. "I know it is a lot to ask of you, but I also know you can do it. You simply have to look at this like any other directive from William Marshal. You must become that agent that is hardened and focused – no emotion, no past, and no future. You live, and remain, in that moment – the moment that Robert FitzRoy becomes your prey. Focus on your task and you will succeed."

She nodded. "I will," she said. "But where will you be?"

"I will be close by," he said. "I am riding with Sean disguised as a royal knight. In fact, we are all going to be with you."

"Who is 'all'?"

"Maxton, Kress, Cai, Bric, Kevin, and Sean," he said. "Your father is not far behind us and he will be engaging the royal soldiers, keeping them occupied while the group of us escorts you to FitzRoy. That way, whatever happens, we can cover our tracks without any witnesses. And we shall cover yours."

"My father is in on this plan, then?"

"He has been trailing us. Kevin rode back to find him, so if he is not aware of the plan now, he soon will be."

"He must be terribly worried."

"I am sure he is. But he knows we would not let anything happen to you. *I* would not let anything happen to you." He looked her over, studying her lovely face. "Nothing will go wrong, Cissy. But we will all be there in case something does."

She felt much better hearing that. Truth be told, she was apprehensive and understandably so. There was so much at stake and the burden of it was heavy, crushingly so, but Alexander was absolutely right – she needed to treat this situation like any other mission. FitzRoy was her prey. When he put it that way, she was able to feel more confident about it.

"I am glad," she said softly, leaning her head against his, feeling him gently kiss her forehead. "I feel much better knowing you will be there. But this… this is my fight, Sherry. I am the target, after all, and I will fight my own battle."

He put a big hand on her head, smoothing back her dark hair as he gazed into her eyes. "But not alone," he said softly. "Never alone, Cissy. As long as I have breath in my body, you will never be alone."

"Nor will you," she said. "I can only imagine that must feel strange for a man like you. You told me that you preferred to work alone."

He smiled faintly as he pinched her chin gently. "Not anymore."

She reached out, touching his face, and he closed his eyes to the flutter of her fingers. Both hands came up and she gently clasped his face, her fingers in his hair. Their warm, gentle conversation turned into something else. The passion that ignited so easily between them flared. Eyes still closed, Alexander leaned forward and kissed her.

There was nothing more to say.

His lips were soft and warm, his tongue licking at her lips until she opened them. She responded to him quickly, comfortable and titillated with his attention. Alexander lay her back against the small bed, covering her with his big body as their kisses became more heated. With no one to interrupt them, he could take his time with her.

But he didn't want to.

Something about the woman inflamed him. He wore full armor, putting him in a logistically difficult position for what he wanted to accomplish. But that didn't stop him. He continued to kiss her as he went to work on his mail.

His belt, his sword, and his tunic were the first things to come off. Christin, swept up by the fervor that was brewing between them, began to help him with his pieces of protection. She pulled the hauberk off, followed by the mail coat. Then it was a matter of stripping off the under tunic and breeches. All the while, she never said a word, a more than willing participant to what they intended to do.

The power of attraction between them was overwhelming.

With his armor and tunics off, he went to work on Christin's shift, pulling it right over her head. She was nude beneath it and, for a moment, he simply looked at her, feasting on her gorgeous form. There was something so surreal and magical about her beauty. Once again, his lips fused to hers, his heated touch speaking more than words ever could.

The more he touched, the more he had to have her. Alexander was so consumed by his passion that he was blinded it by it. Taking her in his arms, he continued to kiss her as he wedged himself between her legs. With one hand, he managed to guide his erection into her warm, wet core.

Christin groaned as he invaded her body. She was tender from earlier in the day, but the pain of his entry only served to enhance the sensations he was creating within her. Alexander tried to be gentle, but his need for the woman was overpowering. He slid into her, with a few tender thrusts, until he was seated. Then, he began to move.

The thrusts were gentle at first, erotic and slow. She was slick and welcoming. But his passion dictated his movements, and they became faster. A hand moved to her full breasts, gently fondling the soft skin as her legs wrapped around him, holding him tightly.

That only wanted to make him thrust harder.

Her soft gasps in his ear threw him over the edge. He could feel himself peaking faster than he ever thought possible. Harder and faster he went, feeling her body stiffen beneath him until she began to twitch and her soft cries filled the chamber. Feeling her release draw at him, demanding his seed, he didn't do what he'd done earlier – he didn't withdraw and spill himself elsewhere. This time, he spilled his seed deep inside her delicious body. He shouldn't have done it, but he didn't much care.

It was the most satisfying thing he'd ever done.

But he was still moving within her. He could not seem to stop moving, making their passion last until it could last no more. Beneath him, he felt her release at least twice more, her body shuddering with delight and her legs trembling uncontrollably. In fact, her entire body was trembling uncontrollably, which excited him beyond reason.

But when the movements finally slowed, he fell forward on her, drawing her into his protective embrace as if to never let her go. He couldn't even fathom the thought of what was to come, where he would have to turn her over to another man and put her in such great danger.

And he would be helpless.

When next he realized, someone was pounding on the chamber door.

CHAPTER TWENTY-THREE

ALEXANDER WAS OUT of bed in a flash.

"Who comes?" he demanded.

"Open the door, Sherry."

It was Sean, muffled on the other side of the door. Alexander glanced at Christin, who was sitting up in bed, wide-eyed at being caught with Alexander in her bed. It didn't even occur to her that Sean wouldn't care because he was the one who told Alexander where to find her.

"A moment," Alexander said through the door. Quickly, he pulled his breeches on from the pile on the floor, tossing Christin the shift he'd snatched off her. "Quickly, sweetheart. Put it on."

She did, yanking it over her head as Alexander went to the door. He made sure she was properly covered up before unbolting it.

Sean appeared. He was dressed in full armor, as if he were going to battle, and he didn't even look at Christin. He was singularly focused on Alexander.

"De Lohr's army has been sighted," he murmured. "They are just coming into the edge of town, so get her dressed and to the livery immediately. We must leave."

"My father is here?" Christin blurted.

Sean looked at her, nodding his head. "They marched through the night to reach the king's soldiers and engage them," he said. "Very smart, actually. There was no way he could catch up with us if he rested the men for the night, so he didn't. He pushed them straight through."

Alexander nodded with approval. "Good man," he said. "He will keep the soldiers busy while we ride on."

"Exactly," Sean said. Then, he looked at the two of them. "Even though he will more than likely not make it to the inn, I would get dressed and get down to the livery. We must leave immediately while the king's army is occupied."

Alexander began grabbing his clothing and mail, putting it on the bed as Christin leapt out of it. Sean closed the door, heading down into the pre-dawn street, as Christin and Alexander quickly dressed.

In fact, there was a bit of a frenzy to Christin's movements. As Alexander put on his own clothing and mail, he could see that she was close to hysteria. It was rather comical the way she was tossing on clothing and frantically running a comb through her hair, but when she tried to put her shoes on and nearly fell in her haste, he put out a hand to steady her.

"Dressing should not be a hazardous sport," he said. "Slow down, sweetheart. We'll make it to the livery in plenty of time."

Christin looked at him, her eyes wide. "Did you not hear him?" she said. "My father is entering the town. Do you know what will happen if he sees us leaving the inn together? Or, worse, comes looking for me and finds us leaving the chamber together? My God, Sherry, he'll cut your head off!"

Alexander bit his lip to keep from smiling. "That is not what he would cut off," he muttered, watching her flush violently. Then, he couldn't help but chuckle. "Not to worry. If I thought that might happen, I would climb back out the window and he would be none the wiser."

"Maybe you should," she said.

"Should what?"

"Climb out the window. There may be people in the common room who would tell him they saw us leaving the chamber together."

She had a point, much as he hated to admit it. He grunted, thinking her paranoia was rather ridiculous, but he was prepared to err on the side of caution.

"Very well," he said. "I'll climb out and you can throw my bags to me."

Christin nodded eagerly. She was dressed in a dark blue wool traveling dress, heavy, with long sleeves and a cloak that was part of the garment itself. She'd braided her hair, making her look rather sweet and lovely, and as he moved in for a kiss, she ducked him and pushed him towards the window.

"*Go*," she demanded. "Out the window before my father sees you."

He grinned, letting her push him to the window. "I told you not to worry," he said. "He will not see me. But I will go out the window and circle around to the front of the inn and meet you there. Do not dally."

He spoke the last few words as he climbed onto the windowsill, but he wasn't moving fast enough for Christin. The fear of her father finding them together was overwhelming, so just as he spoke the last word, she shoved him and he fell out of the window, grabbing a branch on his way down to break his fall. But the branch snapped and down he went, landing heavily as tree branches and twigs fell on top of him.

"Here are your bags!" she said.

His saddlebags came sailing at him, one of them clipping him in the head before they landed beside him. Rubbing his head, he scowled as he looked up at her.

"God's Bones, woman," he said unhappily. "You did not have to throw me from the window, you know."

Christin looked at him, very contritely, before blowing him a kiss. "I am sorry," she said. "Did you hurt yourself?"

"*Now* you ask."

He climbed to his feet, rubbing his left thigh and bum where he'd landed, grumbling as he made his way around the side of the inn. Meanwhile, Christin splashed some cold water on her face, drying it with the sleeve of her dress as she grabbed her satchel and fled the chamber.

Alexander was waiting for her as she bolted from the inn. Grasping her by the elbow, he quickly escorted her across the alleyway to the livery where men were gathering. Kevin was there, having recently come from Christopher's army, and Christin went to him.

"How is my father?" she asked. "Is he very worried over me?"

Kevin nodded. "He was," he said. "But when we told him of our plan, he calmed admirably. You needn't worry."

Christin didn't. She was grateful that her father wasn't hysterical about the situation, instead, moving his army to intercept John's soldiers. She stood there as the knights prepared their horses – Caius, Sean, Kevin, Bric, Maxton, Kress, and Alexander. It was quite a collection of seasoned knights and although she was still somewhat apprehensive about the situation, she knew these men would do everything in their power to keep her safe.

As she watched them, it occurred to her just how fortunate she was. These were men who had been serving England longer than she'd been alive in some cases, and their skills were uncontested. They had accepted her into their network because of her name, but she'd proven beyond the de Lohr name that she was talented enough to be one of them.

And then, there was Alexander.

He was the greatest one of all as far as she was concerned. What she felt for him went beyond adoration. She'd known the man for less than a month and, already, she couldn't live without him.

Perhaps she wasn't meant to.

Perhaps their relationship was simply meant to be.

Christin was staring at him, daydreaming, as he finished with his horse. Glancing up, he saw that she was looking at him and he winked at her. Her heart fluttered as if it had wings. But they were prevented from conversation when the distant sounds of swords could be heard.

Sean dashed to the livery entry, peering down the road in the darkness.

"The battle has begun," he said. "Quickly, mount your horses. We ride."

The knights did, all of them swinging up into their saddles. Christin realized her horse wasn't anywhere to be found and thought, with horror, that she had been expected to prepare it. Just as she began to recall that she had ridden the day before with Sean, he grabbed her by the arm.

"Come with me," Sean said.

She did. He took her satchel, tying it off on his saddle, before lifting her up onto the horse. Alexander directed his horse next to Sean as the man mounted up, pulling Christin's hands in front of him. When Sean saw Alexander's questioning expression, he simply shook his head.

"She must ride with me, Sherry," he said quietly. "That is what everyone expects. She is still my prisoner as far as anyone knows. It makes sense that FitzRoy, when we arrive, should see her with me."

Alexander understood. He smiled at Christin, who smiled in return. He was near her and that was all she cared about. As the horses thundered out of the livery and traveled northwest beneath skies that were beginning to lighten, she fought off the apprehension of what the day would bring. She hadn't allowed herself to entertain her fears, but as the group thundered down the road, she found that she couldn't think of anything else.

She had a man to kill.

CHAPTER TWENTY-FOUR

FAIRSTEAD LOOKED LIKE something out of a ghost story.
The manor home of Robert FitzRoy was large, rambling, and run-down. Stones had fallen from the eaves and vines grew up all around it. It had a sturdy wall, however, and a massive iron gate for protection.

There were dogs everywhere.

Big dogs, little dogs. Dogs that came too close to the horses and got kicked for their efforts, sending them away yelping. The ride to Bishop's Lynn had taken all day, from dawn to dusk, and they were all exhausted from the hard ride, including the horses. The animals were sweating and foaming, and it was big and frightening Caius who dismounted his horse and demanded Robert FitzRoy from the two guards who manned the old, iron gate.

One of them went running inside the manse to summon FitzRoy, who emerged from the front door a little bit later with a jug in his hand. At least, they thought it was FitzRoy. The soldier who had summoned him pointed to the gates, indicating the men outside, and the man with the jug stumbled from the entry door, tripped down the stone steps into the small bailey, and weaved his way towards the gate.

Only a few torches were lit against the darkness, making it difficult to see. But once the man with the jug came close to the gates, his eyes widened and he pointed at the group.

"Royal standards, you fools!" he barked. "Open the gate! They are wearing royal standards!"

The gate was quickly opened, permitting the group entrance. Sean was in the lead, peering down at the man with the jug. He was tall and slender, with a mop of dark, dirty hair. He appeared unshaven and pale and had no resemblance to the king other than the physical trait his father had – one droopy eye.

That told Sean who the man was, but he asked anyway.

"Are you Robert FitzRoy?" he asked.

The man nodded unsteadily. "I am," he said. Then, he clutched the jug against his chest fearfully. "Did my father send you here? What does he want? Why have you come?"

He sounded like a nervous idiot, clearly drunk. Sean eyed the man before dismounting his steed to speak with him face to face.

"My name is Sean de Lara," he said. "I serve your father in the capacity of personal guard. The men with me are also royal guards. We have come with a message from your father."

FitzRoy looked at the collection of very big knights, all of them, and one small lady sitting on de Lara's horse. His fear turned to confusion and he continued to clutch the jug of wine to his breast as his attention returned to de Lara.

"A message?" he repeated. "*What* message?"

Sean indicated the lady sitting atop the horse. "It is your father's wish that you marry this lady," he said. "Her name is Christin de Lohr and her father is a powerful warlord. Your father wishes to be related to de Lohr by marriage, so you must do your duty."

FitzRoy looked at Christin a moment before returning his focus to Sean. "I cannot marry her," he said as if it were a ludicrous suggestion. "I already have a wife!"

That brought a reaction from the group of men, who glanced at each other in shock. This was an element they'd not anticipated.

FitzRoy is already married!

"Your father did not know you were married," Sean said after a moment. "He was under the impression that you'd not taken a wife."

FitzRoy hugged his jug with one arm, scratching his head with the other. "That is because he does not care for me," he said. "He has ignored me most of my life. And now he sends me a bride? He did not even bother to ask me if I had already taken one. I have, you know, but she's a worthless whore. She's inside right now, drinking all of my wine."

No one seemed to know quite what to do, but Alexander did. He wanted to take Christin and get the hell out of there. If FitzRoy was already married, there was no reason to remain. Sean must have had the same idea because he didn't reply to FitzRoy. He simply turned back to his horse and was preparing to mount when FitzRoy stopped him.

"Wait," he said, edging closer to Sean's horse and looking up at Christin. "I want to see what my father sent me. Get down from there."

Christin, who had so far remained silent and stoic, glanced at Sean, who nodded imperceptibly. Without a word, she climbed down and presented herself to FitzRoy, who was seriously looking her over. His gaze raked her from top to bottom, and everything in between.

It was enough to make Christin's skin crawl.

"So, he wanted me to marry you, did he?" he said, his voice sounding very much like John's – lascivious and chilling. "You're quite pretty. Your name is Christin?"

"Aye, my lord."

"How old are you?"

"I have seen eighteen summers, my lord."

Suddenly, FitzRoy didn't seem so drunk. He took another step towards her, looking Christin in the eye.

"My God, you *are* beautiful," he said seductively. "If my father sent you to me, then I would not be rude enough to refuse. I do believe that I will keep you."

Christin's eyes narrowed. "I will not be your whore, my lord."

FitzRoy lifted an eyebrow. "Resistance," he said. "I like that. I like it when my women fight back. De Lara, return to my father and thank him for this exquisite... gift. I will keep her."

Sean eyed the man. "You are meant to marry her, not keep her as a concubine," he said. "Your father wants the bond that only marriage can bring. If you cannot marry her, then I shall return her to your father. He will find someone else for her to marry."

FitzRoy's response was to reach out and grab Christin by her braid, yanking her with him as he took several steps back, away from the knights.

"My father has never done anything for me," he said. "He has sent me this beautiful gift and I intend to keep her. Call it compensation for all of those years my father preferred to pretend I did not exist. Get out of here, all of you. The woman stays with me."

The situation suddenly turned edgy as an unanticipated element took hold. He wasn't really hurting her, but it was uncomfortable. Christin let herself be dragged along because she really couldn't fight him the way he held her. But the advice from Alexander and Sean kept rolling through her head, advice on what she was to do when she found herself in this position.

She knew what she had to do.

Alexander had told her to view the man as her prey, not as her captor. Sean had told her to move swiftly with her actions and not wait. She was going to do both, for the moment he let go of her braid and went to grab her hand, she unleashed on him.

A balled fist when flying at him, catching him in the nose and sending his wine jug flying. As he screamed and put his hands on his face, blood streaming from between his fingers, Christin hit him in the face again, so hard that he fell onto the stone steps of his manse, striking his head.

The blow was enough to daze him, but he was still conscious and Christin was in panic mode. She was terrified of what would happen if she didn't kill the man immediately, terrified that he would get up and try to hurt her. Terrified he would drag her into the house and the battle would continue inside, behind locked doors where no one could help her.

Where Alexander couldn't get to her.

FitzRoy lay on the steps, his head on the first stone step while his body was sprawled out in the dirt. Leaping on his chest, Christin put all of her strength into his neck, using her knee and ramming it into his throat as hard as she could. He tried to scream, but she had crushed his windpipe. When she went in for another blow, however, he lashed out with his long legs, kicking her over so that she toppled into the corner of the stone manse. Striking her left side hard, she fell to her knees.

But FitzRoy was strong. With his windpipe crushed, he was slowly suffocating, but he could still move. He could still kill. He spied Christin crumpled a few feet away and he rolled to his side, reaching towards her with claw-like hands. He was going to grab her and ram her face right into the ground.

But he never had the chance.

Alexander charged.

No one tried to stop him, not even Sean. Alexander moved with the speed of a cat, rushing FitzRoy, who was struggling to rise. Swinging his broadsword in a skilled, tight fashion, Alexander brought the blade to bear right on FitzRoy's neck. In one clean slice, the body fell away as the head remained on the stairs.

With startling speed, the situation was over.

Furious, Alexander kicked the body aside as he went for Christin, who was picking herself up from the ground. He caught her by the arm, helping her to her feet.

"Are you injured?" he asked.

Christin shook her head, though she was holding her left elbow. "I... I do not think so," she said. "Sherry, you killed him!"

Alexander had to force himself to take a deep breath and calm down. Christin was not terribly injured and FitzRoy was dead.

That was all he cared about.

"I had to," he said quietly. "I know we told you that this was your duty, but you belong to me and when the duty became yours, it became mine. I could not stand by and not help you. I hope you understand that."

She looked at him, a weary smile on her face. "Of course I do," she murmured. "I am glad you did."

Alexander didn't have anything more to say, so he pulled Christin against him, comforting her. Or perhaps he was really comforting himself, knowing she was safe and alive and this whole stupid mess was over. As he turned to glance at FitzRoy, a bloody mess on his entry stairs, Sean walked up. He looked at FitzRoy for a brief moment before turning around and motioning to the men behind him.

"Get the body," he said. "De Lohr will want him."

Maxton and Kress came up to collect FitzRoy, one taking the body and one taking the head by the hair, carrying both back to the horses. As Caius helped Maxton heave up the body onto Sean's horse, Kress went to hunt for something to wrap the head in. The two gate guards, who had watched the entire incident unfold, tried to intervene but Kevin and Bric raised their swords to them and chased the men into the darkness.

There was no doubt that the witnesses to the event would be eliminated.

It was a precise, swift operation, not unlike the dozens of operations the knights had completed in the past. No emotion, no fear, no disgust – simply business. They'd had a plan and they'd stuck to it. They would remove the body and remove the witnesses.

No trace.

The Executioner Knights lived up to their name this night.

As FitzRoy was being secured on the back of the Sean's horse, Sean turned to Alexander and Christin. They were huddled together, with Alexander's face on the top of Christin's head. Sean could see in that moment how much this situation had meant to them both. In truth, they'd both been so professional about it that he'd hardly realized it until now.

Now, he could see the fear and relief.

"You did well, Christin," Sean said. "It is rare to see a woman with such bravery and I am proud to serve with you."

Christin smiled weakly, looking over to the body that was being secured. "A pity he could not have simply left me alone," she said. "When he said he was married, I had hoped my troubles were over."

Sean lifted his eyebrows. "That," he said, "was a distinct surprise."

"What will you tell the king?"

"I will tell him that I delivered you as I was ordered," he said. "Beyond that, I know nothing. And neither do you. Let your father handle this from now on."

Christin nodded as Sean's gaze moved between her and Alexander before turning and heading back to his horse. Christin watched him go for a moment before turning to Alexander.

"I will make sure my father knows that you saved me," she said softly. "That was a very brave thing you did."

Alexander gave her a squeeze. "As I said, I could not stand by and watch," he said. "But I thought you might be angry at me for intervening. I did not mean to steal your glory."

She snorted. "Glory?" She shook her head. "I think I have had enough glory to last me for a while. I think I would prefer to be Lady de Sherrington and let that be glory enough."

He grinned. "Do you mean it?" he asked. "You are going to give up serving The Marshal without resistance?"

"You told me you did not want your wife going on missions."

"And *you* said we could serve together like Achilles and Susanna."

She laughed softly. "Mayhap we will, someday," she said. "But for now… now, I simply want to go home. With you."

He kissed the top of her head. "Home *where*? I do not have a home and the only home you have is Norwich Castle."

"Lioncross Abbey," she said softly. "I want to go home to Lioncross and I want you to come with me. Please, Sherry. Take me home."

His smile faded. "As you wish," he said, stroking her hair. "Let's deliver FitzRoy to your father and ask his permission if I may take you home. Fair enough?"

"Fair enough."

"And then I will ask for permission to marry you."

She chuckled. "Hand over FitzRoy when you do," she said. "That way, he cannot deny you. The body of his enemy in exchange for his blessing."

It was the way such bargains were struck in the world of the Executioner Knights. Grinning at one another, the pair headed back to the horses but as they were sharing a special moment, Kevin was having a moment of his own.

Over in the darkness, he was brooding. He'd just chased down one of the stupid gate guards and put his sword through the man's belly to silence him, but as he headed back to the group as they prepared to ride off, he was becoming more and more disturbed.

It had to do with his discussion with Alexander the night before and how the man had lectured him on how he treated his brother. Truth be told, Kevin didn't serve with his brother that much and this ride to FitzRoy had been a rare occurrence. He usually avoided Sean at all costs, but that hadn't been possible over the past couple of days. He'd watched how the other knights seemed to have such great esteem for Sean, something that Kevin used to ignore.

But now, he wasn't ignoring it.

Watching Sean and Alexander interact with Christin and FitzRoy had him thinking heavily on his brother and the man's sacrifice. He served the king, yet he clearly enabled Christin and Alexander to kill the man's bastard son. Kevin had always known Sean walked a fine line between keeping the illusion of Lord of the Shadows and working with The Marshal and his spy ring to keep the country safe. That had never been in dispute. But what he saw tonight… tonight, he realized just how much Sean was risking.

It was complicated, confusing, and dangerous, but through it all, Sean did his duty.

And Kevin had hated him for it.

Perhaps that's why he was so disturbed at the moment. He was starting to see what everyone else saw. Alexander's words had impacted him more than he cared to admit, that stubborn younger brother who was so terribly hurt by his older brother's actions. Perhaps that really *was* the problem all along; Kevin knew how great Sean was. He'd idolized him his entire life, so when Sean became the Lord of the Shadows, Kevin had been hurt and confused by it.

His brother deserved so much better.

But Sean clearly felt what he was doing *was* better.

Kevin had been stewing on it since yesterday and as the men began to mount their horses, he made his way over to Sean, who was tightening up one of the ropes on FitzRoy's headless body. Perhaps Kevin just didn't want to stew anymore, or perhaps he simply needed to get things out in the open, but he came up on the other side of Sean's horse, looking at the top of his brother's head as he bent over the body.

"Sean," he said quietly.

Sean glanced up but when he saw who it was, he went back to work. "What is it?"

"I just wanted to say..." Kevin stopped and started again. "I just wanted to say something. When we were very young, we went into town with Father because he wanted to purchase candied grapes and lemon rinds from the woman in the village of Pool for Mother. She was dying at the time and wanted the sweets. Do you recall that moment?"

Sean paused in tightening the ropes, confused with the topic of conversation at this ill-timed moment. "I do."

Kevin scratched his ear as he tried to think of the right words. "Do you also recall that I stole a stick that had candied apple slices on it? Just because I wanted it?"

"I do, indeed."

"I was very young," Kevin said. "I was nearly four years of age, I think. You were six. I was old enough to know better, however, and I greedily ate the apple slices. You saw what I'd done and you took the stick from me just as Father caught sight of you. He punished you for that and you never told him that I was the one who stole them. Why didn't you tell him?"

Sean returned to his ropes with slower actions now. "Because you were my little brother," he said simply. "It was my duty to protect you."

Kevin spoke softly. "You are still protecting me. Only now, you are protecting all of England, too. You are still the big brother, taking the blame for things that are not of your doing."

Sean didn't look at him, but he was no longer fumbling with the ropes. He was simply fingering them. "What would you have me say, Kevin?"

Kevin could feel the tears stinging his eyes. He didn't know why, but he was close to crying. Perhaps because there was a history of Sean being a martyr for the greater good and he could see that now. He'd put it into a context he could understand and, suddenly, he didn't hate Sean so much anymore. He was starting to understand all of it. He opened his mouth to speak but a sob caught in his throat.

"I hate that you have to take the blame for a man who is not worthy of you," he said, his lip trembling. "I hate that the man I love and admire most in this world is reviled and hated. Mayhap I do not show you the respect you deserve on the surface, but inside, I love you like I have always loved you. I just hate that you have done this to yourself, Sean. I... I am trying to come to grips with it and I will continue to try. I promise I will. But I do not hate you. I just thought you should know."

Even in the darkness, Kevin could see the tears glistening on Sean's cheeks and he turned way, but not before releasing another sob. He simply couldn't help it. Emotions he'd kept bottled up for years were coming to the surface whether or not he wanted them to. Here, of all places. But he quickly wiped his face and took a deep breath, struggling to compose himself as he headed over to his horse.

He'd said what he needed to say.

It was the right thing to do.

As the sky began to cloud overhead, the agents of William Marshal departed the small bailey of Fairstead and headed out into the night, taking the road back to Dereham.

Kevin rode with Sean all the way.

CHAPTER TWENTY-FIVE

IT HADN'T BEEN much of a fight.

In fact, Christopher's army saw about an hour of serious fighting before the royal soldiers began to surrender in droves. Perhaps that was because they'd lost about one-third of their numbers in that hour, or perhaps it was because they'd grown lazy and simply didn't want to fight anymore.

Whatever the reason, Christopher had sixty-one prisoners surrender to him by midday and by nightfall, he decided to send them all back to John with their weapons stripped and their tunics torn up and vandalized. Come the next morning, he planned to do exactly that.

While his men guarded the prisoners in a field south of town, Christopher and David and Peter had supped heartily and slept in The Cock and Bull, a tavern that they found to be a step above most. The food was excellent, the beds soft, and Christopher was awakened before dawn the next morning by Peter, shaking him gently.

"Papa?" Peter whispered loudly. "Papa, wake up."

Christopher had been sleeping heavily, enjoying his first real sleep in days. "I am awake," he muttered. "But you had better have a good reason for disturbing me."

"I do," Peter said. "Christin has returned!"

Christopher sat up so quickly that he nearly hit his son in the chin. "Where is she?" he demanded.

Peter was pulling him out of bed. "She just rode into the livery," he said. "Sherry and Maxton and Sean and the others are with her. They brought her back!"

Christopher was in his breeches and a thin tunic and nothing else. He yanked on his boots, tying them haphazardly as he rushed out of the chamber after his son. He was just passing David's door when he kicked it open, revealing David passed out on his small bed.

"David!" he hissed. "Get up! Christin has returned!"

David struggled to rouse himself, rolling out of bed and ending up on the floor as Peter and Christopher continued down the stairs into the common room of the inn. As David scrambled up and grabbed his boots, Peter and Christopher were already out the door, rushing over to the livery just as Christin and Alexander and the rest were dismounting their thoroughly exhausted horses.

The first thing Christopher saw was the headless body on the back of Sean's sweaty horse. He came to a halt, peering at it and suspecting who it was before he was even told. Sean, seeing where Christopher's attention was, made his way over to him.

"It's FitzRoy," he said as he wearily removed his helm. "Christin and Sherry made short work of him."

"Sherry killed him because he was trying to kill me," Christin said as she came out from between a couple of horses. She went straight to her father and they embraced tightly. "Sherry saved my life, Papa."

Christopher was holding her so tightly that he was certain that he was squeezing the life out of her, but she clung to him tightly as well. The joy of having her back in his arms, safe, was almost more than he could bear.

"Are you well, sweetheart?" he asked. "He did not hurt you, did he?"

Christin shook her head, releasing her father but realizing he had no intention of releasing her also. She had to pry his hands from her.

"I am fine," she assured him. "Did you hear me? Sherry killed him."

Christopher took a deep breath, struggling to compose himself because he was so damned relieved to see her. "I heard you," he said. "Tell me what happened from the beginning."

"We reached Fairstead Manor, which is FitzRoy's home," Alexander answered him. He was standing a few feet away, back behind the butt of a horse, and all attention turned to him as he spoke. "When we arrived, FitzRoy came to speak with us and Sean told him that his father wished for him to marry Christin, but there was an immediate complication with that because FitzRoy was already married."

Christopher's eyebrows lifted in surprise. "He *was*?" he said. "And John did not know this?"

Alexander shook his head. "He did not," he said. "FitzRoy ranted about how his father never cared for him, so he'd evidently married without permission."

That changed the entire dynamic of the situation and the impact wasn't lost on Christopher. In truth, he was stunned.

"Christ," Christopher hissed. "So FitzRoy was already married. But what happened that you had to kill him?"

"Because he considered Christin a gift and wanted to take her as his whore," Alexander said. "She fought against him valiantly. But in the end, I stepped in to end it. I was not going to stand by and watch her fight for her life."

"And that is how he ended up headless?"

"Aye, my lord."

"Where is his head?"

"Here," Kress said, lifting up a bloody tunic he'd wrapped around the skull. "He is in pieces, my lord."

Christopher stood there a moment, pondering the situation, before going to Kress and collecting the head. He opened up the tunic enough to examine the state of the head before wrapping it back up again.

"The damage to his face," he said. "How did that happen?"

"When your daughter hit him in the face, twice," Alexander said. "As I said, she fought valiantly, but I delivered the final blow before he could gain the upper hand."

"I told you that he saved me, Papa," Christin said, wrapping her hands around his forearm and gazing up at him with her big, gray eyes. "Does that not deserve a reward?"

Christopher knew what she meant, the little minx. Like her mother, she knew how to manipulate him. He was so glad to see her that his defenses were down and she knew it. He lifted a disapproving eyebrow at her before handing the head over to Sean.

"You are going to take the head and the body back to John," he told him. "You will tell him that I killed FitzRoy in retribution for the abduction of my daughter. I am the one who delivered the death blow and I captured you and your army and forced you to return the body to the king along with a message."

"What message might that be, my lord?" Sean asked.

Christopher's eyes narrowed. "Tell him that if he ever seeks to touch my family again, in any way, that I will find him and I will kill him. That is my message to the king, Sean, and know that I mean it. If you stand in my way, I will consider you the enemy as well. I will have little choice. Do you understand me?"

Sean nodded. He wasn't offended. In his position, he couldn't afford to be. "I do, my lord," he said. "John… it could go either way with him. He will either single you out for a vendetta or he will leave you alone."

"He hasn't left me alone for twenty years."

"There is always a first time for everything, my lord."

Christopher nodded as if he didn't quite believe that. "We shall see," he said. "In any case, the remainder of the king's troops are south of town, being held captive by my men. I shall have Peter take you over there with a sword to your back so that your men believe I captured you also and gave you FitzRoy's body. That should keep the illusion of your loyalties alive for them."

Sean nodded. "Thank you, my lord."

Christopher reached out, clapping Sean on the shoulder. "You do valuable work for us, Sean," he said. "I would never knowingly betray your position and I would kill anyone who tried. That being said, get back to John and deliver my package. If he is wise, he will let things lie. If not…"

They all knew what was at stake. Sean tied the head off on his saddle and with Peter to his back, led the horse back down the road, towards the group of men being held by the de Lohr army. As he faded into the coming dawn, Christopher turned to the other men around him.

"Thank you," he said. "For helping regain my daughter, I am indebted to all of you. You are all great men in your own right and I respect you for it. Except for Maxton, of course. I reserve a special sentiment for him."

Everyone grinned except for Maxton, who pursed his lips wryly. There was no love lost between the him and Christopher, yet they would die for each other without question. It made for a strange relationship, indeed.

"If Sean is heading back to London to deliver FitzRoy to the king, I do not think it would cause The Marshal too much trouble if the rest of us took the day and night to sleep," Maxton said. "None of us has slept very much in the past few days. I could use a good meal and a soft bed myself."

Christopher waved him off. "All of you need a good meal and some sleep," he said. "I will send Peter to The Marshal to report on what has happened because I am quite certain that my son has slept more than the rest of you have, and also because I doubt Sherry is going to want to take the time to report to the man even though he is the mission commander. He has other things on his mind."

Whenever the Executioner Knights went on a mission, it was usually Alexander in command because he had a natural air of leadership about him and was flawless in his decisions. Technically, Sean may have concocted the plan, but Alexander had commanded the men to it. But Christopher's final comment had Alexander looking at him strangely.

"My lord?" he said.

Christopher looked at him, his eyes glimmering at him. "My daughter says you saved her life," he said quietly. "That, indeed, deserves a reward. Tell me what you desire and you shall have it."

A smile spread across Alexander's face. He wasn't sure if Christopher meant Christin, but he suspected he might. Perhaps the man had finally decided to leave his daughter to her happiness, after all. It couldn't have been an easy thing for Christopher to acknowledge and Alexander understood that. Surely it was difficult for any man to let his daughter go and Alexander hoped to find that out for himself, one day. He hoped to have many sons and daughters with the woman he'd chosen for his wife.

For the man who had been a loner for most of his life, it was truly a time of end.

But it was also a time of beginning.

"My greatest desire is to marry your daughter, my lord," he said, looking at Christin. "I could imagine no greater honor or blessing."

Christopher sighed heavily, realizing that he was, indeed, losing his eldest daughter. It was such a bittersweet moment, but one he had known would come someday. He simply wasn't ready for it, even if she was all grown up. David came to stand next to him and put a brotherly hand on his shoulder.

"Welcome to the family, Sherry," David said before Christopher could respond. "Christin could ask for no finer husband."

Alexander beamed and so did Christin. Realizing she had her father's approval, she threw her arms around Alexander's neck, hugging him tightly as he picked her up and swung her around, joyful beyond measure. As Maxton, Kress, Caius, Bric, and Kevin congratulated the pair on their happiness, Christopher held up a silencing hand.

"Wait," he said, getting everyone's attention. "There is something I must know."

Alexander still had Christin in his arms as he looked at Christopher. "What is that, my lord?"

Christopher cocked an eyebrow in a gesture that looked a good deal like his daughter when she was annoyed. "Are you going to force her to give up serving The Marshal?" he asked. "I do not mind you doing it, or Peter doing it, but for my daughter… I would feel better if she did not. But, of course, the decision is yours."

Alexander chuckled. "Then you know?"

"I know about The Ghost."

Alexander looked at Christin. "Tell your father what you told me."

Christin let go of Alexander and went to her father, her eyes glimmering with the mirth of the situation. So the man knew about her service to The Marshal? She knew he'd find out, eventually. At least he wasn't screaming about it. But she wondered if he had when he'd first been told.

Truthfully, he wasn't going to have to worry about it any longer.

"I told him that I would prefer to be Lady de Sherrington and let that be glory enough in my life rather than serving in The Marshal's ranks," she said. "Truly, Papa, that is the best life I can imagine. Serving The Marshal had its moments and I felt I was making a difference as few women can claim. And mayhap, someday, I shall do it again. But not now. It is time to retire The Ghost for the time being. I am content to be Lady de Sherrington."

Christopher could see the utter delight in her features as she spoke of becoming Alexander's wife. He smiled at her, patting her hands. "Are you certain, Cissy?"

"I have never been more certain in my life."

Christopher kissed her on the forehead, taking one last look at his daughter before he gave her off to another man. "Then it seems my decision is made," he said. He looked at Alexander. "She is yours, Sherry. Pray treat her right or I will do to you what you did to FitzRoy."

Alexander chuckled, knowing it was the zeal of a father speaking but that there was also some truth to it. "No need to worry, my lord," he said. "Or may I all you Papa?"

"You may not."

"Father?"

"*Nay.*"

By this time, Christin was far gone with giggles and Alexander was pretending as if he were very hurt. "Then what am I to call you? My lord seems terribly formal."

Christopher waved a dismissive hand at him. "We have time to decide."

"I much prefer Dada."

Everyone was laughing at that point. Christopher shook his head at the lot of them. "You are a ridiculous fool," he said to Alexander. "But you are a fool my daughter clearly loves. As David said – welcome to the family, Sherry."

It seemed that Alexander had been waiting all his life to hear those words but he didn't realize that until now. He would soon take a wife and with her came a great, noble family who loved each other deeply. His father-in-law was perhaps one of the greatest knights who had ever lived and there was tremendous honor in that.

But no greater honor than in the bride herself.

She was quite a woman.

As Christopher and David headed out of the livery, going to see to their captive army and Sean's delivery, the rest of the knights trickled out of the livery one at a time, each one personally congratulating Alexander and Christin until only Maxton was left. He approached Alexander, taking the man's hand and smiling wearily into his face.

"Marrying my wife was the best thing I have ever done, Sherry," he said. "My advice to you is to let your wife rule your heart and your home. You will be a much happier man for it."

Alexander smiled in return, holding the man's hand for a moment. He considered Maxton one of his dearest friends and since Maxton wasn't good with sentiment, he knew the effort it had taken for the man to speak from his heart.

"You and I have known each other many years, Maxton," he said. "I remember when you married Andressa. I remember thinking you had been somehow weakened by falling in love with a woman, but now I realize how wrong I was."

Maxton snorted softly, gave Alexander's hand a squeeze, and headed out of the livery, following the path of the others as they headed to The Cock and Bull. When they were finally alone, Alexander turned to Christin, noting that she appeared particularly pensive.

"What is it?" he asked.

She cocked her head thoughtfully. "I have been thinking."

"Of what?"

"Ramsbury."

"What about it?"

She looked at him pointedly. "Because this whole situation started when the French spy told me that there was a threat from within, right under our noses. We went to Norwich, which we had to go to, anyway, but everything seemed to take off from there and we never did discover if there was a threat against John from within."

"And?"

"And I think that the king does not need anyone trying to kill him when he is so willing to destroy England himself," she said. "Look at what he has done – he was willing to marry me to his bastard son, knowing my father would try to destroy him for it. It would have torn England apart."

A smile spread across Alexander's face. "You are coming to the conclusion that the rest of us are," he said. "John is his own worst enemy. It is difficult to protect a man from himself, but that is the duty we find ourselves with. All of The Marshal's agents."

"Then you do not think one of the allies is a threat? Someone who might have been at the celebration at Norwich?"

Alexander shrugged. "It is difficult to say," he said. "But I don't believe the French spy had anyone in particular in mind when she said that. I am coming to think she truly did mean the king himself."

That made sense to Christin. She wrapped her hands around his big forearm, smiling up at him.

"Then you can figure it out," she said. "I will be busy being Lady de

Sherrington."

"May I seek your advice on such things, then?"

"I would be honored, my lord."

He laughed softly and patted her hand. "Very well, then," he said. "Now that we have that straightened out, what now? Shall we find a church and marry?"

Her eyes widened. "God's Bones, we shall *not*," she said, pulling him out of the livery. "If you fear my father, my mother will be twice as terrifying if we marry and she is not present. For now, we return to Lioncross Abbey, tell my mother that we have permission to marry, and let her plan such a thing. It is her right, as my mother."

He grinned lazily as she pulled him out into the street. "Whatever you wish," he said. "But I will again ask the question – what do we do *now*?"

Christin came to a stop, looking down the road towards the south, seeing her father and uncle in the distance as they went to find the army. The sun was just starting to rise, the dawn of a beautiful new day, and all was right with the world.

It was the beginning of the rest of their lives.

"I could use food and sleep like the others," she said. "You?"

He nodded. "I am suitably weary," he said. "But your father will be seeing to the army for at least an hour, I would think. There is much to see to. I wonder what we could do with that hour?"

She bit her lip to keep from smiling when she realized what he meant. "Really, Sherry," she scolded softly. "Is that all you think about?"

His smile faded and his dark eyes took on a glimmer that was as warm and pure as when the world was new. A new day, a new life, a new wife.

"Aye," he whispered. "It is all I think about. *You* are all I think about, Christin de Lohr. I love you more than I could have ever anticipated."

Her eyes immediately began to well. "And I love you. Until the end of all things, I will."

His reply was to take her in his arms, out in the middle of the street, and kiss her deeply as the sun rose.

They put the following hour to good use.

And Christopher was none the wiser.

EPILOGUE

Six Months Later
Ashdown Manor

CHRISTIN HAD HER eyes on him.

It wasn't that he'd been showing any signs of nerves or angst during their journey from Lioncross Abbey to Ashdown, because he hadn't. He'd been even tempered and normal as far as she could see. But there was something in his dark eyes that conveyed apprehension no matter how hard he tried to hide it.

Apprehension at seeing his father for the first time in twenty years.

It was just the two of them on this journey because that's the way he wanted it. Christopher had offered to let him take men-at-arms with him, as many as he wanted, but Alexander had declined. When he faced his father, he wanted it to be only him and Christin. He didn't need an escort or a gallery of witnesses.

It was a surprisingly fine day for travel given the season, with a bright sky and the greenery of spring covering the land. The topography was relatively flat but for a few rises now and again, and heavily agricultural. The fields that they passed were covered with shaggy cows, dairy and beef herds as Alexander had explained. He seemed to be pleased that he was back in the area of his birth, pointing out homes or fields or small hills as they passed them, telling her of adventures or memories of his youth.

All the while, Christin simply smiled and listened.

But the chatter was covering up his nerves and she knew that. He spoke of Warminster, which was not far to the northwest, and he spoke of the ponies he and his younger brothers would ride in the fields in spite of their father telling them not to. In the dead of winter, he said. He laughed as he spoke of Andrew being tossed off into a freezing brook and how he was the one who had been punished for the folly.

The memory still brought smiles.

But their journey to Ashdown was for a reason. Alexander had finally decided to face his father, to reconcile with the man, and to assume his rightful place as Phillip's heir. He felt strongly that Christin deserved a home of her own, although she assured him that she'd not married him simply to gain a home, but Alexander had been insistent. He wanted to do everything he could for her and for their unborn child. Christin was two months along in her pregnancy and feeling splendidly, but the coming of a son had Alexander in nesting mode.

He wanted a home for his son – *his* heir.

But there was more to it. Now that he had a child on the way, he'd put himself in his father's position and he could understand what it would mean to him if he and his own child became estranged. That gave him a perspective he'd never had before and he was eager to make amends for his foolishness.

He only hoped his father could forgive him.

They were drawing closer to Ashdown, as evidenced by the fact that Alexander kept craning his neck to see through a copse of trees they were coming to on the west side of the road. He stopped the chatter, too. They came around a bend and, immediately, a large manor home came into view.

Christin looked at Alexander, who seemed riveted to the sight. She didn't even have to ask if it was his home because she could see that it was from the expression on his face. As they drew closer, she could see the great walls surrounding the place and a speckling of flowering trees on the land beyond the walls.

Flowers were everywhere.

The manse itself was built from pale stone, the second floor peeking over the tops of the walls. There was a small moat surrounding it, but the small drawbridge was open, as was the entrance gate, and there were people moving in and out. Some were tending the flowering trees but there was also a field across the road, growing vegetables, and there were several people tending the field as dogs ran about, protecting the field from invaders, both animal and human.

In fact, as Alexander and Christin rode up, one of the dogs ran forward, barking, as a young boy ran up behind the dog with a bow and arrow in his hands. He couldn't have been more than ten years of age.

"Halt!" the boy said. "Who are you? What do you want?"

Alexander looked at the lad with some amusement. "I have come seeking Phillip de Sherrington," he said. "Will you please tell me where I can find him?"

The boy's brow furrowed. "Why do you want him?"

"Will you please tell me where he is?"

The boy was growing confused because the man wasn't giving him any answers. Then, he turned his head, shouting at the field behind him.

"Mam!" he bellowed. "*Mam!*"

A woman at the edge of the field turned in answer to his summons, setting aside her hoe and making her way over to him. The boy, still with the bow and arrow semi-pointed at Alexander, scampered his way back to the woman, pointing to Alexander and whispering to her. She brushed her hands off on her broadcloth skirts as she approached.

"I understand you are looking for Phillip de Sherrington?" she said.

Alexander nodded. "Aye."

"Are you a friend?"

Alexander hesitated. Not knowing who the woman was, he didn't want to tell her too much. "You could say that," he said. "If I could see him, he will know me."

The woman smiled politely. "Do you have business with him?"

Alexander shook his head. "It is a social call."

The woman nodded, taking a step or two closer so she wasn't speaking loudly for all to hear. "I am sorry, but my husband died last year," she said. "May I be of service to you?"

Alexander felt as if he'd been hit in the gut. Not only had his father died, but he'd evidently remarried. In truth, he shouldn't have been surprised by either of those things considering how long he'd been away, but they were still a blow. Grief swept him.

But so did something else.

Realization.

The young boy had called the woman "Mam".

"I am sorry for your loss, Lady de Sherrington," he said. "I did not know."

The woman maintained her polite smile. "It was swift," she said. "An illness took him from us."

"And the lad," he said. "He is yours?"

The woman's smile turned genuine. "Aye," she said. "He is Phillip's son, Alexander. He was named for Phillip's eldest son who was killed in The Levant. If you knew Phillip, then mayhap you knew his eldest, Alexander."

Alexander couldn't help the genuine shock. He turned to look at Christin, who was looking at him with great sympathy. For a moment, Alexander had no idea what he should say or do. He'd come to seek his father and got far more than he bargained for. More than that, he realized there would be no forgiveness, no reconciliation. His father had died thinking his one remaining son had died without ever seeking him out again.

It was a horrible thing he'd done to his father.

"The manse," he finally said, his chest tight with emotion. "It... it looks as if it has been prosperous in spite of Phillip's death."

He said it because he couldn't think of anything else to say, under the circumstances. But the woman nodded.

"It is a wonderful place," she said. "Alexander has a younger sister and it has been an honor to raise Phillip's children here. I am sorry, my lord... I did not hear your name?"

Alexander looked at her. What could he say? She had a bucolic life with Alexander and his little sister, clearly the heirs of his father's estate. It legally belonged to him, but he'd been gone for so long that his father had believed him dead and had remarried. And rightfully so. He'd even named his firstborn son with his new wife Alexander, after him, which broke Alexander's heart. What he had put his father through was unforgiveable and he could see that now.

He didn't deserve Ashdown or anything about it.

It belonged to young Alexander and his little sister.

"This is my wife, Lady Christin de Lohr," he said after a moment.

Though he'd avoided introducing himself, the woman didn't press him. She simply nodded, greeting Christin politely before returning her attention to Alexander.

"How do you know Phillip?" she asked.

Alexander was truthful. "I have known Phillip my entire life," he said. "I have not seen him in many years. I came... I thought..."

"When did you and Phillip marry?" Christin mercifully stepped in because Alexander was struggling. "I never met him, but I have heard he was a kind and generous man. I am very sorry to hear of his passing, for I was rather hoping to meet him."

Lady de Sherrington smiled. "We married twelve years ago," she said. "My father owns lands adjacent to Ashdown, so we have been able to work both lands and make them quite prosperous."

"Then you have lived here your entire life?" Christin asked.

The woman shook her head. "Nay," she said. "My family was originally from Salisbury, but my father purchased the lands right after Phillip's sons left for The Levant. In fact, Phillip often told me that he wanted me to marry his eldest son, but when Alexander did not return, he married me instead. He was a wonderful husband. I am not sure his eldest son could have been any better."

Christin didn't dare look at Alexander. She was waiting for him to tell the woman who he was but, for some reason, he seemed hesitant.

"Then I am glad to hear Phillip was good to you," she said. "Did... did he ever speak of Alexander? He had two other sons, also."

Lady de Sherrington nodded. "Adam and Andrew," she said. Then, she sobered somewhat. "Phillip never got over losing all three sons in The Levant, but that is an old story to families in England. So many lost sons during the quest. But for Phillip, he lost his entire family there."

"Did he tell you that?"

"Aye," she said. "He would often speak of his sons as if they were still living, speaking so fondly of them. In fact, when he lay dying, he spoke of the joy of seeing them again in heaven. That thought has given me great comfort, knowing they are all together again."

Alexander abruptly dismounted his horse and walked away, but not before Christin saw tears rolling down his cheeks. Given that she was pregnant, and emotional, tears stung her eyes as well, knowing how heartbroken her husband was.

It was an action not missed by Lady de Sherrington. She looked after Alexander with concern.

"Is your husband well, my lady?" she asked.

Christin nodded, trying very hard not to display her emotions. "He is," she said. "It is simply that Phillip was an old and dear friend and he did not know of his death. He was hoping... to see him."

"I see." Lady de Sherrington appeared very sympathetic. "Would you like to come into the manse and refresh yourselves? Please let me show you the hospitality that Phillip would have shown an old and dear friend."

Christin forced a smile as she dismounted her palfrey. "I will ask him."

Leaving Lady de Sherrington looking after her with concern, Christin made her way over to Alexander, who was standing on the edge of the road, his back to her. Coming up behind him, she put her arms around him.

"I am so sorry, my love," she whispered. "You could not have known any of this. You must not blame yourself for anything."

Alexander had his eyes closed as tears coursed down his cheeks. "I knew this might be the outcome," he whispered. "I have not seen or spoken to him in twenty years, so I knew. But it is clear he thought I was dead."

Christin hugged him gently. "He could not have known otherwise."

"He named his son after me."

"I think that proves he did not hate you, nor was he angry with you. He did it to honor you."

Alexander nodded and the tears fell faster. He put his hand to his face, wiping away the tears, laboring to compose himself. Christin held on to him, hugging him tightly.

"What do you wish to do?" she asked. "Lady de Sherrington has offered us refreshments. Do you want to go into Ashdown and speak to her? It might make you feel better."

He shook his head. "Nay," he said. "Because she would want to know my identity and I am afraid I would not be able to keep it from her. Something might slip out and she would know."

"Then you are not going to tell her?"

"Nay," he said. "Look around, Cissy; Ashdown is peaceful and everyone seems happy. Why would I disrupt that? Leave them to their little world. Leave it to the next Alexander, the lad with the dog and the bow and arrow. I lost my right to anything twenty years ago when I refused to return home, so it belongs to them now. Not me. Leave them to their paradise, because I have found my own elsewhere."

Christin looked at him intently, trying to see if there was some regret or sorrow there, but there was truly none. He was grieving his father, of course, but not the loss of Ashdown. He seemed genuine about that. Reaching up, she helped him wipe his tears, patting his cheek gently.

"Are you certain?" she asked.

He nodded, taking a deep breath to compose himself. He happened to be facing the manse of Ashdown and his gaze moved over the walls, the home of his ancestors.

"I am," he said. "I was born here, but my home is with you, at Lioncross or wherever we may end up. This... this is my past and I will give it over to the next generation. You are my future."

Christin smiled at him, taking his hand as they turned around and headed back towards the horses. Lady de Sherrington was still standing there, still looking at him with concern. She seemed like a pleasant woman and Alexander was glad his father had found comfort with her in the last years of his life. He was also glad that he'd had the comfort of a son, one who hadn't abandoned him.

Truly, it was all he could ask for.

"My lord, would you like to come inside?" Lady de Sherrington asked as they drew near. "Any friend of Phillip's is welcome."

He forced a smile. "You are very kind, but we must be on our way," he said. "We were traveling home to the Marches, so this was simply a stop along the way. I was very fond of... Phillip and I extend my friendship to you, also. If you are ever in need, or need help, send word to Lioncross Abbey Castle in Herefordshire. I will come."

Lady de Sherrington smiled. "Thank you, my lord," she said. "But I still do not know your name."

Alexander glanced at the lad with his same name, now running in the field with his dog, shooting his bow and arrow. As he watched, the child reminded him very much of Andrew and Adam and he had to grin when the boy tripped and fell, right into the mud. Oh, the memories that vision brought back.

Good ones.

"Your son and I share the same name," he said. "I wish you well, Lady de Sherrington. Peace upon your home and your family."

She simply nodded as Alexander helped Christin mount her palfrey. He swung himself onto his own horse, gathering the reins and giving Lady de Sherrington a nod as they headed out.

The woman stood there for a moment, watching him go and thinking that he looked an awful lot like Phillip. Around the eyes, she thought. But perhaps it was her imagination.

Returning to her garden, she could not have known that her son's destiny remained intact due to the unselfish act of a man and his wife who had been inquiring on her dead husband. She could not have known, in any case.

But Alexander knew. And wherever his father was, he knew, too.

Finally, Alexander de Sherrington had found the peace he so desperately needed.

And a future to be proud of.

Children of Alexander and Christin
Andrew
Adam
Gabriel
Nicholas
Liam
Maxim
Sophia

CS THE END SO

About Kathryn Le Veque

Medieval Just Got Real.

KATHRYN LE VEQUE is a USA TODAY Bestselling author, an Amazon All-Star author, and a #1 bestselling, award-winning, multi-published author in Medieval Historical Romance and Historical Fiction. She has been featured in the NEW YORK TIMES and on USA TODAY's HEA blog. In March 2015, Kathryn was the featured cover story for the March issue of InD'Tale Magazine, the premier Indie author magazine. She was also a quadruple nominee (a record!) for the prestigious RONE awards for 2015.

Kathryn's Medieval Romance novels have been called 'detailed', 'highly romantic', and 'character-rich'. She crafts great adventures of love, battles, passion, and romance in the High Middle Ages. More than that, she writes for both women AND men – an unusual crossover for a romance author – and Kathryn has many male readers who enjoy her stories because of the male perspective, the action, and the adventure.

On October 29, 2015, Amazon launched Kathryn's Kindle Worlds Fan Fiction site WORLD OF DE WOLFE PACK. Please visit Kindle Worlds for Kathryn Le Veque's World of de Wolfe Pack and find many action-packed adventures written by some of the top authors in their genre using Kathryn's characters from the de Wolfe Pack series. As Kindle World's FIRST Historical Romance fan fiction world, Kathryn Le Veque's World of de Wolfe Pack will contain all of the great storytelling you have come to expect.

Kathryn loves to hear from her readers. Please find Kathryn on Facebook at Kathryn Le Veque, Author, or join her on Twitter @kathrynleveque, and don't forget to visit her website and sign up for her blog at www.kathrynleveque.com.

Please follow Kathryn on Bookbub for the latest releases and sales: bookbub.com/authors/kathryn-le-veque.

Printed in Great Britain
by Amazon